Deer Season

Deer Season

AARON STANDER

Publisher's Cataloging in Publication Data
Stander, Aaron.
Deer Season / Aaron Stander. – Interlochen, Mich.: Writers & Editors, 2009.

ISBN-10: 0-9785732-2-6
1. Murder–Michigan–Fiction. 2. Murder–Investigation–Fiction.

Printed and bound in the United States of America

FOR BEACHWALKER

WHO HELPS THIS ALL HAPPEN.

1

G avin Mendicot III finished the pint of peppermint schnapps—pushing his tongue into the opening to get the last drop out of the inverted bottle. He shifted cautiously in his precarious perch, a tree stand strapped to the side of a large oak fifteen feet off the ground. With his left hand he tossed the bottle at the trunk of a tree directly across from him. It bounced off the trunk without breaking and landed in the snow.

Mendicot moved his bow to his left hand and reached into his jacket, a worn and grease-stained camouflage coat, and pulled a Glock from his shoulder holster. He tried to hold a bead on the neck of the bottle, the only part still visible above the snow. A cold chill ran through him, and he started to shiver. The report of the pistol echoed through the woods, its recoil almost causing him to lose balance.

The bottle was untouched. He fired a second round. Another miss. His world spinning, he tried to steady the weapon, concentrating on the target, and continued pulling the trigger until the magazine was empty. Finally, the bottle disappeared from view. He carefully slid the pistol back in its holster.

Gavin looked at the horizon; the light was quickly fading. He hooked his bow to a line and lowered it to the ground. Then he unhitched his harness, turned, and started down the ladder. Three quarters of the way down he missed a step and fell the rest of the way, his descent softened by several feet of new snow. He clumsily brushed the wet snow from his already damp canvas bibs and started up the trail along the river, trudging through the deepening drifts. After a few hundred yards he stopped to catch his breath. He lit a cigarette and opened another pint of schnapps, the third of the afternoon. He shivered as he tightened the cap. The snow was falling heavier. He tossed the half-smoked cigarette in the snow and lit a joint. Leaning against a tree he inhaled deeply, holding the smoke in his lungs for a long moment, then slowly exhaling. He opened the schnapps again and took a long pull on the bottle before he inhaled again.

Gavin retrieved a compass from his upper jacket pocket. "If I go straight east I can get to the road faster than following the river," he said out loud. He looked at the compass; the needle swung back and forth in his shaky hand. Gavin launched himself in an easterly direction. The first few hundred yards were easy; he stayed near the roots of cedars and avoided the soft earth between them. Then the trees thinned as he moved into a marshy plain. His boots sank deeper and deeper as he pushed himself forward. Pulling his boots from the mud became more difficult with each step. He could feel the water beginning to ooze in around his toes. A cold shudder ran through his body.

Then he heard the choppers and the cannon fire. Bullets whistled overhead. Artillery rounds were exploding in front of him, their acrid smell burning his nose. The water continued filling his boots. He froze in place, looking for the enemy, crouching, and then moving forward.

The ground became firmer as he moved into a heavy stand of cedar. He saw something move and dropped to his knees, slid on his stomach, his bow in front of him. A buck lifted its nose into the air and turned toward Gavin. It then raised its tail and moved

in the opposite direction, first a few quick steps, then full flight.
Gavin rose to his knees and sent an arrow in the animal's direction.
Then he pulled out his Glock, pointed it in the direction of the
fleeing deer, and wildly squeezed the trigger. There was only a thin,
mechanical sound; the gun was empty.

Gavin pulled himself to his feet and ran to where he first
saw the buck. He studied the snow in the dull, flat light of late
afternoon, looking for blood on the thick white carpet. He could
see none. He followed the tracks until they were obscured by the
darkness.

He pulled out his compass, illuminating it with a cigarette
lighter, trying to hold it level. He started east again. The snow was
thicker as he crossed a field, his feet burning, his breathing labored.
Gavin could hear a snowmobile, could see the headlights moving
perpendicular to his path. He struggled through the deep snow
until he reached a road.

Heading north directly into blowing snow, he stopped to take
a drink from the nearly empty bottle. Just as he tossed it away,
Gavin was startled by the chugging sound of an engine; a decrepit
pickup paused next to him. He looked over as the window was
rolled down.

"Need a ride, mister?"

Gavin moved to the side of the vehicle and looked at the
grizzled man behind the wheel, his face dimly lit by the yellowish
glow of the instrument panel. "I think my truck is just up the
road."

"Better get in. Help ya find it. Too damn cold and dark ta be
walking."

Gavin came around the front of the truck and climbed in,
pulling the door shut behind him; he had to slam it closed a second
time to get the latch to catch. The interior was warm and smelled
of tobacco and whiskey.

"What's your truck look like?"

"It's a Blazer, black."

"Did ya park it along the road?" the man asked. He dropped his cigarette out of the vent window.

"Just off, at the entrance to the camp ground."

The old man sort of laughed, three audible exhalations, cough-like, mocking. "Well you're a lucky son-of-a-bitch. That's three, four miles up. You'd-a-bin fucking dead in a snow bank 'fore ya got there on a night like this. Yup, just fucking dead in the snow. County plow come through and toss ya sorry ass way off the road. They'd find ya in the spring after the crows got the best of ya. Want a drink?" He pulled a bottle of Jim Beam from under the seat and handed it to Gavin. "Leave the top off, I'll have one after ya."

Gavin took a mouthful of the whiskey, swirled it around, swallowed, and took a second sip, larger than the first. "Good," he said handing the open bottle over to the driver. "Name's Gavin, what's yours?"

The driver took the bottle, lifted it to his lips, sipped, and handed it back. "Jake, Jake Janson. First time I had Beam I was in the army."

"Where?"

"Korea. I was an eighteen-year-old kid. Weather like this— fucking freezing, no hot food for days, taking lots of casualties. I didn't think I could stand it no more, so my sergeant gives me some Beam, stuff like this. Never had any before. Think I was drunk as hell with a swig or two. It helped me get through the night. Next day we got sent to the rear. Always like having a sip of whiskey when it storms like this. Reminds me of that time. You serve?"

"Yeah."

"Where?"

"Iraq."

"No snow there."

"No, just fucking sand and smoke. Not much whiskey. Lots of beer."

Gavin went silent. He closed his eyes. He was in the chopper again. They were coming into the target area. He ran his hands over his gun. He was trying not to think. Just waiting for the order to get out of the chopper. Just waiting to hit the ground, hoping to survive the day.

"That ya car over there? Can't tell it's black, being covered the way it is."

Gavin opened his eyes. "Yeah, that's it. Thanks for the ride."

"You okay to drive?" the man asked.

"Yeah, sober as a judge."

"That's not saying much. Fucking judges. Where ya stayin?"

"Grand Marais, got a motel room there."

"Better get moving; road won't be open much longer," the old man said. "I'll wait til ya get on the road. Don't want ya out here alone. Probably die before someone else comes along."

Gavin slogged though the snow to his vehicle, pulled open the driver's door, tossed his new composite bow in the back and got the motor started. He rocked the Blazer back and forth several times, then locked it into four-wheel drive, finally making it back to the highway. The old man waved and slowly drove away.

Gavin lit a cigarette and waited for the defroster to clear the mist from the inside of the windshield. By the time he started down the road, the truck and the old man were long gone. He looked for his bow, trying to remember where he'd put it. It wasn't on the seat next to him. He turned on the dome light, but couldn't see it in the jumble of gear in the back of the vehicle. "Fuck," he said groggily, "I must of left it in that old fart's truck. Fuck hunting."

He reached under the dashboard and retrieved a small brown plastic prescription bottle. After struggling with the cap momentarily, he poured the capsules in his hand. He counted them twice, picking up two, one at a time, and putting them in his mouth. He cupped his hand and returned the remaining pills to the bottle. After secreting the bottle again, he washed the already half-dissolved pills down with a few gulps from a newly opened bottle of schnapps.

"Fuck hunting. I'm going home," Gavin said, putting the car in gear. He made a clumsy u-turn, almost getting stuck, and started south toward the narrow ribbon of steel and concrete that connects Michigan's two peninsulas.

2

Clay Bateman was having a party, not a big party, just his two best friends, Drew and Zack, all high school seniors and members of the Cedar Bay football team. They were well into a case of beer and had another in reserve. Of the group, Clay was the biggest drinker; his two hundred and forty pounds of muscle and fat could absorb huge amounts of alcohol.

They had started to party about 6:00, just after football practice, and by 10:00 they had collapsed on the couches and the floor in the living room of the Bateman's modest home. A Rambo movie—the second of the evening—was running on the TV, the sound turned down; no one was really watching anymore.

Gavin—Clay's mother's boyfriend—was in the U.P. deer hunting. His mother, Donna, the evening bartender at the Last Chance, was at work and probably wouldn't be home until after 1:00 a.m.

The increasingly inarticulate conversation focused on the physical attributes of the Cedar Bay cheerleading and pom-pom squads, starting with Ali Bealman and working through the ranks to Wenonah Zapinski. When the boys had exhausted that topic— one that they had discussed countless times before—they moved onto the next game, Friday night, the last game of the season, and their last game as high school players.

"We should keep their fucking quarterback in the mud. We should blitz on every play. That's all they got. We knock him outta the game, and they ain't got shit," Clay said.

"Since when do we blitz every play?" asked Zack, his speech badly slurred.

"Well, we could. It's our last game; we can do anything we want."

"Ya got beer on the brain," Zack responded. "Coach Fronz would put your butt on the bench for the rest of the night."

"What's he gonna do? Play some skinny-assed sophomore? If he pulls any of us he doesn't have a chance of winning. He sure as hell doesn't want to lose to Sand River three years in a row."

"Ya got a bug up your butt if you think he'd keep you in if you're not following the plan. He'll pull you right away. Hell, if he could see us now, none of us will be playing on Friday, and if he knew about the mail boxes over in Sand River…."

"Was that brilliant or what? How many mailboxes do ya think we got? Wake Drew up and ask him. He was supposed to do the counting."

Zack pushed the lifeless body next to him, "Drew, wake up. How many mailboxes did we get? Wasn't it about twenty?"

"Let me sleep, I don't care about your mailboxes."

"He can't do weed," said Clay. "Right after he smokes he always falls asleep. That's why Wenonah stopped dating him. They'd blow a joint, and he'd conk just when she wanted some good loving."

"How are we going to get him home?" asked Zack. "He's totally out of it, and there's a hell-of-a storm blowing."

"I'll call his mom. Drew told her he was coming over here for dinner after practice. I'll just say he fell asleep, extra hard practice tonight and the roads are too bad to drive him home. That dumb bitch won't suspect anything. She just loves me; she believes anything I tell her. God she's got big tits. I bet she's a great…."

"You asshole," said Zack. "You got sex on the brain."

Clay went to the kitchen phone and dialed Drew's number. Waiting for an answer, he looked out of the window over the sink. "What the hell," he yelled to Zack hanging up the phone on the second ring.

He hurried into the living room. "There's a car out there, and I think they're fucking with our mailbox."

"Whataya gonna do?" asked Zack.

"Scare the hell out of those fuckers." Clay disappeared into a back bedroom and emerged a few moments later carrying a worn shotgun.

"Don't do anything stupid," begged Zack.

Clay ran from the house, leaving the front door open. As he raced toward the road, his gait unsteady, he yelled, "What are ya doing?" He stopped and raised the gun over his head in a menacing gesture. In his intoxicated state, he saw a vision of Rambo, glistening with sweat, bandoliers hanging across his naked chest, defiantly shaking his gun at the entire Red Chinese army.

Car doors slammed and the car sped away, fishtailing wildly on the snow-covered road.

An explosion jarred Clay just as he reached the side of the road, the tan plastic mailbox a few feet to his right tearing open and flying apart. Momentarily stunned, he staggered onto the road. He saw the brake lights of a car flash on. The car had reached the end of the road and would have to come back his way. "What are you doing?" asked Zack.

"They cherry bombed our mailbox."

"Get rid of the gun."

"No, I want to scare them."

As the SUV came back in their direction, four headlights blazing in the blowing snow, Clay stood in the center of the road and raised the heavy weapon over his head so they could see him clearly. He was Rambo again, a squadron of black helicopters descending upon him.

All at once Clay felt himself being hauled backwards off the road. He stumbled and fell backwards into the snow. "Why did you do that?" he demanded as he scrambled to his feet.

"Getting your ass out of the way so you don't get flattened," Zack yelled.

The large vehicle went flying by, throwing a thick sheet of slush in their direction. Clay ran back out onto the road, waving the shotgun, Zack grabbing Clay's arm just as he aimed it at the receding taillights.

The gun kicked violently as he fired both barrels.

"You're crazy," Zack yelled.

"I didn't know it was loaded."

"What if you hit them?"

"I didn't. I was aiming way off to the side."

"That sounded like a war. Sure as hell one of your cranky old neighbors is gonna report the gunfire. The sheriff is going to be out here."

"It's hunting season."

"It's bow season, asshole. You can do the talking when the cops get here. I'm taking Drew home."

Clay didn't offer to help as Zack half-carried Drew to his rusting pickup. After they were gone, Clay collected the beer cans scattered around the living room and tossed them in a black garbage bag that he pitched near the sink before crawling into bed.

3

D onna Bateman stood behind the bar at the Last Chance looking through one of the large windows on the opposite wall. Beyond the windows, snow swirled through the beams of the floodlights in the parking lot. And much to her surprise and relief, the three old timers who spent almost every evening at the Last Chance nursing a few beers—Willie, Ken, and Franklin—headed out into the storm soon after the eleven o'clock news. She cleared their bottles and glasses, wiped the bar and the counters. Then she locked the front door to prevent any more customers from coming in for a nightcap, not that there was much chance of that late on a stormy weeknight. She emptied the meager contents of the till into a zippered bank bag and locked it in the safe in the small office next to the kitchen. Then she turned down the lights and went into the back kitchen area to do some final cleaning and washing up.

"The first snowy night," she said, as she wiped and dried the long stainless steel counter. She hadn't seen her longtime lover, Dirk Lowther, the one constant man in her life, in months. But he had promised he would see her the night of the first big storm, sort of an anniversary. And it would be so easy tonight; her current companion, Gavin, was in the U.P. hunting. She wouldn't have to lie about why she was late coming home.

Their last assignation had been in late August on the beach at Otter Creek; it was one of the warmest nights of the summer. The encounter followed a pattern she had known for more than half her life. Usually they'd have a few quick drinks followed by torrid lovemaking. And then he would be gone with no contact for six weeks, or sometimes six months. And this arrangement had continued over the years, uninterrupted by romances, affairs, or marriages.

Their first tryst had taken place in the back seat of the big maroon Pontiac he drove back then. She had been baby-sitting the two small children he had had with his first wife. That night Donna could tell the couple had both been drinking heavily when they returned from the party. The woman asked her husband to drive Donna home, saying that she was too drunk to get behind the wheel. In the course of the evening Donna had been doing some drinking of her own, helping herself to small glasses of Baileys Irish Cream. There was always an open bottle in their refrigerator, and they never seemed to notice that any was missing.

Donna remembered how snowy it was that night, the first storm of the season. Halfway down the long drive, he turned off the lights and stopped the car. He grabbed her, pulled her over to him, and kissed her hard. It wasn't her first sexual experience; she'd lost her virginity the summer before ninth grade. But somehow this was so much more exciting than anything that had happened before. She kissed him back, pushing her tongue deep in his mouth, and then plunging it into his ear. She knew that made her boyfriends go crazy. He didn't have to undress her, she tore off her clothes and helped pull him out of his.

Hours later, when she was home in her own bed in the old farmhouse that had been in her family for three generations, wide awake, her body still tingling, she tried to remember everything that happened, the chronology, all the things he'd done to her and had her do to him. She wished they could have spent the night

together, nothing had ever felt so good, none of her boyfriends
had ever given her that kind of pleasure.

And that was the start; all these years later it was still the
same. And it was their secret; she had never told anyone, not even
her closest girlfriends. And she knew he never would. And even in
a small town where secrets are hard to keep and tongues are quick
to wag, she didn't think there was the slightest suspicion that there
was anything between them.

And there was one more part of this secret that she had never
shared, the truth about her son's paternity, conceived a year after
their first encounter. Donna stopped her cleaning for a moment,
thought about her boyfriend at the time, dear sweet Herbie.
When she got pregnant he assumed that he was the father. She
remembered Herbie talking about "honor" and not wanting his
child to be considered a "bastard" by everyone in town. "Herbie."
She said his name out loud. She liked saying his name. He wasn't a
bad guy, and for a couple of years he worked hard to support them
and help with the baby. And she tried hard to love him and be
faithful, not that she was very successful. Her grief was real when
Herbie died, less than a mile from their home, colliding with a deer
late one night as he was coming home from work, his damaged
Harley and mangled body ending up in the woods a few dozen
yards off the road.

Donna closed her eyes for a second. She could see the whole
scene again. The flashing lights in the fog, Herbie's lifeless body on
a gurney, the rumble of the engines running at idle, the faces in the
crowd lit by pulsating strobes.

The next day, as her mother looked after her toddler, Donna
walked back along the highway where the accident took place. In
the silence of a radiant autumn afternoon, she walked the area.
Donna could see the skid marks, the path through the brush the
bike had created as it careened off the road, breaking saplings until
it stopped against a large red oak. Near the bottom of the tree the
bark was battered and torn, showing the force of the impact. She

knelt in the grass and could see small pieces of glass reflecting back the soft autumn sunshine in the sandy soil close to the tree.

And although Donna was not given to introspection, she stayed there a long moment, wondering what she was supposed to be feeling. Wanting to be able to look down upon the whole scene and perhaps get some understanding of the meaning of Herbie's death, she wandered up the hillside. Near the ridgeline she found the deer, a buck, the shattered ends of a bone sticking through the skin of a deformed rear leg, its flank torn, flies working the open flesh. She knelt near the head of the animal and reached out and touched an antler. She ran her hand over the hard, bony surface.

The sound of an engine and the slamming of a car door, followed by a sharp rap on the steel back door, interrupted her thoughts. She peered through the peephole and undid the lock and deadbolt. It was the first snowstorm of the season.

As he drove east on Route 2 in the swirling snow toward Saint Ignace, Gavin Mendicot could see the lights on the bridge glowing across the dark tumult of waves funneling through the Straits. Snow and cold had taken away his passion for bow hunting, and now he was trying to beat the storm.

****

Gavin pushed a half empty bottle of Glenfiddich from view just before he reached the tollbooth. Then he pulled behind an eighteen-wheeler and crept across the bridge. At Gaylord he pulled off the interstate and slowly worked his way back to Cedar County on snow-covered, two-lane highways, consuming the rest of the scotch along the way.

When Gavin finally reached the Last Chance, the lights were out in the bar and the parking lot was empty. He plowed through the heavy snow in the parking lot to the back of the building to see if Donna was still finishing up. He stopped just short of crashing into a sheriff's car, parked just behind Donna's battered pickup.

Gavin's synapses, which for most of the day been slowed by alcohol and weed, were now firing rapidly, albeit haphazardly, driven by the continued ingestion of amphetamines as he drove south. Pausing, he looked at the police car and the dark building, his damaged brain still functioning well enough to understand what was happening.

Slowly he backed up. His first impulse was to ram the police car and drive it into Donna's pickup. Then he remembered the last time he had crashed into a police car. The lawyers hired by his trust were barely able to get him out of the charges; a conviction would have led to his being declared a habitual offender.

Gavin drove around for a while, finally pulling into a space at the far end of the Village Market parking lot. He got out and climbed into the rear of his vehicle, pushing clothing and gear out of his path. He kicked off his boots and slowly pulled himself into his sleeping bag. As he squirmed to find a comfortable position, he settled against something sharp. He pulled one arm out of the bag and fished around for the offending object. His hand surrounded the cold surface of his composite bow. "Fuck," he said, tossing the weapon toward the front seat.

4

Late night calls usually meant something was seriously wrong; it wasn't that the watch command and the available personnel couldn't handle such situations, but Ray had made it clear from his earliest days as sheriff that he wanted to be kept abreast of any significant events involving the department.

"Sheriff, Lisa, dispatch," came the voice on the other end of the phone.

Ray pulled himself awake. "Yes, go ahead."

"We have a shooting, male, late teens. He's currently at the medical center. I've dispatched two cars to the center."

"Where did the incident take place?"

"Don't know. We just got a call from the ER saying they had a shooting victim. He came in by car with a couple of other kids. I have no other information."

"Who's there?"

"Lawrence and Reilly are en route."

"How are the roads?" Ray asked.

"It's slow going. They're doing their best to keep main roads open," came the response.

"I'm on my way," said Ray. "I'll let you know when I get there."

Ray pulled himself out of the chair in which he had fallen asleep and switched on the light. He picked up a now cold mug of herbal tea from the table next to him, drank the last of it, and stopped at the bathroom. After pulling on a well-used pair of duck boots and a heavy jacket, he headed toward the garage. Ray carefully maneuvered the winding, snow-covered road down the highway, then switched on the overhead flashers and headed for the Cedar Bay Medical Center, a place where earlier in the fall he had spent several weeks recovering from a serious gunshot wound.

Ray pulled into a parking place at the ER entrance. There were two patrol cars but no other emergency units. Mort Loftman, known to everyone as Doc, dressed in green scrubs, no coat or hat, was standing outside, just beyond the perimeter of the emergency entrance, smoking. As Ray approached, Doc said, "Don't say a goddamn thing, I get to do this when I need to."

"What do we got?"

"It could have been worse. A teenage boy with shotgun pellets in his arms, neck and head. He also has some facial lacerations from flying glass."

"Do you know what happened?"

"Just got bits and pieces. The victim and a couple of friends were driving around. God only knows what they were up to—teenage boys cruising at night, never a good thing. They did something or were just in the wrong place and someone shot at their car. The kid riding in the back seat is the one that got hit. Guess the other two thought he was kidding when he said he was shot. When they figured out he was really hurt, they brought him here. We probably got him twenty minutes after the shooting.

"The kids are from Sand River," Doc continued. "I just got off the phone with the parents of the injured boy. The other two kids are okay, one of your guys is talking to them."

Ray followed Doc into the building. He found his deputies with two teenage boys in the otherwise vacant ER waiting room.

Ben Reilly was sitting with the boys at a table and filling out an incident report. Detective Sue Lawrence was standing on the perimeter, following the interview. Ray could see the two boys answering Reilly's questions. He walked to Sue's side and looked at the kids; one was lank and wiry with thick brown hair, a thin face and delicate nose; the other boy was brawnier—big shoulders, a thick neck, and a solid visage. Both were wearing maroon jackets with the raised letters "SR" on the right side. Gold footballs were pinned at the intersection of the S and R on each jacket.

"We'd heard that they were the ones that spray-painted our stadium and bombed some mailboxes last weekend. It was just sort of a payback; we didn't mean to hurt anyone," said the bigger of the two, the sandy haired kid with a round, pimple-covered face. Ray noted that Todd was embroidered in bright yellow thread on his jacket under the varsity letter.

"We were on White Oak Trail. One of Shane's cousins told us where this kid lived. Guess he was bragging all week at school 'bout what he done last weekend."

"Who was that, Todd, who was bragging?" Reilly asked.

"I don't know the kid. His name is Clay something. He's on the team, plays center. Supposed to be their toughest kid."

"What exactly happened?" Reilly pressed.

"We had a cherry bomb," said the other boy, Shane embossed on his jacket. "We found the address on the box. Chris was hanging out of the rear window with a flashlight checking addresses as we drove down the road. It took us awhile to find the right box; it was snowing like snot. When we finally found the right one, Chris got out of the car, lit the fuse and threw it in the box. He jumped back in the car, and I took off down the road; somehow I hadn't noticed it was a dead end on the way in. I turned around, and when we came back there was this kid in the road yelling at us and waving a gun. I heard some shots after we got by him. The window in the tailgate exploded. I ask Chris if he's okay, and he says he's shot. I thought he was kidding at first, but his voice was real funny, so I pulled over and put on the light. He was bleeding. I had noticed the hospital sign along the highway when we were driving up, so I just drove straight here."

"Did you see who was shooting?" Reilly asked Shane.

"I think it was the guy in the road. I didn't see anyone else."

"Could you identify him?"

"I don't know. Everything was happening so fast. And like it was a whiteout. I was just trying to stay on the road without running the kid over."

"How about you," Reilly asked Todd. "Could you identify the person in the road?"

"I just saw him for a few seconds, sorta like a deer darting out into the road."

"How many shots were fired?" Reilly asked.

"Couldn't tell you, we had the music cranked," said Shane.

Reilly looked over at Todd.

"I heard this boom, one, maybe two."

"What kid of gun did the person in the road have?"

"I didn't see the gun," said Todd.

"I don't know much about guns," said Shane. "It was big, some sort of rifle I guess."

"And the address, do you remember the address?" Reilly asked.

Todd fished in his jacket pocket and pulled out a scrap of paper. He handed it to Reilly.

"1084 White Oak Trail," Reilly passed the slip to Sue with a questioning look on his face. She moved away from the group and opened her phone.

"I think we're just about done with these boys," Reilly said. "Unless you have other questions, Sheriff."

"No," Ray responded.

"Deputy Lawrence has talked to both of your parents," Reilly continued. "Your fathers are coming in one car to get you. We will be impounding your Durango for the near future."

"How long?" asked Shane.

"Just a few days. It's important evidence."

"Are we in trouble?" Todd asked meekly, looking as though he was just beginning to understand the enormity of the evening's events.

"In addition to putting yourselves into harm's way, you broke a number of state and federal laws. We're going to let you go home with your fathers, but you will be coming back for more questioning and possible prosecution," Reilly responded sternly.

"Please stay with the boys until their fathers arrive. I'm sure they will have some questions for you," said Ray to Sergeant Reilly as Sue Lawrence returned to his side. She handed him a notepad. He looked at the name and address on the otherwise blank page. He handed the notepad on to Reilly, who looked at it and nodded his comprehension.

5

~~~~~~~~

White Oak Trail, unpaved and with a low priority for plowing, was covered by more than a foot of fresh snow. Using a spotlight, Ray checked addresses on the widely separated mailboxes. As expected, the box he was looking for wasn't on the post. He spotted the torn, blackened remains lying half covered with snow at the side of the road. He pulled into the drive, stopping behind a dilapidated Chevy pickup, and put his spotlight on the numbers next to the door. There were only three numerals; there was a space where the fourth number should have been. The other three numbers conformed to the address he was seeking. Ray climbed out of his Jeep and started for the front door. As he paused to wait for Sue Lawrence to catch up to him, Ray observed that the windshield on the truck was clear, and there was only a light dusting of snow on the hood. He pulled off a glove and touched the sheet metal with a bare hand, feeling the warmth radiating out from the engine.

Light shone from the windows, and he could see someone peering out at the vehicles in the drive. As Elkins and Lawrence trudged through the snow toward the house, a yellow bug light came on at the entrance. The front door opened before they reached it, and Donna Bateman stood in the open door.

"Sheriff, what brings you at this hour? It's not Gavin, is it?" asked Donna. Ray remembered that Donna had bailed Gavin Mendicot out of jail the previous summer after he was arrested for public intoxication.

"No, Donna, we're not here about Gavin."

"He's in the U.P. hunting," she continued nervously. "When I saw your car, I was afraid that something might have happened to him."

"Can we come in, Ms. Bateman?" asked Sue.

"Be my guest," she replied without enthusiasm, as she backed into the small living room.

"Just get home?" asked Ray.

"Twenty, thirty minutes ago. I drink so much coffee in the course of the evening that it takes me a while to wind down. I was just having a drink and cigarette before I tried to sleep."

"So you haven't been here all evening?"

"I was tending bar at the Last Chance, as usual. What's this all about, anyway?"

"It was reported that someone was firing a weapon in this area late this evening."

"Where?"

"It was reported to be at this address. Who else is in the house, Donna?" Ray asked as he surveyed the shabby and littered interior. The walls, soiled and damaged in places, were textured and painted soft yellow. Long dead shag carpeting in a bilious green covered the living room floor. The place reeked of beer, cigarette smoke, and years of neglect.

A large TV stood at the end of the room; a beat-up vinyl couch faced it, a second couch in a faded floral print leaned toward the wall at its right. Pizza boxes were stacked on the side of the sink in the kitchen area at the opposite end of the room.

"It's just me and Clay. And there was no shooting going on here, I can assure you of that."

Ray looked around the room a second time as Donna spoke. He noted a double-barreled shotgun partially visible in the far corner at the right of the TV.

"Would you get Clay for us; we'd like to talk to him," he asked.

"Sheriff, the boy is sound asleep. He had football practice today; he always comes home dead tired. I'm sure he's been sleeping for hours."

"Donna," Ray moved close to her, looked directly into her eyes, and repeated firmly, "We want to talk to Clay."

She bristled and stepped back. Her tone became hostile. "You have no right to come barging in here and demanding that I...."

"Donna, get Clay out here right now."

She stood and looked defiant for a long moment, then turned, but before she had taken more than a step, a door from an adjoining room opened. Clay stood in the opening wearing a football jersey that hung half way to his knees.

"What's going on, Mom?"

"Sheriff's here. Says someone reported hearing gunshots. You don't know nothing about that, do you?"

Looking at his mother he said, "I think I've been asleep since about 8:00."

"Who else was here?"

"No one, I was here alone."

"Do you have any firearms in the house?" Ray asked, his eyes fixed on the shotgun.

"Gavin's got some; he keeps them locked up in a trunk in the pole barn," Donna answered.

"How about that shotgun?" Ray asked, pointing to the one in the corner.

"Oh," she said, a few seconds passing as she took in the gun, "that's just an antique. Clay likes to fool with it when he watches his movies."

Ray stepped forward and picked up the weapon with a gloved hand and carefully sniffed at the end of the barrel. "Smells like it has been recently fired, Clay. What do you know about it?" Ray opened the weapon; the chambers were empty. He held it so Sue could see.

"I don't know shit about nothing. Like I said, I've been sleeping."

"And you don't know anything about mailboxes?" pressed Ray.

"No," he countered, his manner becoming increasingly hostile.

Ray approached him. Clay backed into his room and then lunged at Ray. He caught him with a glancing blow to the left shoulder. Ray grabbed Clay's arm and twisted it behind his back. He cuffed the right wrist and with Sue's help secured and cuffed the other arm.

"Sheriff, what's this all about?" Donna demanded.

"Some boys from Sand River were cruising around the area this evening. Seems they were getting even for some vandalism that took place in their community last Saturday night. Your address, Donna, was one of their destinations. They blew up your mailbox. They allege that as they were coming back down the road someone fired a weapon at their vehicle."

"Well they can allege any goddamn thing they want. Clay told you he was in bed. You heard him tell you so."

"Donna, a boy Clay's age has been wounded. That weapon," Ray pointed toward the shotgun, "has been recently fired."

"Who was with you tonight, Clay?" Sue asked.

"I was here alone, and I don't know nothing about any shooting," he responded defiantly.

"Let's get a blood alcohol," said Ray to Sue, noting that Clay reeked of beer. "And check his hands for gunpowder residue."

Ray repeated the question, "Clay, who was with you tonight?"

"Like I said, I was here alone."

"And you had two large pizzas." Ray picked up a plastic trash bag at the side of the sink and peered in at the contents. "Looks like you washed them down with two or three six packs."

"I don't have anything more to say."

"Donna," instructed Ray, "do you want to pull some pants on your boy, or do you want us to take him in bare assed. I think a night sitting in a cell will help restore his memory."

"Clay," she said, moving close to his face, "you don't tell them nothing. Wait till I get you a lawyer. Don't say a word. You hear me."

"Yeah," Clay said without enthusiasm.

Donna disappeared into his bedroom, returning a moment later with a large pair of sweat pants. With Ray on one side and Sue on the other, they put Clay on a kitchen chair so Donna could pull the pants on her son.

"What are you going to do now?" Donna demanded.

"We're going to take Clay in and put him in a cell. Tomorrow morning we will seek an arrest warrant."

Donna moved in front of Clay, her face a few inches from his. "Don't answer any questions. I'll have a lawyer there tomorrow morning and get you bailed out. You hear me?" she asked, her voice filled with anger and fear.

"Get a coat for him, Donna," said Ray.

She took a large Minnesota Vikings jacket off a hook near the back door and tossed it at Ray. With Sue's help they draped it over Clay's shoulders. Sue grabbed the shotgun with her free hand and they marched Clay out into the snowy night.

As they were approaching Ray's Jeep, another police vehicle pulled into the end of the drive.

"Dirk's here," said Sue. "Let's have him take Clay in."

Passing off the shotgun to Ray, Sue helped Deputy Dirk Lowther get Clay belted into the back seat of his Ford.

"Dirk," said Sue, "see if you can find out who was with Clay tonight. Be subtle, just weave the question into a conversation."

They stood for a moment and watched the vehicle disappear into the swirling snow. "Let's catch up for a minute," said Ray.

After they climbed into her Jeep, he said, "I liked the way you asked Dirk to be subtle."

"I want to know who was with Clay, but I don't want Dirk to pound it out of the kid with a Maglite." Without really discussing it, Ray knew they shared a similar view of Dirk Lowther.

Sue called the jail on her cell phone, asking them to check Clay for traces of gunpowder as soon as he was booked. She also asked for a sobriety test. Then she talked briefly with dispatch, requesting that Deputy Jamison be sent to her location.

"What do you need Jamison for?" Ray asked.

"I am going to work this scene now," she said. "I would guess the shotgun casings are in the snow, and I want to recover them before Donna comes out and tries to clean up the scene. And I need his help because you're going home. You're just off medical leave; I want you to get some sleep."

"Who's in command here?" Ray asked.

"I'll make sure there's nothing on your calendar until 1:00 p.m. With enough sleep I know you'll be in complete command," she said. She flashed him a quick smile.

"See you at noon," said Ray, as he got out of her Jeep and headed for his vehicle.

6

Although physically exhausted, the adrenaline produced during his physical confrontation with Clay Bateman still swirled in Ray's system long after he climbed into bed. Ray became aware of some tenderness in his shoulder caused by Clay's clumsily thrown punch. And there was also the nagging pain in his thigh from his recent wounds, something he could push into the background during the day, but an annoyance during the night when he struggled with insomnia.

He tried reading a long piece in the *New Yorker* but had trouble following the story, his mind preoccupied with everything that had transpired in the last few hours. He reflected on how lives can be forever changed by thoughtless actions, how adolescent boys don't seem to have the capacity to anticipate the consequences of their deeds, and what might have happened if Clay had had a deer rifle in his hands rather than a shotgun. He thought about the parents of the injured boy and then about Clay's mother, Donna. He knew she was a scrapper, doing her best to support and protect her son. But her best was probably misguided and not enough to keep Clay out of trouble this time.

And then he looked back on his own teenage years. He remembered taking risks and doing things that from an adult perspective were foolish. But those were more innocent times, he said to himself.

Ray called to mind the time he fell through the ice on the lake near his home when he was fourteen or fifteen. His father had warned him to stay off the ice, but he was in a hurry to get to a friend's house, and it was much faster to cross the lake than follow the country roads around the lake. Fortunately he was near the shore in waist deep water, and he was able to scramble back onto the ice. When he came back to the house fifteen minutes after he left, soaking wet and shivering, his father led him to the bathroom and started the shower. When he finally emerged from the steaming water, he found his bathrobe on a hook next to the shower and his wet clothes gone. The incident was never mentioned again.

He reflected on the other scrapes he got into as a teenager, like the time he skidded off a gravel road and smashed up the family car—an old, dented Ford. And then there was his first experience with too much beer and the effects of a hangover. Every time he got into a scrape, his parents helped him work through the experience without lectures or punishment. They seemed to accept the fact that he had to get into difficulty to learn about the world. And they were always ready to offer advice and counsel, but only if he asked for it. He wondered how they would have acted it he had ever gotten into real trouble.

Sometime during his musings on adolescent life, sleep had come, and he woke with a start, sunlight streaming into his bedroom. He looked over at the clock on his nightstand; it was past noon. He started to reach for the phone, to call in and say he was on his way, but he stopped and settled again. He looked at the designs made by the shadows of the half-open blinds on the wall near him. The midday sun was low on the horizon, the winter solstice being little more than a month away. Without raising his head he gazed around the room. He had spent so much time there in the past month while recovering from the serious physical and emotional wounds suffered earlier in the fall.

Somehow things seemed different this morning. He wondered if it was just the cheering effect of sunshine. He closed his eyes for a few moments and then looked around again. He was feeling different. The pain medications he had been taking after he was released from the hospital were now well washed from his system, and the almost overwhelming depression that had held him in its grip for weeks seemed to be lifting.

He climbed out of bed, hobbled off to the kitchen—the muscles of the injured leg still stiff, especially in the morning—to start the coffee. Then he headed for a shower.

Later, with a large travel mug of coffee carefully positioned on the seat next to him, Ray backed out of his garage. He locked the vehicle in four-wheel drive and descended his long, curved driveway. He stopped at the end and looked both ways; deep furrows had been cut in the still unplowed road by passing motorists.

Sudden movement in one of the snowy trenches caught his eye. He kept his foot on the brake, waiting for a cat or small dog to pass. And then the unexpected, a skunk waddling alone slid in front of him, stopped for a moment to look at him with ebony eyes, and then hurried on. A few yards beyond his drive, the animal climbed out of the track and started down a sharp ravine.

Ray watched as the skunk struggled in the deep snow, surfing down the incline in something akin to a breaststroke. He sat and observed until the Mustelidae finally disappeared in the thick underbrush.

"Omen?" he said out load. "What does it mean when a skunk crosses your path on a snowy morn?" He chuckled as he pulled onto the road and started the slow descent down the hill.

7

Gavin Mendicot III wakened cold and stiff, his head throbbing, his mouth dry and foul tasting, his bladder on the edge of bursting. The windows on his Bronco were covered with a translucent mist, the moisture from his respiration frozen to the glass.

Feet first, he clumsily slid into the driver's seat from the back of the vehicle and started the engine. Gavin scraped at the windshield with his long fingernails, eventually switching to a battered credit card he dug out of the litter on the passenger's seat. Once he had managed to clear a hole in the frost big enough so that he could navigate, he turned on the wipers and waited as a heavy layer of snow was pushed away. Then he pulled out of his parking place.

Less than a quarter of a mile down the road, he pulled into the Cottage Inn. In large letters the word EAT, highlighted by red fluorescent tubes, glowed brightly against the gray landscape. As soon as he got inside the restaurant, he headed for the men's room. After taking care of his most immediate needs, he washed his hands and face in the basin and attempted to comb his long blond hair with his fingers. He rocked close to the mirror and looked at his blood-shot eyes and rubbed his three- or four-day beard with his right hand.

On his way to an empty booth at the rear corner of the restaurant, Gavin grabbed several sections of the Free Press from the counter. He was in the middle of an optimistic opinion piece on how the Lions might make the playoffs when a waitress placed a mug of coffee in front of him and asked for his order. A few minutes later a plate of eggs, bacon, hash browns, and toast was pushed in front of him, and Gavin momentarily gave up reading as he started to devour his breakfast. As he focused on the food, he tried to remember his last real meal.

Gavin peered across the restaurant. First he noticed the hair— in a military style, close-cut, salt and pepper; then the uniform, the brown of the sheriff's department. He watched as the man pulled on his winter jacket, a heavy nylon affair, in a slightly lighter shade of brown than his shirt. Gavin could see the deputy's head in profile as he chatted with the woman at the cash register. Then, as the man turned toward the door, Gavin could see him clearly. It was a face that had been burned into his memory years before.

The waitress, a large, taciturn woman, laid his check on the table after filling his coffee cup a third time. He tossed a ten on the table when he left, not bothering to take his bill to the register.

Gavin had anticipated some kind of confrontation on his return from his hunting trip. His departure from the home of his girlfriend, Donna Bateman, had not been a peaceful one. The tensions had been building, most of them caused by her son, Clay. Gavin knew the kid resented his mother sharing her bedroom, but he rationalized that the kid might as well get used to the ways of the world.

Gavin thought about buying a bottle before he confronted Donna, but decided against it. He would need his wits about him in this face-off. Donna was smart and always seemed to argue better than he did.

He could feel his anxiety rising when he turned onto White Oak Trail. He pulled into Donna's drive, parking behind her truck.

And as he walked toward the door, he considered what he was going to say, how he was going to handle the situation. He knew what he had seen at the Last Chance. Now he had to figure out what to do about it.

Gavin stopped at the front door. This was the place he had been living on and off for the last eight months, but for some reason he felt compelled to knock. When Donna opened the door, she seemed stunned to see him.

"You," she said in an accusatorial tone.

"Who were you expecting?" Gavin responded, thinking he should go on the offensive. "Maybe a visit from the sheriff. Pick up where you left off?"

"It's because of you the sheriffs were here," she responded angrily. "You and that old shotgun...."

"I stopped in to see you last night and...."

"What are you talking about?" Donna demanded.

"Last night. I was going to surprise you. Pulled in after closing, but it looked like you were taking care of some business," Gavin said, thinking that he had her trapped.

"Yeah," she said, her anger palpable. "They came to tell me that my son was involved in a shooting. That he was going to jail." After a pause, she said, "What did you think was going on?" Donna followed quickly with, "You dumb shit. I know what you were thinking. Look, Clay was playing with one of your guns. He shot at a car with some other teenagers in it. He's in jail. And I think the police are looking to have a little chat with you too, asshole."

"What are you talking about?" Gavin demanded.

"The guns, your guns. The ones in the pole barn."

"I had them locked in a steel box," he countered defensively.

"Well genius, you didn't have it locked up very securely."

"So what happened?"

"Some kids from Sand River blew up our mailbox. Clay was going to scare them with a gun of yours. He didn't know it was loaded. It was an accident. Some damn kid got hit."

"Loaded," protested Gavin. "It wasn't loaded."

"Yes, it was, and it's all your fault, asshole," Donna yelled at him. "And now I want you out of here. Just take your things and go. I don't want you here any more. And take all the fucking guns you got locked up in the safe in the pole barn with you."

"You want me to take that deer rifle, the one I bought you last year, too?" Gavin asked, thinking that he'd like to have the gun back.

"No, leave it. It was a gift. It's mine. I can hock it or use it on your sorry ass if you come sniffing around." She paused briefly, "And before you go, I want some money."

"I don't have any money," he said.

"You lying sack of shit. If you don't have any, ask your keepers. I'm sure you can get some."

"How much you need?"

"Two grand for openers. That's what the lawyer wants as a retainer. I'll need more later."

"The kid that was shot...?"

"He was just nicked. The little bastard probably deserved it. Now I want you gone. Get your stuff, anything I find is going out in the trash." She directed him toward the bedroom they had been sharing.

Gavin tossed the few clothes and other possessions that he had been keeping at Donna's in a couple of garbage bags. As he was leaving, she stopped him at the door, moving into his space, her body almost touching his. "Bring me a check. At the Last Chance. I don't want you here again. Ever. Understand?"

Gavin pushed past her without answering. He tossed the bags in the back of the Bronco and climbed behind the wheel. He looked back toward the house; Donna was standing outside, holding a cigarette and glaring at him.

"I'll get even with you, bitch," he mouthed in her direction before backing out of the drive.

8

Ray was not surprised to find Maggie Engle, the superintendent of the Cedar Bay Schools, waiting for him at his office when he finally arrived a few minutes after 1:00 p.m. Over the last few years, since he had moved back to the area and been elected sheriff, he and Maggie had been in constant contact. She initiated most of their meetings. Not that Maggie ever wasted his time, but she was on the phone or making a personal visit to his office any occasion when the safety or welfare of one of the district's students was in question.

Maggie had arrived in Cedar Bay twenty years earlier, coming to the area with her husband, many years her senior, who had just retired from Columbia University. His roots were in the region, and he was delighted to be returning to the family farm to tinker with raising grapes and apples. Maggie, however, while not completely immune to the bucolic pleasures of rural life, was bored and restless. She was a fish out of water: Jewish, a devoted city dweller, a regular at the opera, symphony, and museums. She liked strong black coffee; short, thin cigars; and reading the *New York Times* the morning it was published, something that was not possible in Northern Michigan in the mid 1980s.

So when the chemistry teacher at Cedar Bay High fell ill and retired unexpectedly, Maggie was delighted to be back in the classroom, even if students weren't as intellectually aggressive, urbane, and diverse as the kids she had taught during her tenure at Horace Mann.

That first semester she thought she'd only teach until the district found a replacement. They didn't. In fact, the board and subsequent boards—farmers, owners of small businesses, housewives, and an occasional professional—quickly understood what a treasure Maggie was. Not that she didn't ruffle feathers and challenge local values, which was something she did almost daily. But her skill as a teacher, and then a principal, and then the superintendent—the administrative positions thrust upon her by the board and community—reflected their appreciation for the transformation she brought to the schools.

Maggie believed with few exceptions every kid could go to college and that opportunity and mobility came through education. And as principal of the high school, and later as the superintendent, she recruited the best teachers she could find to replace an aging faculty.

She all but eliminated the district's dropout problem; more than a few parents were surprised to find her at their door demanding to know why their sons and daughters were not at school. She was brave, direct, and unflappable. And she didn't hesitate to use law enforcement if she thought any of "her kids" needed protection or, her phrase, "enforced enlightenment."

Under her guidance most kids who graduated from Cedar Bay went to college. If they needed financial support, she and her staff would help them find scholarships and grants. And Maggie would follow up on the grads, providing additional assistance and encouragement when it was required. The college matriculation rate of the district's graduates looked more like that of a fairly tony suburban school than that of a small, class "D" rural school.

"Hey," Maggie said, her voice gravelly from years of heavy smoking, "Late start today. I thought crime never sleeps."

"Up here in the woods it occasionally naps. What can I do for you?"

"What's happening with Clay? What's he been charged with?"

"Initially he will probably be overcharged—assault with intent to commit murder. Who knows what he'll end up with— possession of a firearm while intoxicated, reckless use of a firearm, minor in...."

"Then what?" Maggie asked.

"Can't tell you for sure. But I can say with great confidence that Clay is going to get more than a slap on the wrist. But he's lucky it isn't an election year. Right now the prosecutor, John Tyrrell, won't need to go for the maximum to show he's tough on crime."

"How long are you going to keep Clay?"

"He may be out on bail later today."

"So he could be in school tomorrow?" she asked, rhetorically, her grey eyes locked on Ray's. He knew the high school kids called her the owl, and the name fit. Her thick, gray-black hair surrounded her face, and the black-rimmed glasses perched on her stubby nose magnified her unusually large eyes.

"Do I let him go back to...?" she stopped.

Ray remained silent, allowing her to muse over her question.

"Maybe I should have him go to the alternative program for a few weeks, at least until Thanksgiving," she said more to herself than to Ray.

"Tell me about Clay, what kind of kid is he?" Ray asked.

"He's not a bad kid, but he's incredibly lazy. We're constantly monitoring his progress, trying to keep him focused. It's been a bit easier in the fall because he needs to keep his grades up to play football."

"Is he a good player?"

"Coach Fronz says Clay could be if he worked at it. He's big and strong, but Fronz says he never really gets in shape, he's always carrying a gut and doesn't spend enough time in the weight room."

"So he's not too good?"

"Fronz says Clay has great physicality," Maggie paused for a moment. "I have no idea what that means. Physicality," she repeated the word, carefully enunciating each syllable. "Fronz also says that if he could find a log as big as Clay, he'd play the log. He'd always know where the log was. He never can count on Clay. The kid doesn't seem to follow the play or keep his blocking assignment.

"I've heard from some of the students that Clay was partying with a couple of friends," Maggie continued.

"Yes," Ray responded. "I think we will be able to identify them. Perhaps, that has happened already."

"How about dope?" she asked.

"Wouldn't be surprised."

"It's part of the ritual, isn't it," Maggie said. "They drink some beer, smoke some grass. It's the complete evening. I can't control what they do away from school, but I want to be damn sure it's not being sold or used at school. I'm passionate about that."

"I know you are," said Ray. "You're vigilant, and you're very close to the students. You do a wonderful job with that problem."

"I do my best," she shot back, "but there are so many ways kids can screw up their lives. And kids like Clay, they just don't get it. They don't understand that there are consequences for their actions.

"Donna, Clay's mother, she was one of my special projects early in my tenure here. And the fruit didn't fall far from the tree. She had so much promise, but…" she stopped and looked at Ray. "You ever miss smoking?"

"Tobacco?"

"Yes, of course."

"Sometimes," he responded.

"Yeah, me too," she said. "It's almost an essential part of a good bitch session. Some smokes, some black coffee, some profanity—you feel so much better after. A real catharsis. And now

I do my damnedest to make sure kids don't touch the rotten stuff. It's a different day."

"And the football game?"

"Fronz and the AD at Sand River worked everything out with the league. We're canceling the game and trying to send a message that there are things more important than football. Unfortunately, all the kids get penalized for the actions of a few." Maggie paused for a long moment and took a sip of coffee. "What a mess. Maybe I'm getting too old for this."

"How have the parents and students reacted?"

"For the kids, this has been a shocker. It's sort of like when Pete Dekker ran his car off the road and hit the tree the night before graduation a few years back. This is real. A few of the ball players, especially the seniors, are very disappointed. And I appreciate their feelings, but almost everyone understands how this event is bigger than any game. Fronz has had a few angry calls, but most of the players, parents, and the community are very supportive. You were in education for many years, you know about teachable moments," she paused briefly. "We're having a staff meeting this afternoon to talk about how we can try to make something good come from this mess."

Maggie got up and gathered her newspaper, "Hey, gotta run." She stopped for a moment in the doorway and looked back at Ray. "We do what we can, all of us. Sometimes it's just not enough."

Ray nodded his agreement.

9

"How's Maggie?" said Sue Lawrence, entering the office a few seconds later.

"Passionate, as always," Ray responded. "And upset. And wanting to make something good come from something bad."

"She's an amazing woman; that's who I want to be when I grow up." Sue paused, her tone changed. "Did you get some sleep?"

"More than most nights. You?" he inquired.

"I'll catch up tonight."

"What did I miss?" asked Ray.

"Lots," Sue responded.

"Are you going to tell me about it or just give me that Cheshire cat grin?"

"First, the crime scene. We found two spent shells buried in the snow. Sure glad we bought that metal detector. They were tossed in the ditch at the side of the road. And Clay's blood alcohol was 0.15, and his hands and arms were covered with gunpowder residue. You know," Sue said, "he didn't act too drunk; the kid can hold his alcohol."

"He's got a lot of bulk to absorb it. And the other kids?"

"Dirk got the names. And he gave them to me when I got back. I waited till 5:00 a.m. before I called the parents. They live in the village. Both sets of parents came in, each with a scared kid in tow."

"What did you learn?"

"I had an informal interview with each boy, their mom and dad sitting at the table with them. The gravity of the situation really hit when I told them about the injured boy from Sand River. I questioned Drew Chappone first. He readily admitted to being at Clay's. He says he drank too much and fell asleep. His buddy Zack drove him home, dropped him on the front porch, rang the bell, and took off. That's how his parents found him. So he was already in a lot of trouble with them before he got here."

"Does he have any priors?"

"None," said Sue. "He seems like a nice kid with two very concerned parents. He was in the wrong place at the wrong time."

"Who's the other kid?"

"Zack Jacobik. He was a bit more edgy and defensive than Drew, and his parents looked like they were ready to kill him."

"What did you learn?"

"He substantiated Drew's story. They went over to Clay's after football practice, both boys had told their parents they were studying for a chemistry test. They ate pizza and drank beer. Then they watched a Rambo film. Sometime during the film, Zack didn't remember when, Drew fell asleep."

"How about drugs?"

"Zack was a bit elusive about it. Finally his father said, 'Tell the lady what you know.' Dad's got a great gravelly voice; he sounds like Brando in The Godfather. Zack admitted they had shared one joint, but even when pressed he wasn't about to tell me the source. I let that go, I was more interested in getting his version of what happened."

"And his version?"

"Like I said, they were partying and watching a movie. Suddenly Clay was running out of the house with a gun, there was an explosion, and Clay was out in the road waving the gun. This car almost ran over him, and he fired at it as it drove away."

"How many shots?"

"Zack only remembers one. Clay probably pulled both triggers at the same time. Zack initially said he didn't think Clay was shooting at the car. He thought Clay was shooting over it. But when I pressed him on that point, he wasn't sure."

"Did you ask him about the vandalism last weekend in Sand River?"

"Yes. At first he said he didn't know anything about any vandalism, but again his father admonished him to tell the truth. He said the three of them painted the sidewalk in front of the school, did some spray painting at the stadium, and blew up a few mailboxes. His memory seemed to fail him on the actual number."

"Anything more?"

"With his parents' permission we checked him for gunpowder residue; there was none."

"And then what?"

"We sent both kids home with their parents. I told both sets of parents that we would be in touch. And it's interesting, they each thanked me as if I had done something important for their kid, the anger was directed at their sons, not at me, not at the police. But that situation didn't last long."

"How so?"

"No sooner had they left than Donna Bateman arrived with Mr. Smiles, the friend of all victims of police brutality."

"How was he today?"

"A real poster-boy for Vitalis, Aqua Velva, and the blinding effect of bleached white teeth. I was afraid he was going to kiss my hand. That dude gives sharkskin suits a bad name. And I think he was wearing the last pair of spit-polished wingtips in the north."

"Enough," interrupted Ray. "Just tell me what happened?"

"I took them into the interview room and asked that Clay be brought down. In the few minutes we had before he arrived, I told them we had the weapon, matching finger prints, the brass, and Clay's hands and arms were covered with gunpowder residue."

"His reaction," pressed Ray.

"I think he's beginning to mellow. He didn't fall into his usual tough-guy persona. He let me interview Clay with few interruptions. Donna was more of a problem."

"And Clay's story?"

"His account was remarkably like Zack's until we got to the part with the gun. First he said he didn't know it was loaded; he contended that he only took it out to scare the kids in the car, but when they tried to run him down he used it in self-defense. When I pointed out that the vehicle was hit from the rear, he changed his story, saying the gun went off accidentally. And that might have been caused by Zack trying to pull it out of his hands. When I mentioned that we didn't find any powder residue on Zack, Clay said everything happened so fast, that Zack might have caused the accidental firing but wasn't next to him when it actually fired."

"Sounds like he had enough beer not to be clear on anything, and then he's also trying to cover his ass."

"That's my take. And I don't think Clay would hesitate to move the blame to his friend Zack if he could think of a way of doing it," Sue observed. "Anyway, my report is typed up, and the transcripts of the interviews are being keyed. They should be available for you to review later this afternoon."

"Thank you for doing this," said Ray, feeling a bit guilty that he had gone home to bed and left Sue to complete the investigation. "One question. How do you know about Vitalis and Aqua Velva, those old-time brands?"

"Isn't that what you use?" she asked, giving Ray a wry smile.

10

~~~~~

Ray pulled off the highway and followed the long two-track drive back to an old family cottage on the Lake Michigan shore. His friends Marc and Lisa lived there and had been remodeling and modernizing the place in the years since they ran away from their careers and moved to the woods.

Ray had called earlier, saying he was behind schedule, which was often the case when he was invited for dinner. And since Marc, the one who did the cooking, was always running late with his culinary experiments, Ray's pattern of belated arrivals seemed fortuitous rather than an irritation. Ray parked near a small SUV covered with a thin dusting of fresh snow that stood near the back door of the cottage.

Without knocking, Ray entered through the door into the small mudroom at the rear of the kitchen. Like most of the old cottages, the more formal entrance, the one that opened to the living room, was at the front of the house on the lakeside, seldom used during much of the year. He hung his coat on one of the wooden pegs that lined the back wall of the room and opened a second door into the kitchen.

"Ray's here," announced Marc, working at a chopping block at the side of the stove.

Lisa and Sarah James came to greet him. Lisa—thin and athletic, dressed in her usual uniform of jeans, a navy t-shirt, and one of Marc's chambray shirts, worn out and hanging like a jacket—slid under his right arm for a quick embrace.

Sarah followed, in a black sweater and skirt, her work clothes, the dress of a private school administrator. Her embrace was slower, softer, and extended. Ray held her for a long moment, enjoying the intimacy. He had been looking forward to seeing her all day.

Sarah was a recent acquaintance. He had met her earlier in the fall, within hours of beginning the murder investigation of a young faculty member from Leiston School and her lover, an event that had profoundly shaken his life. During the course of the investigation he was in almost daily contact with Sarah. And after he had been seriously wounded, she was a frequent visitor at his hospital bedside and later at home when he was recuperating.

"What took you so long?" Marc asked, briefly looking up from his work.

"Phone calls," Ray answered. "I was just trying to respond to any message that looked urgent before the beginning of the weekend."

"Well, the women are way ahead of you. They've already gone through part of a bottle of that lovely wine you dropped by yesterday. I imagine you're curious about the menu."

"I can smell the lamb," Ray said. "What's the rest of the fare?"

"A medley of locally grown root vegetables, slowly roasted in olive oil and sprinkled with sea salt. A salad of mixed greens with walnuts and dried cherries, and an apple tart." Ray leaned against a counter, watching the two women in a lively conversation and his friend Marc putting the finishing touches on dinner. He felt much of the tension for the last few days beginning to drain away.

"There is also this peasant bread," said Marc, lofting a large loaf like a football. "I've been trying to turn a large Dutch oven into a steamy environment where I can bake crusty bread."

"How did it work out?"

"You be the judge."

With little further conversation, Lisa guided the four of them to the table.

"Did you know Lisa was an alum of Leiston?" asked Ray, a few minutes into the meal.

"She was telling me that before you arrived," responded Sarah.

"But I don't quite understand what your role at the school is now?" Lisa asked, looking at Sarah.

"After the horrible events involving the headmaster's wife, the board decided that it would be best for Dr. Warrington to leave. At first they were going to let him finish the semester, but some of the board members just wanted him out of there. So they bought his contract.

"I ran the business operations at the school for four years, that's my background. What I know about education, especially private school education, I've learned working at Leiston. But the board is comfortable with me running the school for the remainder of year. They are forming a search committee and hope to have a new headmaster in place for the next school year. At their last meeting they named Harrison Davids, our veteran social science teacher, to be acting academic dean. He's been released from half of his teaching duties to handle the academic side of the administration, the things Ian used to do."

"So does that make you the headmistress?" quipped Marc.

"It's okay to kick him under the table," said Lisa. "I do it all the time."

"Wonderful meal, Marc, thank you," said Ray. "And the bread is a noble experiment."

"Does that mean it was successful?"

"Absolutely. The crust is equal to the kind you get with a steam injection oven." Ray looked over at Marc and Lisa. "Thank you for all of this. It's a wonderful transition into the weekend after a difficult week."

"We had a sense of that," said Lisa. "And those kids we saw on the news…."

"Now it's my turn to do the kicking," said Marc, cutting Lisa off. He looked across at Sarah. "We, the three of us, for the last several years have had dinner together at least once a week. And I always get Lisa to promise that she's going to leave Ray alone, no work-related questions. She's not going to ask about what she's seen on the news or read in the paper. And she's made good progress. This evening I was so impressed that she didn't start her questions as soon as Ray came through the door."

"Have they been in trouble before?" Lisa finished her question.

"No," answered Ray. "Not even a traffic ticket. That's unusual for three teenage boys. These guys have never been on our radar. Unhappily, we've got some kids their age who already have substantial criminal records."

"The kids in serious trouble, the ones with the criminal records, at what age do you start seeing them?" Marc probed.

"Usually they're in middle school before they do anything bad enough to involve law enforcement. In most cases it's boys who are in trouble, although in recent years we've started to see girls, too. And I often hear from neighbors and teachers about these kids after the fact. They tell me they could see problems early on, often when they were six or seven."

"Do you think that's true or just talk?" ask Lisa.

"It's probably true. The literature supports that a certain percentage of the prison population exhibited very negative personality traits during childhood. But these kids, the three local boys who were involved in the incident the other night, they have no previous run-ins with law enforcement. Two of them come from solid families. The kid who is in real trouble, the one who did the shooting, his home life is less than ideal. His father died when he was an infant. His mother works nights, and the kid is free to roam."

"So what's going to happen to him?" asked Lisa.

"I'm not sure how the prosecutor is going to play this."

"You don't have any kids like this at Leiston?" said Lisa in a slightly mocking tone, looking over at Sarah.

"Not at the moment," Sarah responded, everyone at the table well aware of the irony of her response, given the recent events. "We do our best to screen out kids with serious behavioral problems, not that we always succeed."

"Rifle season starts next week," Marc said to Ray. "Are we going to restore some old traditions this year?"

Ray chuckled and addressed the two women. "He does this every year. Reminds me that my dad and his grandfather were deer hunting buddies."

"Well, are you?" ask Sarah.

"When I was a kid, hunting and fishing provided most of our meat," said Ray. "My father worked a lot of odd jobs, mostly during the summer, and they were few and far between in the winter."

"And one of the things Ray's father did," continued Marc, "was accompany my grandfather deer hunting, even when he was very elderly. Ray's father was a skilled hunter and made sure my grandfather had a good chance at getting a buck. He also made sure Grandfather got home safely."

"So every year," said Ray, picking up his part of the conversation again, "Marc asks when we're going to restore that old tradition, that bond of the hunting brotherhood. In truth, I don't think either one of us is nostalgic for the joys of deer camp."

"Is deer hunting still a big thing around here? I've been isolated from what goes on by living on campus," Sarah noted.

"It's a big part of the region's economy, but not as much in this area. There's been so much development since we were boys. We don't get the hunters like we used to. I think most of the dyed-in-the-wool hunters want to go somewhere that's more remote, like the tip of the mitt or the U.P. That said, many of the locals still hunt deer. Some of the farmers get their buck right on their own property. But we'll still see a lot of hunters when rifle season starts in a few weeks."

The conversation moved to lighter topics as coffee and dessert were served.

"This tart is wonderful," remarked Sarah.

"Marc really hit it," said Lisa. "He spent one fall perfecting it. He experimented with different apples and recipes for the custards and crusts. I think I gained about five pounds while he was trying to find the perfect combination. But the final result...." She looked across the table at Marc. Ray noted the affection in her smile. He admired their joy in being a couple.

"I hate to break up the party," said Ray. "But I'm starting to fade."

"Understood," said Lisa, rising from the table.

After clearing dishes, glasses, and silver to the counter and the hugs and goodbyes, Ray and Sarah walked into the cold winter evening. After Ray helped her brush the snow off her vehicle, she caught him in an embrace.

"I have someone covering for me at school. I'm not expected back at Leiston tonight. In fact, I could be gone all weekend."

Ray pulled her close and kissed her gently. "That would be wonderful."

11

Ray didn't go into the office on the weekend, a rare event. And on Monday morning his arrival there was a few minutes after eight, late by his standards. He and Sarah had had an early breakfast and then lingered a bit too long over coffee—trying to hold onto the happiness they had shared the past two days—before hurrying off to their respective jobs.

Ray had barely attacked the waiting pile of paperwork when he was interrupted for the first time. Jan, his secretary, who also shared duties as the department's receptionist, called to ask if he could be interrupted. Lynne Boyd, a local TV anchor, was here to see him. He peered at the work in front of him, and then told her to send Lynne in.

Ray was always surprised when he saw Lynne Boyd face-to-face. In real life she looked quite different from the face he occasionally saw at six and eleven on the local news. Without the makeup and TV lights, Lynne was a bit less glamorous, but Ray liked her unadorned look. In person she was more animated and expressive; she used her hands, body, and face as she communicated. He always found Lynne effusive, genial, and very pleasant.

"Hi, Ray," she said, her voice warm and resonant. "Your gatekeeper said you weren't to be disturbed."

"Obviously you charmed your way past her. I see you're going to be a hunting widow in a few weeks," Ray said holding an Away From Duty form up for Lynne to see.

"Dirk's annual Thanksgiving trek to the woods with his brother and some friends."

"In the U.P." said Ray looking at the form.

"They've got a big old dilapidated log cabin in the woods near Seney. I've been there a couple of times in the summer—swamps, woods, mosquitoes, black flies, and an occasional black bear rummaging for food—not my cup of tea."

"What can I do for you?" asked Ray, changing the subject.

"Mind if I shut the door?" she asked.

"Go ahead," Ray responded.

Lynne pulled a chair close to his desk and sorted through a large designer bag. She pulled out a small pack of envelopes held together by a rubber band and set it on the desk in front of Ray. "These came in the last few days. I've never had anything quite like this before."

"How so?" Ray asked, peering at the envelopes. Then he reached into a desk drawer and extracted a pair of latex gloves from a cardboard carton. As he pulled them on, he waited for her answer. Lynne seemed lost in her own thoughts, like she was considering her response. She hooked some of her long blond hair between her thumb and index finger and brushed it away from the right side of her face.

"I was going to say that I'd never gotten a death threat before, but that's not quite true." She gave Ray a knowing glance. He remembered their first meeting; Lynne was being stalked by Jesse Buehle, a college boyfriend who had flipped out when Lynne broke up with him when she first took the anchor job at the local TV station. The stalking had gone on for months before Lynne finally came to Ray and asked for help, and then only after she had become acquainted with him over the course of several news conferences and interviews. Ray had guided her through the court system to get the proper legal safeguards in place and then put her in contact with Charlene Stoddard, an ex-nun who ran the local women's resource center. Lynne moved into a safe house owned by the group, and seldom traveled alone.

But just as Ray thought the problem was contained, the situation spun tragically out of control late one snowy evening when Lynne was driving home from the station alone. Buehle rammed her car and forced her off the road. The officer responding to her frantic 911 call, Dirk Lowther, confronted the stalker, who by that time had smashed the passenger-side window of her car, unlocked the door, and was in the process of trying to pull her from the vehicle.

In the ensuing battle, first to free Lynne from her assailant, and then to suppress and cuff him, Lowther's side arm was fired. Lowther later testified that Buehle had managed to pull the weapon from its holster, and the pistol had gone off as he struggled to regain control of it. Moments later Buehle was dead from a single shot that had pierced his heart.

In the subsequent investigation of the shooting, conducted by the prosecuting attorney of a neighboring county, Lowther was exonerated and found to be acting within the guidelines of the department. But Ray was always a bit bothered by the incident, not that he could find anything in the final report that suggested Lowther had deviated from department procedures.

But then Ray had never been comfortable with Lowther, one of the officers he had inherited from the previous sheriff who had staffed the department with relatives and cronies. In the first couple of years of his administration, Ray had done his best to counsel most of the veteran officers into early retirement or other careers. But he couldn't retire or fire everyone as he rebuilt the department with younger, better-trained officers. He looked on Lowther as the best of the worst, someone he could put up with if he had to.

That said, Ray felt Lowther possessed most of the negative characteristics often ascribed to law enforcement by its critics.

Lowther was arrogant, often hostile, and ruthless. His politics seemed to be a weird blend of conspiracy theories and long-standing prejudices. He preferred working the third shift, 11:00 p.m. to 7:00 a.m. And Ray was happy with that arrangement. The long nights on road patrol in a rural area meant that Lowther would have little contact with the public, keeping possible problems to a minimum.

Lowther—tall, muscular, with a rough-hewn profile and thick salt and pepper hair and mustache—was a good-looking man. And Ray knew many women found him rather charming, at least initially. He was also a braggart and a notorious womanizer, with several marriages and numerous girl friends in his past. Shortly after the shooting incident, Ray was surprised to learn that Lowther was dating Lynne Boyd. Ray thought she must be at least twenty years younger than Lowther, and he couldn't imagine that they had much in common. He was even more surprised when he learned that they had wed, the nuptials following the shooting by only a few months.

"And these letters, it's not only the threats. It's…" Lynne paused a long moment and then continued. "Well, look at them. I think you will know what I mean."

Ray removed the rubber band holding the letters together. He carefully examined the top envelope and then noted the others. They were all standard size white business envelopes, all addressed using a poor-quality inkjet printer.

He removed the first letter. The text was composed of letters and words cut from newspapers and magazines. The note was obscene, threatening, and violent. Ray looked at the rest of the letters. As he worked his way through them, he saw that they were all constructed in the same way, assorted print pasted haphazardly and then Xeroxed. The messages were all variations on the same theme. While the writer's meaning was clear, Ray was struck by the almost childlike quality of the letters.

"Well," he said, "I understand your concern." He looked at the postmarks. "So these have all come in the last few days?"

"Yes. The first one I sort of laughed off. But when they kept coming I became rather frightened." As she was talking, her phone chirped. She looked at the screen and then back at Ray without answering the call.

"The writer seems to be referencing something you did on gun control?"

"I did a series a few weeks ago on gun deaths in America involving children and adolescents. It was in five parts and ran each day during the news at 6:00 and 11:00. Do you know what I'm talking about? Have you seen any of these?"

"Lynne, I hate to admit it, but lately I haven't seen much television. I'm seldom home before 7:00 and by 11:00 I'm reading or sleeping."

"Let me explain, then," said Lynne. "The series followed the same format that I've used for several years on our special issues section. I'll develop a topic over a week or two to provide a more in-depth report on a matter that is currently of interest to our viewers." She paused, held Ray in her gaze, and then continued, "Like after the migratory bird die-off in October along the Lake Michigan shore; I did a series on invasive species and how they affect our local ecology. In August I did two weeks on global warming."

Again her phone chirped.

"Do you need to take a call?" Ray asked.

"No," she responded, after looking at the ID of the caller.

"These other series, did they produce any threatening letters?"

"No. In fact I seldom get letters, letters like that, snail mail," she motioned toward the stack of envelopes. "Who writes letters? I get lots of e-mails and a few phone calls."

"Threatening, obscene?"

"Never. After the global warming piece I received a few e-mails that were fairly hostile. I was accused of being part of the liberal press that peddles junk science. One writer said I was an 'Al

Gore, Michael Moore fellow traveler,' whatever that is. Like I said, hostile but not obscene."

"Since the letters seem to address this last series you did, can you tell me about it? Was there something that might have set this person off?" Ray asked.

Lynne pondered the question before she started to answer. "Like I said, it was on gun deaths in children and adolescents. We've had three tragic deaths like this in our viewing area in the last six months. In each case the guns were left around the house where the child could easily get their hands on them; they weren't locked up. I researched this topic on the web, most of my data came from the Centers for Disease Control and various medical groups. I also provided some comparisons between the U.S. and other industrial countries."

She stopped for a moment and looked directly into Ray's eyes. "I am passionate about this subject, but I was doing my best to let the numbers do the talking and not do any preaching. The last couple of segments of the series dealt with gun safety, things like trigger locks and storage safes. My thesis for the whole series was that if adults acted responsibly and kept guns under lock and key, we could really do something about this problem." She paused briefly. "That tragic wounding of the high school kid from Sand River ...." She let her sentence hang.

Ray nodded his agreement. "And you got these letters," Ray responded. "Anything else?"

"Like I said, lots of e-mails, most were very positive. Then there were a few from NRA types. You know, the kind of people who get upset if you mention guns and laws in the same sentence. They don't listen to what you're saying; they just send you some of that old, tired propaganda. 'Guns don't kill, people do,' and that other one about outlaws ending up with all the guns."

"Have you shared these with your husband?"

"I don't want Dirk to know about them. It would only make things worse."

Ray didn't respond. He held Lynne in his gaze and waited.

"Most marriages have some rough times," Lynne finally said.

Ray watched a wave of emotion sweep across her face. He wasn't sure if it was fear or sadness, or a combination of the two.

"We're not going to be together much longer." She paused for a long moment, then continued, "He seems to care about the twins; he's good to them and occasionally spends time with them. But he's not happy with me." Another long pause followed. Lynne played with a strand of hair. "He's been very upset with me, especially since I've started seeing a psychiatrist. Dirk accused me of having an affair with…."

"The psychiatrist?" Ray finally asked.

"He's a lovely older man. He's in his late sixties, but Dirk won't let go of it. He also complains about the au pair."

"What's the problem there?"

"He doesn't like the idea. Says people should raise their own kids, not that we could both work without this kind of help. And he doesn't like the au pair we currently have, Marie. She's a lovely young Frenchwoman who has just graduated from college. She wanted to live in the States for a year and work on her English before she started graduate school in international business. I think she's a real find. The twins are four, what a great time to start them learning a second language. They're having so much fun with French. But Dirk hates France or anything French. And Marie is smart and sophisticated; when Dirk has tried to flirt with her, she's just put him down. He's not used to that. So she's one more thing he's angry about."

"You don't think Dirk sent these."

"Can you imagine him taking the time to cut all those letters out?"

"I just needed to ask. I would like to send these to the State Police lab, perhaps they can find some prints or something else that might lead us to the sender. We'll need a set of your prints, also. We use a kind of scanner now, it will just take a few minutes."

"No problem," Lynne responded.

"What can be done to increase your security?"

"I've already talked that over with the station manager. In fact, I would not be here if he hadn't insisted on it. I can ask for a driver if I feel one is needed. And when the kids need to be chauffeured, I'll let Marie do most of that. But I don't want Dirk to know."

"That makes things difficult for me. If I can't make people aware of these threats and ask them to be especially vigilant...."

"Sheriff, can I call you Ray?"

"Of course."

"Send the letters to the State Police lab, but don't do anything else, please. I promise to be very cautious. Look at those letters. The guy is a crackpot, probably a middle school kid."

"Crackpots can be very dangerous," Ray responded with some obvious irony that wasn't lost on Lynne.

"Please, just send the letters." Lynne pleaded.

"I'll share these letters with Sue and have her send the letters to the lab. We will respond quickly if we find anything. It's very important that you let me know if you see anything unusual or suspicious. Will you promise to do that?"

"Yes," she responded.

"Are you afraid of Dirk?" he pressed.

"No, not really. He has a lot of anger, but he has never been physical with me. I don't think it would ever come to that."

"But you're not sure?" Ray asked.

"I'm not alone, Ray. Marie is there all the time. And I don't think Dirk would hurt me." Lynne's phone chirped a third time; she looked at the display. "Listen, the station is trying to reach me, something must be going on. I better run. Thank you for your time," she said, getting out of her chair and gathering up her purse.

Ray stood and took her extended hand. "Please keep me in the loop."

"I will," Lynne responded. "I promise."

Ray watched her depart, then settled back into his chair. He had a sense of uneasiness as he started to read through the letters a second time.

"Ray, sorry to disturb you again," came Lynne's voice from the open door. "I just wanted you to meet Marie Guttard, our au pair. Marie, this is Sheriff Ray Elkins."

Ray came around his desk and accepted Marie's extended hand. She was his height, or perhaps slightly taller, very slim, but muscular, with unnaturally reddish hair in a stylish cut. "Welcome to our community," he said, noting the strength in her handshake and her alert, intelligent manner. He wondered how much of a culture shock Marie was experiencing in rural Michigan.

"Thank you. I am happy to be here. It is very beautiful."

"We'll let you get back to work," announced Lynne. "I just thought it would be good if you met Marie."

"Yes. Thank you for bringing her in. Good to meet you, Marie." Ray fished for an appropriate phrase from his college French, but couldn't quickly retrieve one.

"Goodbye," called Marie, as Lynne led her away.

12

~~~~~~~~

Donna Bateman rammed the Chevy pickup down the unplowed two-track, the rear wheels spinning in the deep snow. She finally brought the vehicle to a halt where a heavy cable strung between two steel posts blocked the road.

She reached behind the seat and retrieved a gun case and a box of shells. "Come on," she demanded in an irritated tone.

"But Mom, I promised the judge I wouldn't get near a gun. You were standing right next to me in the courtroom. I don't wanna get my ass thrown in jail."

"Clay, just shut up and do what I tell you. I've got the gun, not you. Besides, who will see us out here? Bring that bag of beer cans."

"Why are we doing this," he asked as he tagged along after her. "You were totally pissed when Gavin gave you that gun. You told me he should have got you something nice, not a goddamn deer rifle. Why do you want to learn how to shoot it?" he asked, following her into the abandoned gravel pit.

"Gavin is crazy as hell. I may have to use it on that son-of-a-bitch if he comes bothering us. The trouble he got you into leaving that shotgun around."

"Shit, it wasn't his…."

"And maybe I'll take up hunting."

"You're going fucking weird."

"Stand those cans out there on that bank," she ordered. When Clay returned to her side, she had the rifle out of the case. "How do you load this damn thing, anyway?"

Clay released a clip from the rifle and held it out. "You've got to load this first," he explained, handing the rifle back and taking a box of shells from her other hand. He filled the clip and then demonstrated how it slipped into the rifle."

"Can I shoot now?" Donna asked.

"No, you've got to get the first bullet into the chamber. Push that rod back and let go. Good, now you are ready. Look through that sight. Is it in focus?"

"Pretty good."

"Get the crosshairs on one of the cans and release the safety." Clay guided her hand, and she pulled the safety off. "Pull the stock against your shoulder and gently squeeze the trigger."

Donna jumped at the sound of the explosion. She rubbed her shoulder with her left hand. "Damn. That hurt like hell," she said.

"You need to pull the gun tighter to your shoulder."

"Did I hit anything?"

"Yeah, Mom. You got some snow. Here, let me show you." Clay took the rifle from her hands, slid his left arm through the sling, stopped momentarily to alter its length, raised the rifle to his shoulder, and adjusted the telescopic sight. "God are you stupid, you didn't put the safety back on. The gun could have gone off when you were handing it to me."

"Shut up and shoot."

Clay pulled the trigger; one of the cans went tumbling off into the snow. He pushed the safety on and handed the gun back to his mother.

"You didn't tell me about this strap," she said. Clay helped her adjust the sling.

"Pull it tight to your shoulder," he instructed, "and take the safety off."

"Did I hit anything?" Donna demanded as she recovered from the kick of the rifle.

"Which one were you shooting at?"

"The one on the left."

"It didn't move. Try this," said Clay, as he readjusted the sling. He got in a prone position and carefully sighted the rifle. Donna watched as two cans disappeared, one after another.

"You want me to get down in the snow?"

"It's easier to steady the rifle, Mom. Just do what I tell you."

Donna followed his model, sending four beer cans flying in rapid succession.

"Good job," said Clay.

"That's not hard at all," Donna responded, scrambling to her feet. "I thought there was some big deal about shooting a deer. It's a piece of cake. Anyone could do that with a gun like this. Where did you learn all this stuff?" she asked, looking at Clay.

"Gavin taught me," he responded, pulling the clip from the rifle and checking to make sure the chamber was empty.

"Good old Gavin, a regular Boy Scout," she responded bitterly. "Let's get the hell out of here."

13

~~~~~~

Ray woke suddenly from an uneasy sleep, startled by the brightness; the moonlight, reflecting off a carpet of fresh snow, poured through the large window on the side-wall near his bed. Ray pulled himself out of bed, glancing at the clock on the dresser on his way to the bathroom; it was a few minutes after 3:00 a.m. Returning to the bedroom, he stood at the window and gazed at the snow-covered slope below. The moon, more than three quarters full, hung in a dark blue sky. The oaks and maples, skeletal-like without their foliage, cast gray shadows across the otherwise glistening blanket of snow.

Ray had checked the weather on his computer before retiring. Another large storm system was heading into the Great Lakes region from Canada, the leading edge of the massive front having already crossed the southern shore of Lake Superior.

But as he looked out at the sky halfway through the night, there was no hint of the approaching storm. He changed his sweat-soaked t-shirt for a clean one and climbed back into bed, repositioning a large block of foam under the knee of his still tender leg.

As he lay there looking at the moon in the trees, the memory of a dream he was having just before he awakened started to come back. The dream wasn't new; it was a variation of one that he had had many times since discovering that he had fathered a daughter years before. In the dream Ray is trying to hold onto a relationship with the girl's mother, a relationship that in reality had been a brief summer romance. He had been home on leave from the army; he was in his early twenties.

In the dream he is a young man again and has prophetic powers. He is trying to persuade Ashleigh's mother not to go back to California; if she will stay with him, their daughter will be protected from a horrible tragedy later in life. The dream always ends with him standing alone on a Lake Michigan beach just before the sun drops below the horizon, possessing prescient knowledge but powerless to change the future.

It took Ray a long time to fall back asleep. Later he woke to the sound of the wind, a howling gale. As he opened his eyes he could see the snow being blown into the thick woods in the gray dawn. The storm had arrived.

14

Monday was preschool yoga morning, a salubrious respite that Marie especially enjoyed. Lynne and the twins seemed to enjoy it as much as she did. They would eat a light breakfast and drive to the yoga studio at the narrows, a strip of land where the shoreline of one of the largest lakes in the region is squeezed down to little more than a river for almost a mile.

The yoga studio was in an old brick building with a stone foundation that dated from the lumber days. In its original iteration the structure had been a bank, the only masonry building in a thriving lumber town that once had two railroads and three mills. The mills closed, their equipment and most of the workers and their families moving up the coast to untouched stands of timber. Farmers settled in the verdant hills, and soon summer communities began to develop along the lakes, the cottagers first coming from the big cities to the south by lake steamer, later by rail, and finally in larger numbers by Mr. Ford's Model T and the automobiles built by his competitors.

And this morning, like many yoga mornings, they were running late. When they rushed out of the house, they discovered that Dirk had taken Lynne's SUV, leaving his truck. They found the girls' car seats tossed in the mudroom and secured them in the back seat of the crew cab. Marie could tell that Lynne was angry, but was doing her best to control her rage.

Marie parked next to the building, and she and Lynne waited as the twins scrambled out of their car seats and collected their yoga mats. The girls knew and followed the routine of the class. They rolled out their mats between Marie and Lynne and settled into Savasana, corpse pose, and did their best not to look around and greet the other children who were entering the studio. They knew that they could socialize with the other kids after the class.

Marie enjoyed watching the girls take various poses over the course of the hour, their pliable, petite bodies easily assuming some poses, yet usually having difficulty with the balance positions, often tumbling to their mats in a chorus of giggles.

At the end of class, after the twins greeted the other children, Marie and Lynne herded them off to the truck and the next stop, a special treat following yoga, a visit to the Bayside Bakery. The twins had muffins and hot chocolate. Marie had tried the muffins early in the fall and found them too sweet and gooey. But she happily discovered that the bakery made acceptable croissants and offered strong, rich dark coffee, one bit of home that she found difficult to replace on the American frontier.

Lynne, aware that Marie was still uncomfortable driving in heavy snow, took the wheel for the trip home. The strong winds were creating blizzard conditions, greatly reducing visibility, and a thick blanket of new snow made the still-unplowed back roads almost impassable.

The last mile on the small country road that led to their house was the most difficult. Lynne had to punch through large drifts that had formed in low spots on the narrow lane. She slowed as they approached the end of the long drive that ran up the hill to their ridge-top home. She pulled a few feet into the drive, stopped, and put the car in park in preparation for getting out to gather the mail. She stepped out of the vehicle, leaving the door slightly ajar, and trudged through the deep snow to the mailbox—a handcrafted, carefully painted structure that closely resembled the restored barn that stood on their property. Lynne pulled a stack of envelopes and catalogs from the box and then turned toward the car.

As she waited, Marie momentarily became lost in the music, a medieval French ballad. She was puzzling over the words, trying to tease the meaning from the five-hundred-year-old phrases composed in an ancient variant of her mother tongue. She could tell it was a song about unrequited love, but she was having difficulty fleshing out the story line, although she had a sense it was about the unfaithfulness of men.

Marie didn't hear the shot; it was obscured by the sound of the idling engine and the music. But she did see Lynne at the moment she was struck. She saw Lynne's knees buckle and her arms drop as she fell backwards into the snow. For a few seconds Marie was paralyzed, trying to comprehend what was happening. Then she was out of the car and at Lynne's side, the blood starting to stain the heavy tan canvas of Lynne's barn coat. Marie slid her arms under Lynne's shoulders and dragged her toward the car. Mustering all her strength, she lifted Lynne into the passenger's seat, bringing her legs in last and closing the door. Then Marie sprinted to the driver's side of the truck. Once back in the vehicle, she reversed out of the drive and followed the tracks in the new fallen snow. As she raced toward the village, she pulled Lynne's phone from the tray between the front seats and dialed 911. Her first sentence was in French, then she switched to English. The girls, still secured in their car seats, were crying hysterically for their mother. Marie was struggling to understand the instructions of the calm, female voice on the other end of the line. Finally she got it. The woman was asking her to pull to the side of the road, emergency vehicles would be sent to her.

"I am not stopping," she said emphatically. "I am coming to the village."

"Do you know where the fire station is?" came the voice after a brief pause.

"Yes."

"Drive to that location. I will have vehicles waiting. Do you understand?"

"Yes," Marie answered.

Marie traversed the five miles on the ice and snow covered roads in less then six minutes, but later she would remember it as the longest six minutes of her life. She would occasionally get quick glimpses at Lynne, crumpled in the seat next to her. Marie couldn't tell whether or not Lynne was still breathing. As she came around the final curve into the village she could see an ambulance and a police car idling in front of the public safety building. She pulled to a stop between them, ran around the car, and opened the door. Two women and a man, all in dark blue coveralls, took control of the situation, quickly moving Lynne onto a gurney and into the waiting ambulance. Two more police cars arrived just as the ambulance, escorted by a police car, both with sirens wailing, roared away from the scene.

Marie felt faint; she wanted to scream and cry and beat her fists on something. Then she remembered the girls.

15

~~~~~~

Sheriff Ray Elkins and Detective Sue Lawrence were at Marie's side as she freed the hysterical little girls from their seats, something that they usually did for themselves. Marie held Amanda, who had leaped into her arms as soon as she was released from her seat. Ray caught Breanne as she slid out of the vehicle. He carried her into the fire hall, followed by Sue and Marie holding Amanda. They settled in a small lounge area of the station on two sagging couches.

The first order of business was to calm the girls and reassure them that their mother would be all right; the adults worked on wiping noses and drying tears.

Both Ray and Sue had met the twins several times before at department picnics and holiday parties, and while they couldn't distinguish Amanda from Breanne, they knew the girls' names and had some rapport with them. The twins kept asking for their mother. Ray explained to them that their mother was hurt, and they would see her when things were better.

Ray shuddered after the words were out of his mouth, not knowing what the next few minutes, hours, or days would bring. He didn't know how seriously Lynne was wounded, or if she was even still alive. And he wondered how anyone could explain this kind of violence to a child, when it was almost inexplicable to the adult mind.

With the arrival of several more of his officers, Ray was able to slide away from the girls for a few minutes. He called dispatch, checking on the whereabouts of Dirk Lowther and was reminded that Dirk was on vacation. He asked the dispatcher to try to reach Lowther on his cell phone.

Then Ray maneuvered Marie Guttard to the side as Sue Lawrence tried to comfort the girls with some cocoa.

"Where did this happen?" Ray asked in a low tone, keeping Marie within the sight of the twins, but beyond their earshot.

"At the house, just at the end of the drive," she responded. "Lynne got out to get the mail. I saw her fall, but I didn't understand what was happening. I went to help her; I could see blood and thought she must have been shot. I got her in the car, and we're here."

"Did you see the shooter?"

"I saw nothing. I was just trying to get her away."

"Did you see any other vehicles?"

"None. I think there had only been one car that way. I remember seeing the tracks of the postman, where he had stopped at the box. He must have been there a few minutes before us. It was snowing and difficult to drive."

"And you saw no one, no other vehicle?" Ray rephrased his earlier questions.

"No. I told you," she responded with obvious irritation. Then she collapsed in tears and sobbed uncontrollably. She reached out, and Ray held her. Slowly she regained some composure, eventually stifling sobs enough that she could answer Ray's questions. "I saw no other cars."

"Where did the shot come from? Do you know where the shooter might have been?"

"No."

"Was she hit in the front, the back?"

"I do not know. Suddenly she was down. I thought she had slipped. I got out to help her. She was bleeding, going unconscious. I pulled her to the car. I drove fast here. I almost crashed. The girls' crying was breaking my heart. I was afraid she'd die in the car." Marie started sobbing again.

"Before this happened, did she tell you anything? Was she afraid of something?" he asked.

"She seemed like always. She didn't tell me anything."

"Lynne's husband, Dirk?"

"He left this morning to go hunting. He came home from work about six; he had all his gear packed in the mudroom. He came in, got his things, and went away."

"And you haven't seen him since?

"That is correct."

"Marie, the truck outside, isn't that Dirk's truck?"

"When we came outside to go to yoga this morning Lynne's SUV was gone, and Dirk's truck was sitting there. We had to find the girls' car seats and get them in place. That's one of the reasons we were running late, that and the snow."

"Did they trade vehicles often?"

"Not often, but Lynne would use Dirk's truck when she was getting gardening supplies or other things too big or messy to carry in her car."

"Marie, I'm going to have you and the girls driven to my office. You will be safe there. People will be staying with you and looking after your needs. I'll be back in a few hours and we'll figure out what to do next."

Ray and Sue moved off to a corner of the station. "I'll start organizing our search of the crime scene. While I'm doing that, would you get an APB out on Lowther as a person of interest in a shooting. Also, have both ends of Wildwood Road closed off to protect the scene."

16

On a large, clear, workbench at the back of the fire hall Ray laid out a detailed map of the section of the county where the Boyd/Lowther residence was located. A four-tube fluorescent fixture suspended by small chains from the ceiling illuminated the top of the bench. A group of deputies, including Sue Lawrence, stood in a semicircle around Ray peering at the map.

"At this point we don't know whether this shooting was accidental or intentional, but I want all of you to use great caution. And we're going to be hampered by heavy snow and poor visibility.

Sue and I will follow the Wildwood Road in from the north. Given how much time has gone by, I assume the shooter is long gone. But just in case, we will take the time to secure the area before we start examining the scene. Ben, I want you to follow us and be in a position to provide backup as needed." Ray pointed to a point on the map. "This is a lightly traveled road, and I'd like to be able to work the scene of the shooting without any traffic going through. Jake, I want you over here at the other end. If anyone comes along, explain that an investigation is in process and that the road will be closed for several hours.

"As you can see, we've got state forest on the east and federal land on the west. Brett, I'd like you to cover these roads on the west side of the area; it's mostly second-growth forests and old farmland. As I remember it, there are a few houses along this road," he said running his hand along a small wiggle line on the map. And Peter, cover this road on the east. There are some seasonal roads, two tracks, in the area." Ray traced the area on the west side of the road. "It's low and swampy in here, and given the rain and snow we've had the last few days, this would be tough land to cross. That said, this is prime hunting land, and I imagine there will be some people trying to get through these woods. I don't know if you guys know this area?" Both men indicated that they didn't. "Well," Ray continued, "as you can see this is mostly cedar swamp over here. At the center here is Little Mud Lake. On the other side of the lake, near the victim's home, the terrain changes and it starts to become hilly; the glaciers churned this land up a bit."

"Could you do it on an ATV?" asked Brett Carty, new to the area and youngest member of the department.

"I don't know," Ray responded. "I haven't rambled through there since I was a teenager. My memory is that it's an almost impenetrable bog, lots of standing water, old stumps and debris, and there are some springs and sink holes. I don't think you'd get a machine through, not now. Maybe in the dead of winter when everything is frozen, someone who knew the area might be able to get through there on foot."

"What are we looking for, Ray?" asked Brett.

"Anything suspicious. This is not going to be easy. The shooter had lots of time to get out, and what tracks they might have left are now covered with snow. If they didn't come up Wildwood Road and park nearby, they could have walked in from a variety of places, perhaps used a snowmobile. Like I said, there are lots of small trails and roads into the area that they might have used." Ray pointed these out on the map. "And please," said Ray, turning and making eye contact with everyone in the group, "be careful. We'll all be close by. If you run across anything suspicious, call for backup. If you run across any hunters, ask them if they've seen anything and get their names and addresses.

"While you're covering the outside perimeter, Sue and I will start working the scene. We will try to determine where the shooter was and perhaps how they got into and out of the area. Eventually we may need most of you at the scene if we decide to do a line search. So winter boots and snow shoes."

The group split up and headed toward their assignments. Ray and Sue, in separate vehicles, drove to the area where the shooting took place. As Ray turned into the narrow country road, he could see that it had recently been plowed. Ray swore under his breath as he visualized the damage the plow had done to the crime scene.

Stopping thirty yards short of the mailbox and driveway to the Boyd/Lowther home, Ray climbed out of his car. Sue parked behind him and came to his side carrying a camera.

As they moved forward along the newly-plowed road, they noted the shoulders on both sides were covered with a thick layer of snow thrown by the plow. Any footprints or tire marks had been obliterated in the wake of the massive truck. They stopped short of the mailbox, its door hanging open, its interior packed with snow from the plow. Envelopes and catalogs—now only partially visible in the snow—were scattered for several yards up and along the hillside near the road.

Sue pulled the lens cap from her camera. She studied the scene through her viewfinder, and started snapping pictures, picking up all the details visible in the scene. Ray held his position and let her move around the area as she photographed relevant landscape. Finally she looked over at Ray.

"Bad luck," he said.

Sue nodded her agreement.

17

Ray returned to the office thirty minutes after Sue Lawrence. He had gone over to the road that ran parallel to Wildwood Road on the east and slogged through the heavy snow on foot looking for a possible trail the shooter might have used to get across the swamp. By the time he got back to his vehicle, the thigh muscles in his recently injured leg were aching, and he was feeling dispirited.

Ray found Sue Lawrence and Marie Guttard sitting at the small conference table in his office, Marie at the head of the table, Sue at her left. There was a tray of still untouched sandwiches in the center of the table, a pot of coffee, three ceramic mugs, and two bottles of Diet Coke.

"Where are Amanda and Breanne?" he asked, settling into the chair at Marie's right.

"They're with Lynne's parents," Sue explained. They arrived last Saturday to get their place ready for a Thanksgiving gathering. Marie called them to let them know what had happened, and they were here with Marie and the girls when I came back. After checking with protective services, I released the twins to their custody."

"And how are the kids?" he asked.

"They are calm, but very frightened. They kept asking to see their mother," Marie answered.

Both women looked at Ray.

"I was on the phone with the hospital as I was driving back. Lynne's alive, in surgery, and in very serious condition. I couldn't learn anything more." Looking at Sue he asked, "Has Dirk been located?

"No. Dispatch has been trying to call him. His cell phone must be turned off. There has been no response to our APB yet."

"The grandparents?" Ray asked, looking at Sue

"The Boyds, Prescott and Dorothy." Sue gave Ray a knowing look as she continued. "The Crescent Cove—Round Island Hunt Club, I guess they own it now." Ray was familiar with the location, a gated and fenced enclave that held the largest tract of private land in the county.

"I know the area," responded Ray. "The girls will be staying there?"

"At least for the next day or two. A lot depends on Dirk and what develops in the near future," she paused for a long moment. "The girls often spend the night there. They even have their own bedroom. Actually it's a suite they share with Marie," she added, looking over at Marie.

"It's a flat, a sitting room, two bedrooms, en suite," continued Marie. "They want me to stay with them and the twins."

"Now Marie," said Ray, turning toward her. "We sort of touched on this before briefly at the fire hall, but we'd like to go through it again. Would you tell us about your day from the time you woke up until we met you there?" As he asked the question Ray poured a cup of coffee, asking by gesture if anyone else wanted some. The two women reached for the Diet Cokes. Sue passed the plate of sandwiches around.

"What are you looking for?" asked Marie.

"Was there anything unusual this morning, something that caught your eye, something that was different?" Ray probed.

She looked pensive and then answered, "Yes and no."

"Tell me about the 'yes,'" said Ray. "What was different?"

"Dirk came home very early," she explained. "Usually after he finishes work, he goes out for breakfast. Lynne has told me there's a group of men who meet at this place every morning."

"Do you know where?" asked Ray.

"The Cottage Inn," she answered. "I've never been there. Lynne says the place is a…what is her phrase…greasy spoon. All I know is he comes home mid-morning, sometimes later, smelling of cigarettes and fried food."

"But this morning was different?"

"Yes, like I told you before, he was home not long after 6:00," she said rather tartly.

"Marie, in the course of the investigation, we may ask you the same question more than once. We're just trying to get all the information clearly sorted out," explained Sue. "Let's start again with this morning."

"I always wake up early, and I was in the kitchen making coffee. I could hear Dirk collecting his deer hunting things in the mudroom. I thought he was going later this week, but this morning he came in, got his bags and gun case, and went away."

"About what time did he leave?"

"6:15 or 6:20. No later. He seemed to be in a hurry."

"Did he talk to Lynne?" Sue asked.

"No, no one else was awake."

"So he didn't tell his wife he was taking her vehicle."

"No."

"Do you think they had a conversation about this; that would be normal for a couple to do?" pressed Sue.

"They are not a…a normal couple. I do not think they are talking much."

"So why aren't they a normal couple?"

"I do not know. Lynne does not talk about that to me."

"But you live there, you see what's going on. Do they spend time together? Do they seem to like each other?" Sue asked.

Marie's answer was slow in coming. "In France, people who like each other share a bed and a life."

"And they don't?" said Sue.

"No."

"How do you feel about your employer?" Sue asked.

"You mean Lynne?"

"Let's start with her."

"I like her. She is intelligent and professional, very competent. A wonderful mother. I have learned much from her."

"How do you and Lynne get along?"

"Very well." She hesitated briefly. "I have heard horror stories about how some American women treat au pairs, use us as servants and maids. This is not true with Lynne. We had rapport right from the beginning. She is very considerate, very fair. We have shared the care of the girls. I never felt like I was considered an inferior."

"And Dirk," Ray asked, "how do you feel about him."

"A strange man. He does not like me. I do not think he likes the French."

"And you don't think he and Lynne were getting along?" asked Ray, coming back to the topic a second time.

"No, they are not. They do their best to avoid one another."

"You said you don't think he likes you. How do you feel about him?"

"He is old, unpleasant, and I think he is a fascist or whatever you would call them here. I do not understand why a young, beautiful woman like Lynne would be married to an old man like that," Marie stated emphatically.

"How about the girls, what kind of a father is Dirk?"

"The girls, they seem to like him, but he doesn't give them much time. He lives his own life, and he just isn't around."

"Has Lynne told you about a possible separation or divorce?'" asked Ray.

"Not in those words. She is a very open person, but not about all things. But I do not see that they would stay together."

"Do you think that Lynn might have another romantic interest?" asked Sue.

"What do you mean?" asked Marie cautiously.

"As you noted, Lynne is a very attractive woman, and she's in a high visibility profession. And you've suggested that her marriage doesn't appear to be working. It would not be too unusual for a woman like Lynne to find someone else."

After a long silence Marie answered. "I do not think so. Her work schedule is so busy, and Lynne does her best to spend as much time as possible with her daughters. I do not think she has any time for a liaison." She took a deep breath and slowly exhaled, "She gives so much of herself; I think she deserves a good man."

"Friends, does Lynne have many close friends?" Ray asked.

"Lynne is very busy, she spends her time working and attending to her daughters."

"How about women friends?" asked Sue.

"She knows many people," Marie answered.

"Special friends," elaborated Sue, "people she spends time with, someone with whom she might share her thoughts and feelings."

Marie looked thoughtful, then answered, "There is one woman Lynne is close to, Elise Lovell. I think they talk on the phone every day. I know they often meet for lunch, and she brings her children to Lynne's house or we go to her house, usually on weekends."

"Elise Lovell, where does she live?" asked Sue.

"Here in the village."

"We'll need to talk to her," said Ray, looking over at Sue. He turned back to Marie, "Do you know if Lynne thought she was in any danger; did she tell you about any threats she might have received?"

"No."

"Did she seem wary, or perhaps more cautious than she had been in the past?"

"What do you mean? How might she be different?"

"Things like being especially careful about locking the exterior doors," said Sue, picking up the line of questioning, "or looking around as you were coming and going to see if there were any strange vehicles in the area."

"If she was, as you say, more wary, I did not notice it."

"Lynne's parents, you've gotten to know them."

"Yes, many weekends we have spent with them. I like her mother a lot. She is very nice, and the girls adore her."

"And the grandfather?"

"He is, I think you would say, curmudgeonly. But he can also be charming. It is hard to know. No one has said anything, but I do not think that he is well."

"But you will feel safe being there with the girls?" Ray asked.

"Yes. They are very wealthy, the Boyds. They arrive with a staff. There are lots of people around. I think we will be fine." Marie paused and looked at Ray. "Lynne, will she survive?" she asked, her composure starting to slip.

"I don't know," Ray answered. "Her wounds are extremely severe. We may not know if she's viable for several days." Ray looked across at Marie; he was afraid his face might be giving away the pessimism he was feeling.

"But if she survives," continued Sue, "it's because of your bravery and the way you quickly handled the situation. Your actions gave her a chance at life."

"I only wish I could have done more," Marie responded, clearly on the edge of tears again.

18

It was mid afternoon by the time Sue Lawrence had returned from driving Marie Guttard to the Boyd family compound at Crescent Cove. Ray had already completed a graphic outline for the early stages of the investigation on a large whiteboard.

"How are the roads?" he asked as she flopped into one of the chairs at the conference table, still wearing a heavy outside jacket, which she slowly unzipped after pulling off her gloves. Her rosy cheeks showed the effects of the frigid weather.

"Not good. High winds and lots of drifting, especially when you get near the shoreline. Driving conditions are going to be marginal the rest of the day. At this point it looks like all they're trying to do is keep the main roads open." Sue pulled her jacket off and dropped it on the chair at her right.

"Anything new on Lynne's condition?" she asked.

"No," Ray answered, and he rubbed out a few words on his chart and rewrote them. Looking at Sue he asked, "Did you learn anything more from Marie on the drive?"

"Not much. She seems very protective of Lynne, and I think she is somewhat wary of police. She did tell me one thing that was interesting and sort of adds to the picture."

"What's that?" Ray asked.

"She doesn't like Dirk at all."

"Didn't we hear that during the interview," Ray noted rhetorically.

"Yes, but I wasn't finished." Sue stopped and waited until it was clear that Ray was giving her his full attention. "Sometime early on in her stay Dirk put a move on her. She said she tried to make it clear to him that she wasn't interested. It's really neat how she shows her absolute disdain; she sort of wrinkles her face and drops her voice. 'Can you imagine making love to that old man?'" Sue said, trying to imitate Marie's accent. She continued, "But apparently Dirk isn't used to being rebuffed. She said one morning when they were alone in the kitchen—he was just back from work, and she was the only one up—he caught her from behind and cupped her breasts."

"Then what?" asked Ray.

"Bad move on Dirk's part; Marie is a martial arts freak. She told me she carefully set her mug of coffee on the counter, and then tossed Dirk on his back, put a knee on his neck, and told him if he ever got close to her again, she'd do some real damage."

"Did she share this with Lynne?"

"I asked her that. She said no. She didn't want to upset Lynne, and she was perfectly capable of taking care of herself. But Marie did say after that encounter Dirk became increasingly hostile toward her."

"How about the Boyd family home?"

"What a joint. Have you been there?" she asked.

"Just on the perimeter, beyond the fence that separates it from the rest of the world. But I've seen some of the complex from the water when I was kayaking down the coast last August. There used to be a big old hunting lodge there, and they've replaced it with an enormous structure."

"Well, I only got as far as the entryway, but it certainly looked and smelled new."

"What did you learn?"

"The estate—I don't know what else you'd call it—is gated. Security cameras are at the entrance, along the drive, and on the exterior of the main building. The place looks like a small hotel. I walked Marie to the door; a man opened it and invited us in. He was clearly not a member of the family."

"How could you tell?"

"How could I tell?" Sue pondered the question. "He didn't introduce himself, and I just sort of thought he had employee written all over him."

"So what does an employee look like? Are they in livery?" Ray asked, amused by her description.

"They probably should be," Sue shot back. "This guy is in his middle twenties, blond, brush-cut hair, very trim. He looked like he just walked off a Marine poster. I would guess he's part of the security detail. Once we were inside the girls ran to greet us, and I was introduced to their grandmother."

"What's she like?" Ray asked. He was always interested in Sue's impressions of people and how they sometimes varied from his own.

"Not like my grandmother. Dorothy, that's her name, gives meaning to the phrase, sixty is the new forty. She is trim, blond, and athletic looking, an older version of Lynne. But she didn't look that much older. I would guess her face has been redone by a really good surgeon."

"And Lynne's father?"

"I was told that Prescott was at the hospital. I was able to get Lynne's mother aside and asked if we could interview her soon. She said now that Marie was there she was available at our convenience. I'll get back to her after we establish our priorities."

Ray nodded.

"It looks like you've been busy," said Sue, perusing the carefully drawn chart. It had taken her a while to get used to Ray's graphical way of organizing an investigation, but the longer they worked together, the more their styles had begun to blend. She knew he counted on her to bring his attention to logical errors and omissions. He recognized that she was much better at organizing the detail. And she often offered an entirely different interpretation of facts and evidence.

"Look over what I've done," Ray said, gesturing toward the whiteboard. "Wrap your brain around it and tell me what I've missed." Then he went silent and waited. He had learned to give Sue time. She would respond when she had digested the information, occasionally asking questions along the way to get additional details or have him unscramble his handwriting for her. He waited patiently, his own brain racing.

"So we start with Dirk," she finally said, her eyes returning to the left-hand column on the board. "Convenient of him to be out of town and impossible to reach when his wife gets shot. We both know the statistics on this; he's the most likely suspect."

"The challenge here is to keep our own feelings about Dirk in check," said Ray. "You don't like him much."

"And neither do you. You're just so damn professional, you stay away from personalities," Sue responded.

"You almost seem angry at me," said Ray, responding to her tone.

She gave Ray a quick smile. "I just don't like the guy. The Grecian Formula hair, the artificial tan, the spit-polished boots—not part of our uniform, and that heavy gold chain around his neck. He's just creepy. Did you know he hit on me the first week I was working here?"

"Why didn't you say so, it would have given me grounds to help him into retirement."

"I was new. I didn't know the lay of the land. But I got real nasty; he never bothered me again." She paused for a moment, and then continued, "And now that I've got that out of my system, as I was saying, it's convenient that he appears to be out of town when there's a family emergency."

"Yes, convenient," agreed Ray. "Maybe the bullet was intended for Dirk?"

"He seems to have lots of enemies. But I think it would be hard to confuse the two," said Sue.

"Here's his Away from Duty form. I've just reviewed it again." Ray passed the form to Sue. "He worked this weekend, and then he's on vacation this week and next. The form says he'll be in town through Thursday and then he's going to the U.P. to do some deer hunting. Looks like he might have changed his plans without updating the form. He says he'll be at the Four Roses Resort north of Seney. I can't find anything by that name in the region. Do you know the area?" he asked.

"I've only been up to the U.P. twice in my life, family vacations when I was a kid."

"I just checked NOAA, blizzard conditions along the southern Lake Superior shoreline." Ray put a map of the U.P. in the center of the table, orienting it for Sue. "Dirk said he would be north of Seney," Ray leaned over the table pointed to a dot on the map. "Three counties come together there: Luce, Schoolcraft, and Alger. I've called the sheriffs in all three. A snow emergency has been declared across the whole region. And no one has heard of the Four Roses Resort. Two of them suggested the name came from the whiskey of that name, long a popular drink in the deer camps."

"So it doesn't sound like they're offering immediate help in finding a fellow officer."

"You got it. The consensus was that it would take several days after the snow stopped falling before they started plowing secondary roads. If we hadn't heard from Dirk by then, they would do what they could."

"Did you ask about cell phones?"

"Yes. The coverage is spotty. And many of these deer camps are off the grid and don't have landlines. They heat with wood and use propane or kerosene for lights."

"How about the State Police?" Sue asked.

"Same response."

"So," said Sue, "we know things aren't good in the marriage, they're heading for splitsville. But Dirk can't be so dumb to think he could get away with this, even if he could get the boys in the deer camp to give him an alibi."

"Dirk has an almost inexhaustible supply of hubris, but you're probably right, he wouldn't be that stupid. Even with an alibi, he knows he is going be suspect number one."

"And what would be his motive?" asked Sue. "Like it's not the first time he's been divorced."

"We need to get him in here and let him give us his story. And once we get in contact with him, you would think he'd want to be with his kids. I've left two messages, so if he turns on his phone or gets someplace with a signal…."

"The other items you think we should pursue immediately?" started Sue, looking at the whiteboard.

"The letters that Lynne got. Anything from the State Police lab yet?"

"No," said Sue, opening a notepad and starting a list. "I'll call them as soon as we're done and let them know this has become a priority. What's next?"

"I would like to talk to the station manager and see if he's got any ideas. I want to know if there is anything more on those letters, and then I want to question him about other possibilities like professional jealousy and office romances."

"Psychiatrist?" said Sue, pointing to white board. "What's that about?"

"When Lynne came in with the letters, she told me she was seeing a psychiatrist. There's a chance he might have some useful information."

"Did she give you a name?"

"No, but based on her description of the man, I've a good sense of who it is."

"Description? Why didn't she just tell you his name?"

"Lynne was telling me about problems in her marriage. Dirk didn't like the au pair and accused her of having an affair with her psychiatrist, who she said was in his late sixties. Dr. Ruskin fits that description. I'll call him and confirm that she was a patient. And then I'll see if he...."

"Aren't you going to get into a physician/patient confidentiality problem?"

"I don't think so, given what's happened and the kind of information we're seeking."

"Sounds like they have a wonderful marriage," said Sue. Her gaze returned to Ray's diagram, "And next you have family. I assume you're referring to Lynne's"

"Yes. I think we need to see if she's told her parents anything. If she and her mother are close, perhaps Lynne shared something that might be useful."

"I'll set up an appointment to talk to her mother," Sue said.

Ray pointed to an area in his chart. "I'd also like to know more about the family. Might there be a sibling or relative who would benefit by Lynne's death? I'd like you to work that angle. And would you carefully peruse this chart and see what I missed?"

"What are you going to do?" Sue asked.

"I'm sort of stir-crazy. I'm going to the hospital. I'll see if I can learn anything about Lynne's condition, and if I can find him, perhaps have a word with her father. I'll also try to visit with Dr. Ruskin."

"You okay?" said Sue, noting the fatigue in his voice.

"Why do you ask?"

"You just seem tense and very tired."

"The cold weather, my leg has been uncomfortable today, and this...."

Sue cut him off, "There are certain parallels." Her sentence hung briefly.

"We better get started," said Ray, using his arms to help lift his body out of the chair. After Sue left, he stood for a long moment looking at the chart and thinking about what Sue had said, the parallels. He pushed those thoughts from his mind. He needed to keep his focus on the case at hand.

19

~~~~~~~~

Ray parked in the ramp near the emergency entrance. He walked under the large canopy that joined the two structures. The wet pavement glistened under the lights in the otherwise gloomy dusk.

Two large glass doors slid open as he approached the building. Stopping at the registration desk, Ray told the female attendant, a graying woman in a green smock, the name of the patient he needed information on. She keyed the name into the system and looked at the flat screen monitor on her right.

"That patient has been moved to surgery. Follow this hallway," she gestured with her arm, "to the end and take one of the elevators to the second floor. Then follow the signs to the surgical information desk."

Ray followed the directions and waited for an elevator. When one of the doors opened, Saul Feldman, his close friend and internist, was coming off the elevator in his direction.

"How are you?" said Saul extending his hand. "Staying out of trouble?"

"Trying to. I stopped by to see if I can get some info on…"

"Young woman, the TV woman."

"Yes," Ray answered, "Lynne Boyd."

"I was just coming from the OR, I can tell you what I heard in the doctor's lounge. How about a coffee?"

Saul Feldman led the way to the cafeteria, and after getting two mugs of coffee they settled at an empty booth in a deserted area of the large, brightly lit room.

"So, what's her condition, is she going to make it?" Ray asked.

"She's still alive. And if she makes it, well, all the planets lined up for her," Feldman offered.

"How so?"

"The newest physician on our trauma team is a young woman. In the last couple of years she's worked both in a mobile field hospital in Iraq and Landstuhl Medical Center in Germany. She's spent months stabilizing badly wounded GIs so they could be evacuated to Landstuhl, and then she spent time at the other end, at Landstuhl, as part of a surgical team.

"So today she was on call when the shooting victim came in. I heard that the victim was almost gone by the time the ambulance arrived. Hanna Jeffers, that's the young surgeon's name—little woman, ninety pounds at the most, and really intense. And she's gutsy as hell, and not afraid to take chances to save a patient. In the few months she's been here she's earned the nickname 'fearless and fast' Hanna.

"Jeffers has them run the patient to surgery, she wanted to get a CT of the wound, but the patient was too unstable. So Hanna goes ahead and cracks the woman's chest and starts administering NovoSeven. That's something they used in Iraq to control bleeding, but it's not FDA approved for use here. Well, that raised some eyebrows. But that's only the beginning. Then Hanna puts the patient on a heart-lung machine and starts repairing the damage. I talked to a couple of the scrub nurses, and they said she's fantastic. She's got incredible hands, she's very fast, and she can sort of improvise as she goes.

"So she did things the military way?" asked Ray, as he visualized the scene in the OR.

"Yes. Military, that's the perfect phrase. I guess she was ordering people around. Everyone was expected to move in double time. And she didn't show proper deference to some of her distinguished colleagues. Some of the old boys are a bit upset by her less-than-conventional approach to surgery, but I can't fault her. No one comes close to having the experience she has at salvaging patients with this kind of horrific wound."

"But she's rubbing people the wrong way?"

"The cardiac group, it's the last exclusive boys club left in the local medical community. In the last ten years about half of the new physicians coming to town have been female. In family medicine and some of the specialties, it's now mostly female."

"So she's breaking new ground," Ray observed.

"More than that. She's really stirred things up. The old boys, they don't like anyone who doesn't respect the pecking order, and Hanna, hell, she doesn't know a pecking order exists. And they don't like the way she's breaking all the long-standing paradigms. Most of my colleagues have become quite comfortable doing the same thing year after year. They're smart, competent people, and they usually get good results, but they're slow to change. In comes this pretty, young woman who challenges much of what's considered standard practice."

"So what's happening with Lynne?"

"The patient's in intensive care. Hanna will probably be living in the hospital the next few days watching over her."

"Prognosis?"

"It's hard to say. I've been told there was a lot of tissue damage. I guess it all depends on whether the repairs hold together, and there's no infection or other complication. This patient won't be out of the woods for a long while. But let's talk about you," said Feldman. "Are you still getting physical therapy for that leg?"

"I finished last week. The PT said I was good to go."

"How about the psychiatrist, Dr. Sandlow?"

"I'm seeing her twice a week. And to be frank, Saul, I don't know where the therapy's going." Ray reflected on therapy sessions, the long silences when he didn't know what to say.

"Do you want to talk about it?"

"I'm okay during the day when I'm busy at work. It's when I'm trying to go to sleep, or when I wake at 2:00 or 3:00 and can't get back to sleep. That's when the enormity of it all hits me. I'm struggling to even understand what happened. I have this sense of loss and sadness. And I don't think I've ever really been depressed before. Not like this."

"You really had a double whammy. The physical and emotional stress from being shot, well, that's enough for anyone. But then the discovery of your relationship to the victim, that's almost beyond comprehension. It's going to take time, Ray. And it goes without saying that there are some things we never completely recover from. But we do get to a place where we can go on with our lives. You like Dr. Sandlow?"

"You always refer me to good people."

"How about that pretty woman who visited you in the hospital. You seeing her?"

"Occasionally, but I don't know if it's fair to date someone when I'm feeling so…what… down…confused?"

"Look Ray, you won't feel any better isolating yourself and waiting for a time when you have everything figured out. We've got piles of literature that says people are healthier when they are involved with other people. I know that this is easier to say than do, but you need to try to get on with your life."

Ray nodded, indicating his understanding of the advice.

"And come in and see me this week or next. I'd like to closely monitor your health for the next few months. Let's see if we can find ways to mitigate some of the physical effects of this stress."

"What can I say, Saul. I'm forever in your debt. But I'm really busy right now…."

"And when you fall over dead, people will remember your dedication to your job for at least two weeks after the funeral. If

I don't see you in a few days, I'll come looking for you. Where are you going now?"

"I wanted to know about Lynne's condition. You've helped with that. Now I'd like to find her father."

"He's probably in the surgical waiting room."

"That's where I was heading when I ran into you."

20

There were only two people in the surgical waiting room, a large man talking forcibly on a cell phone and a much younger man sitting attentively at his side. As Ray approached the pair, the man on the phone looked up briefly, his eyes magnified by the thick lenses of his glasses, and continued on with his conversation. Although Ray had yet to get the drift of the conversation, he could tell by the man's commanding tone that he was used to getting what he wanted.

The young man—thirty-something, with brown hair in a Princeton cut, button-down shirt and tie, and blue blazer—rose and extended a hand. "I'm Harry Hawkins, Mr. Boyd's personal assistant and lawyer."

Ray felt Hawkins' muscular grip and noted his height, about 6'4" or 6'5" he guessed, as he gave his name in return.

"And you, sir, are the Cedar County Sheriff?" Hawkins asked before releasing Ray's hand.

"Yes," Ray answered. "Ray Elkins."

"Have you arrested that bastard yet?" asked the other man, the person Ray assumed was Lynne's father, coming to his feet, still holding the cell phone to his left ear. "Or do we have to deal with cops protecting their own?" he asked, anger in his voice. The man was quite stout, and Ray guessed he was close to six feet tall. His head was large and round, mostly bald with a ring of pepper-gray hair from sideburn to sideburn, and flushed cheeks. Before Ray could respond, the man demanded in an angry tone, "Do you know who I am?"

Ray held the man in his gaze for a long moment, slowly filled his lungs in a effort to control his anger, and replied, "I assume, sir, that you are Lynne Boyd's father."

Ray's response seemed to further enrage the man.

"You haven't answered my first question," the man demanded, poking a finger into Ray's chest. "Do you have that bastard behind bars yet?" His voice was gravelly, that of a person who was still or had been a heavy smoker for most of his life.

Harry Hawkins gently pulled his employer's hand down. "Sir, I'm sure you can understand how upset Mr. Boyd is."

"What are you people doing?" Boyd demanded, his tone indicating that he was sure nothing was happening.

Ray took his time to respond. He wanted to slow down this exchange, to get a sense of this man and his world, but he was in no mood to be bullied.

"The investigation is well under way," Ray responded.

"Have you questioned Dirk? If he's not the shooter, he's the one responsible," Boyd said. Suddenly his attention shifted back to his phone, still held to his ear. "Well, where is he? I need to talk to him. This is an emergency. If I give you my number, will you have him call me as soon as he's available?" Boyd asked, bringing the phone around and yelling into the mouthpiece. He gave the number, repeating it twice, and snapped the phone shut. He went back to his original question, this time with his full focus on Ray. "Do you have that bastard under arrest yet?"

"Sir, let me say again, the investigation is well under way."

"Let's not play around. What I want to know is if you've got Dirk in custody yet."

Ray noted how Boyd was sucking air. His wife, Lynne's mother, as Sue described her, might be an archetype of sixty being the new forty, but the man in front of him seemed to be in poor health.

"Dirk Lowther is on vacation this week. We believe that he is in the Upper Peninsula deer hunting. We've been trying to reach him. Thus far we have had no success."

"You've called his cell phone?"

"We've left messages on his voice mail."

"Tell me what you know so far," Boyd demanded. "After the first call this morning from your department, I've heard nothing."

Without disclosing any details, Ray briefly described the crime scene investigation, noting the difficulties caused by the extreme weather. He also explained that they were in the early stages of the investigation and the full resources of his department and cooperating police agencies would be used to find the person or persons responsible for this crime as quickly as possible. But before he had finished, Boyd was responding to the ringing of his cell phone.

He snapped the phone open and yelled, "Yes," at the mouthpiece. He listened for a few moments, and then, clearly interrupting, said, "That's all fine and good, but what I want to know is…" His sudden silence, mid-sentence, suggested that someone who was not about to be intimidated had cut him off. "Yes, Doctor," he finally responded, his tone a fraction meeker. "I didn't mean to," he paused again and listened. Then he said, an edge coming back into his voice, "If I call the people at Mayo, do you think that they will give me the same answer?" Boyd listened for a few more minutes, his countenance reflecting his anger and frustration. Finally he responded quickly, "Thank you, Doctor," and snapped the phone shut.

Boyd looked up at Harry Hawkins, "He said if I wanted to know if they'd do something different in Rochester, I should call them. Bastard."

"What was their recommendation?" asked Hawkins calmly.

"It's my cardiologist," Boyd explained to Ray. "He's one of Cleveland Clinic's best, but he's got no people skills." Turning to Hawkins, he continued, "He says he discussed the case with the young surgeon here, and he says she's done everything right, and Lynne shouldn't be moved until she's more stable. And he said he's too busy to fly up here, even if I send the Gulfstream."

"Are you going to call Mayo?" Hawkins asked.

"The hell with it. I don't want another runaround. For now we'll go with his recommendation." Boyd's focus shifted back to Ray. "So what were you telling me again?" he asked, irritation in his voice.

"I had described for you the current state of the investigation."

"Which is what? I didn't hear that you knew where Dirk was, and I didn't hear about any other suspects."

Ray listened to the words and the tone in which they were delivered. It was clear that this man was powerful enough, rich enough, or both that he felt he could heap verbal abuse on those around him with impunity. Ray had no intention of caving into Boyd's demands.

"Your cooperation would speed the investigation," Ray said, moving right into a question without giving Boyd time to respond. "Has your daughter, Lynne, said anything to you recently that might suggest that she felt she was in any kind of danger?"

"No."

"What is the nature of your relationship? If she were apprehensive, is this something she might share with you or her mother?"

"Sheriff, my daughter is a fully functioning young woman. She is absolutely capable of taking care of herself."

"So if she were worried about something or someone, she wouldn't seek your counsel?" he asked the same question a second time, slightly altering the language.

"Probably not."

"And you've had no indications that anything is greatly amiss in her life."

"There are things," he paused and looked at Ray, "to use your word, amiss in her life. There have been things amiss in her life since she hooked up with that bastard. But she was finally going to do something about that, she was finally getting out." He stopped and caught his breath, then continued. "So, Sheriff, how can I have confidence in your investigation if Dirk is representative of the kind of people you employ?"

Harry Hawkins intervened before Ray could respond. "I'm sure the Sheriff has some competent people."

Ray anticipated that Boyd's ire would be directed at Hawkins, but Boyd seemed to accept his comment.

"Is there anything else Mr. Boyd could help you with?" Hawkins asked.

"One thing, going back to what you said a few minutes ago. You suggest your daughter was getting a divorce. Could you tell me at what stage she was in this process?"

"I know she's been meeting with a lawyer."

"Was Dirk aware of this?" Ray asked.

"I don't know."

"Do you know the grounds?"

"She was going with irreconcilable differences," answered Harry.

"But I'm sure she could have nailed him for…" Boyd stopped.

Ray waited for a moment, and then asked, looking at Boyd. "Might you know where Dirk's hunting camp is? Did you ever go up there with him?"

"Why do you ask?"

"We're having trouble finding its exact location."

"No, I don't know. He asked me to go hunting with him the first year or two that they were together. He described the place to me. It didn't sound like the kind of place I'd want to be. It's off in the sticks without electricity or water. Not my kind of hunting."

"Is there anything else?" asked Harry, resuming his role as moderator.

"In recent years I've gotten to know your daughter. I admire her greatly as a journalist and a person. We will find the person who did this."

"Thank you," said Boyd, his tone softening for the first time. "I appreciate that."

"Here's my card," said Ray, handing it to Hawkins. "If anything comes to mind that you think might be helpful in the investigation, please call me."

Harry took the card. "We will do that, Sheriff. And here's my card, the number on it is for my cell. If you need to talk to Mr. Boyd again, please call me."

Ray started for the corridor, stopped at the door, and looked back. Boyd was talking on his cell phone, Harry sitting patiently at his side, listening to his boss rant. As Ray walked down the long corridors toward the exit he could feel the tension that had built up during his exchange with Boyd.

21

The turbulent circumstances of the day had propelled Ray forward, his energy focused on the rapidly unfolding events. After leaving the hospital he stopped at the office, now mostly empty and dark, to read over the notes he and Sue had made during the day and to type in a summary of his interview with Lynne's father. He had learned early in his career of the importance of getting interview notes on paper quickly, while the person's answers, facial expressions, and body language were still fresh. Ray had found that the truth was often more apparent in the nuances than in the spoken message.

Then he turned his attention to the whiteboard and his diagram outlining the possible strands in the investigation. And as he stood there looking at the board with its lines and circles, a wave of weariness ran through his body. Suddenly all of the adrenaline seemed drained from his system. He knew he needed to go home and get some rest.

Carrying a pizza he picked up on the way, with the mail he had just retrieved on top of the box, he entered the house, switching on the kitchen lights. He set the box on the counter, took off his coat and put it on a hook near the door, and filled the teakettle. Ray started looking through the mail, then got pulled into the opening piece in the *New Yorker*. The whistling kettle pulled him back to the moment. He took it off the burner and turned on the hot water in the kitchen sink to wash his hands. The flow of water slowed, dribbled for a few seconds, and stopped. He pushed the handle farther back—nothing. Then he moved it to the cold side; there was a small trickle, then it ceased. "Damn," he said out loud. It was one more frustration in a difficult day.

After putting the pizza in the oven, he went to the equipment room, opened the door on the electrical panel and checked the list until he found the well. He looked at the breaker for the pump. It didn't appear to be tripped, but he pushed it off and reset it a couple of times just to make sure. Then he stood next to the pressure tank on the outside wall. There was only silence, not the usual hum transmitted up through the pipe when the pump was running deep in the well. When Ray got back to the kitchen he called the well drilling company and left a message on the voice mail.

Ray was eating a slice of pizza and a small salad, when a knock at the door was quickly followed by the door opening and then a shout, "Hey, Ray, can I come in?"

Ray greeted his old school friend, Billy Coyle. "What do you mean, 'can you?' You're already in." They both laughed. Not so much at this exchange, but at a long history of jokes and mischief they had shared from kindergarten through twelfth grade.

"Does Neptune Wells guarantee their work?"

"Damn straight. Three hours or thirty gallons, whichever comes first."

"In my message I said that you didn't have to come tonight," Ray said.

"No problem, and I was just completing a service call near here. As soon as we get some real cold weather, like now, the phone rings off the hook," said Billy. "Most of the time it's frozen pipes, nothing wrong with the well or pump. And it's usually the goofy summer people who didn't winterize yet. They come up for the weekend and can't figure out why they don't have any water.

"That won't be the problem in your case since everything is protected, and it's a heated building. I'll have a quick look; it's probably something simple." Billy headed off toward the equipment room.

"What do you think?" asked Ray, when Billy returned.

"I should have the part in the truck," Billy replied, "I'll be right back."

By the time Ray had put the plates in the dishwasher, Billy had reappeared and turned on the faucet at the kitchen sink. "You're back in business," he said, closing the valve.

"What was wrong?"

"Do you want an impressive answer or the truth?" Billy asked.

"How about the truth?"

"The pump pressure control switch failed. These units used to be completely mechanical. They occasionally needed some adjustment, but they lasted for years. Now there's a little circuit board in the box, too. And that's usually the problem. It's non-serviceable, you have to replace the whole control."

"And you did?" asked Ray.

"I didn't have a new one, so I put the one I keep in the truck for testing purposes. It works fine. I'll come back in a few days and replace it with a new one."

"Want a beer?" asked Ray. He was pleased to know he could have a hot shower in the morning, and he always enjoyed Billy's cheerful personality.

"Sure," said Billy, going to the refrigerator, pulling one out. "You want one?" he asked Ray.

"I'm going to make some herbal tea."

Billy collapsed into a chair at the table, unzipping a grease-smeared Carhartt jacket, his ample belly filling a faded red sweatshirt.

"You done with this pizza?" Billy asked, inspecting the half that remained in the box.

"Yes," said Ray. "You want me to warm it up?"

"Warm food, now that's a concept. This is fine, thanks," he responded, fishing a piece out of the box with his large, thick fingers.

"Fork, plate?"

"Perfect," he said, shaking his head, indicating that he needed neither. He quickly finished the first piece, and started on another. When Billy came up for air, he said, "Lots of excitement today. Everywhere I stopped, that's all they were talking about, the shooting. How she's doing, that TV woman?"

"She's in critical condition."

"She going to make it?" Billy asked.

"Don't know," said Ray, pouring some boiling water into a cup with a bag of chamomile tea.

"What a shame," said Billy. "Pretty woman. Not enough of them around. Why would anyone want to shoot her?"

"Wish I knew," answered Ray.

"Surprised no one ever shot Dirk," said Billy, picking up another piece of pizza. "If they did, you'd have a shit load of suspects."

"How's that?" asked Ray, knowing that Billy was an authority on local lore.

"Back in the bad old days, when Orville was still sheriff, Dirk, his brother Danny, and Kenny Obermeyer sort of ran the department. They were all young then; I don't think any of them were thirty yet. They played tough, made lots of enemies, and were dirty as hell."

"I've heard stories," responded Ray. "For over twenty years I was only up here occasionally. And I never knew if the stories about Orville and his deputies were just talk, or if there was more to it."

"You know I went down on possession and sale?" Billy asked.

"Yes," answered Ray. "I did hear that."

"I was surprised when you asked me to bid on your job," Billy said. "I thought you might not want to be associated with an ex-con."

"Billy, that was decades ago. You've never been in trouble again."

"Yeah, but it was stupid. I was twenty-one."

"We really lost touch after high school. What were you doing then?

"I went down to Central to play football. I got into partying, joined a frat, had lots of fun, and flunked my ass out royally my sophomore year. So I came back up here, and my dad took me into the business. Then he had a heart attack and died, and I took over. He had built a good business, and I was young, working lots of hours, and making some real money. I was also spending it, too.

"I had this real fast Olds convertible, candy-apple red. Dirk nailed my ass a couple of times for speeding. Both times he tore the car apart, saying he knew I was dealing."

"Were you?" Ray asked

"Not much, just enough to cover my costs, and just to friends. But Dirk said he was going to get me, and he did."

"How?" asked Ray.

"Okay to have another beer?"

"Help yourself," said Ray. "How did Dirk nail you?"

Billy returned to the table, settled in the chair across from Ray, and scooped up another piece of pizza. "I was stupid, just fucking stupid. I got a call from someone I didn't know wanting to buy some coke. The guy was offering about twice the street price. I should have seen instantly that it was a setup. So I got some stuff and showed up at the place. As soon as the money and dope were exchanged, Dirk comes out of nowhere, cuffs me and takes me to jail."

"What happened then?"

"I got convicted for possession and sale, went to the intake center at Jackson, and then got sent to the farm system. When I got out the business was still here. Herb Eibler—you remember him, he'd worked for my dad—kept it going. So that was it; I learned my lesson, I'd rather die than go back in. But, you know, every time I've run into Dirk over the years, he's always had some smart-assed comment about how he got me."

"The other two, Dirk's brother and Kenny Obermeyer, I've heard some stories. What happened to them?"

"That's one of the great mysteries. Kenny Obermeyer got gunned down late one night; it was July or August. The paper said it happened during a routine traffic stop, but one of the EMTs told me they picked up the body in the middle of a cherry orchard."

"Any arrests?"

"Never. Orville put out the story that it was a random act, committed by someone from downstate, probably Detroit. They all wanted this case to go away. The rumor was that the three of them had worked out an arrangement with an out-of-state mob—Chicago, Miami, it depends on who is doing the telling. Anyway, those people got exclusive rights to sell in the region and protection in exchange for a percentage of the take. Word was Dirk and friends were getting too greedy. Kenny's death was the mob's way of canceling the agreement."

"Then what happened?" Ray asked.

"Dirk's brother, Danny, got real scared, moved his family up north. I hear he's got a bar or a package store somewhere near Seney. But Dirk decided to stay around and take his chances. I think he learned not to mess with those people." Billy took a long pull on his beer and started chewing on the last piece of pizza. Finally he said, "I bet with all the county records being destroyed in that rather suspicious fire, there's no way you can research this?"

"Let me go back to one thing," said Ray. "You said there are a lot of people who…."

"Would love to do great bodily harm to Dirk," said Billy with a chuckle. "There are lots of rumors. And Ray, I don't know how many of them are true. But those three guys were pretty violent, and Orville just let them run the department." Billy paused and rubbed the stubble of his heavy beard with his left hand. "I heard about kids being slapped around at traffic stops. Drugs disappearing after arrests, I don't know if they sold the stuff or used it. And there were a lot of stories about women, including ones that were being held in jail. I think people were sort of relieved when Kenny got blown away. Our local reign of terror was over." Billy tipped up the beer and finished it. "I better let you get to sleep," he said, looking across the table. "If the well isn't working when you get up in the morning, give me a call. I've still got your key."

"One more thing," said Ray, "you don't seem to harbor great bitterness toward Dirk."

"I hate the fucker," responded Billy. "But in a strange way, he might have saved my life. I was just a wild kid into drugs and booze. While I was inside the place, I finally started to grow up. But it was a hell of a price to pay." He gave Ray a final wave and headed out the door.

After Billy left, Ray rinsed out the two beer bottles and his mug, flattened the pizza box, and carried it to the trash bin in the garage. The conversation with Billy had given him a second wind, but now he was feeling very tired and his leg was beginning to cramp.

He went into his study and pulled his journal and favorite fountain pen from under the top of his standing writing desk. Several years before Ray had had a local cabinetmaker design and build it. At the time he was plagued with back pains and was more comfortable standing than sitting.

Ray opened the journal and read through his last entry. Before he began to write, he reflected a few moments on how the focus of his life had changed since the first 911 call came in midmorning.

The account of events, including the interviews, that Ray typed at his office earlier in the evening had been clinical, the repetition of facts, and a timeline of events, all carefully documented. In his journal Ray was free to loosen the reins, to allow his emotions to blend with the facts, to give body and texture to the events, to reveal the tragedy that was unfolding. He described his feelings in the few brief seconds when he saw Lynne, her clothing soaked with blood, as she was lifted from the truck, moved to a gurney, and loaded into the ambulance. He wrote about holding Breanne, hearing her cries and feeling her tiny body in spasms of fear and grief. As he stood at the desk, Ray thought about the fact that he had not been part of his own daughter's life when she was that age, but he wasn't ready to write about that yet. He moved on to describing his frustration when he and Sue discovered that the crime scene had been all but obliterated when the snowplow had gone through the area.

He thought he would only write a few paragraphs, but once he got started and into the story, the words flowed onto the paper. By the time he finally screwed the cap back on his pen, he had filled more than five pages in his small, meticulous hand. With his last thoughts recorded, he felt his energy flagging. Before he went to bed he called Sue Lawrence's voice mail and left a message that he had heard that Dirk's brother, Danny, had a bar somewhere near Seney. If that were true, Danny would probably know how to find Dirk.

22

~~~

Sue Lawrence woke up shortly before 5:00 a.m. On waking she knew she had been dreaming about the shooting. In that dream she was hovering over the crime scene as Lynne Boyd's vehicle came up the road and stopped in the drive. With prescient knowledge, Sue scanned the woods, looking for the shooter. But before she could spot the shooter, her eyes were open, and the vision had vanished.

Sue crawled out of bed, filled and turned on the coffee maker, then showered, dressed, and toasted the last English muffin in the package, which she hurriedly consumed before filling a thermos with coffee and starting for the office. She stood for a long moment at the side of her car and scanned the horizon. The sky was still dark blue, brilliant with stars—the storm had moved east. Sue reminded herself that she needed to try to keep grounded in the emotions triggered by this scene of peace and beauty. She couldn't allow the harsh realities she would be facing the rest of the day to dominate her psyche.

Settling at her desk, Sue switched on her computer and then checked her voice mail as she waited for the system to boot up. There was one message, Ray's. The phone rang just as she set the handset back in the cradle. She waited for the second ring before she answered.

"Sue, this is central dispatch. I noticed you were in early."

"Hi, Jim," Sue responded.

"We had a call from the Munising Police Department about fifteen minutes ago. They've spotted a silver Honda Pilot with a trailer attached carrying an ATV parked on a residential street. The vehicle is registered to Lynne Boyd, and the trailer is licensed to Dirk Lowther. They have the vehicle under surveillance with backup coming from the state police and the sheriff."

Sue sat in silence; she could almost visualize the scene.

"Sue, are you there?"

"Yes. I'll be staying at my desk for a while. Direct all the calls here until I tell you otherwise."

"Will do," came the response.

Sue closed her eyes and inhaled deeply. She wished she were up there, sitting in an unmarked car waiting for Dirk to return to his vehicle. She wondered where he was and with whom.

She thought about driving to the U.P., but that would take far too much time, especially with the current road conditions. All she could do was focus on work that needed to be done and wait for things to develop.

Sue created a folder on her hard drive, attached her camera to her computer, and started to import all the photos she had taken at the crime scene. When that was completed, she burned a CD of the photos, and checked the quality of the CD by opening several photos. After removing and labeling the disc, Sue placed it in her carefully ordered storage file of crime scene photographs.

Once the archival task was completed, Sue began looking at images she had captured the day before at the site of the Boyd shooting. She had hoped to see something new, something she had missed when was she was standing by the side of the road. But as she looked through the images, one by one, displayed on the large, high-resolution screen on her desk, she could see that there was little that could be gleaned from this data. The scene had been completely disturbed by the plow. Any pattern of blood that might have provided clues to the location of the shooter had been obliterated.

She viewed the image showing some of the mail that Lynne had dropped. It was half-buried and scattered along the roadside. Then she looked at the photos she had made of two possible sites where the shooter might have found cover. The first, while showing what appeared to be a path from the road, was drifted over by the time she found it. There were no apparent footprints or other recoverable evidence at the site.

The second area a shooter might have used was on a bluff that provided a good view of the front of the Boyd/Lowther home, but here again there were problems. When she started up the path to the top of the hill, two snowmobiles with deer hunters, one on each machine, passed her going the other direction. And while her fellow deputies had managed to limit traffic on Wildwood Road, cutting off access to all the trails and two tracks was impossible. When she got to the ridgeline that would have offered the assailant a good view of the mailbox, she did her best to visualize where a shooter might have been, but the area was covered with a blanket of new snow.

Sue had had her young colleague, Brett Carty, go over the area with a metal detector. He recovered a surprising quantity of brass, indicating that this summit was a favorite place for hunters. Most of the shell casings were heavily tarnished and filled with debris, suggesting that they had been there for years. One bullet case, however, was shiny. Was it from the gun of the assailant or some deer hunter?

All the things that might provide some real leads to the shooter—a dropped glove, a footprint she could cast—were not to be found. Her efforts to understand the crime scene and collect usable evidence had been totally frustrated by the weather, a snowplow driver doing his job, and deer hunters crossing the land, unaware that an investigation was in progress.

Sue was startled by the chirping of her phone.

"Sue Lawrence."

"Yes."

"This is Sergeant Reynolds, Michigan State Police. We have Dirk Lowther in custody."

"Custody?"

"Yes, we waited until he moved his vehicle, then we pulled him over. He had an open container of beer next to him, and he was clearly inebriated. He blew a 0.30 and is a rather mean drunk. We have him under arrest, and he's going to be charged."

"We need to question him, and I would like his vehicle impounded," said Sue. Then she went on to explain the circumstances. Reynolds agreed to transport Lowther to the Mackinaw City State Police headquarters and hold him there until she arrived to collect him.

23

Early that morning Ray called Nora Jennings—a woman in her eighties, an old friend of his, and someone who had helped look after him during his recent convalescence—asking if he could come by and have a quick cup of coffee on his way to the office, explaining that he needed some background information. Nora asked if Ray had eaten breakfast, and when he indicated he hadn't, she said she'd give him more than coffee.

While Ray Elkins' roots ran deep in Cedar County, Nora's ran deeper. Her great-grandfather was one of the early European settlers. And her parents were active in business and politics of the region through the first half of the twentieth century. Nora got a degree from Ann Arbor just before the war, married, and eventually settled in Grosse Pointe. After Hugh, her husband, returned from the service, they built a summer home high on a bluff above Lake Michigan.

With her knowledge of people, her interest in the history of the region, and her amazing memory, Nora was an important resource for Ray. She had started working on an oral history of Cedar County in the fifties, when most of her parents' generation, and remnants of her grandparents' generation were still alive.

And her knowledge cut across socioeconomic lines. She knew the farmers and the residents of the small towns and villages. She also knew the summer people, the people who had had cottages and family compounds for generations. Nora was a collector of stories, many of them in print in three volumes of local history.

When Ray arrived at the house she was sharing for the winter at the edge of the village, Nora was outside with her two dogs, Falstaff and Prince Hal. He was greeted by a cacophony of barks and wags.

Ray followed Nora and the dogs into the back entrance to the house. He left his coat and heavy boots in the mudroom and walked into the kitchen.

Nora was already working at the stove.

"Where's Dottie?" he asked, looking about for the woman with whom Nora was sharing the house for the winter, a concession to her daughter who didn't want her mother living alone in an isolated cottage on Lake Michigan.

"She's in Grand Rapids with her kids for Thanksgiving. They picked her up on Sunday, and they're bringing her back next Sunday. She didn't want to be gone that long, but they insisted on it."

"What are you going to do?" asked Ray. "Is your daughter coming up or are you going downstate?"

"We are discussing it," Nora replied, some aggravation in her voice. "She was going to come up and get me and the guys, but given the weather, she wanted me to put them," she motioned toward the dogs, "in a kennel and fly."

"The dogs could stay with me for a few days," offered Ray.

"I don't hear you," she responded with a laugh. "I'd rather be here sharing a frozen turkey dinner with these two guys than being a captive in Detroit playing at being a matriarch. Besides, I love these big storms, and we don't get them much anymore."

"What's for breakfast?" asked Ray.

"Buckwheat pancakes, something you used to love." She looked over at Ray, "I got some good local maple syrup and some of that thistle honey, too.

"Sounds wonderful," he responded with a laugh.

He helped carry things to the table, including the coffee pot. Ray attacked his plate of pancakes and Canadian bacon, washing them down with Nora's dark, strong coffee. When they both had consumed most of their breakfasts, Nora asked, "So what do you need to know? You didn't tell me much on the phone, just enough to get my curiosity up a bit."

"You heard about the shooting yesterday?"

"I turned on the news to get the weather, and that's all they were talking about. Horrible thing. And the woman has those two precious little girls. I often see them at the market with her. They're just wonderful. Do you know who did this?" Nora asked as she started to clear away the plates. Ray got up to help her.

"It's still early in the investigation." Ray heard himself giving out the same line, a tired and painful cliché meaning that he didn't know anything yet.

"So what can I help you with?" Nora pursued.

"Lynne Boyd, what can you tell me? Not so much about her, but about the family," Ray explained.

"I don't think I've ever been introduced to her, formally," started Nora, "other than, like I said, chatting with her and the little girls in the checkout line."

"The family," pressed Ray, "you know the family, Prescott and Dorothy Boyd. They own that big estate near the top of the county. I think it was a hunting club at one time."

"I don't know them," responded Nora. "They're rather reclusive, at least when they're up here. I knew his parents, Nick Liago, the wife's name was Lillian."

"I'm confused," interrupted Ray. "Who are the Liagos?"

"That's Prescott's parents. He shed the family name, had it changed, wanted something more Anglo."

"Okay," said Ray. "Tell me about his parents and this piece of property he owns."

"It wasn't really his parents, it was his grandparents who were part of the original group that developed that property. And it even goes back further than that."

Ray was getting frustrated with Nora. She knew so much about people and places in the region, but it was hard to keep her focused. And she always wanted to tell the whole story in minute detail.

"Can you tell me about the property, how did it come into Boyd's hands?" asked Ray.

"I can't really start there, or you won't get the big picture. You need to have the complete history."

"How about a summary, Nora. I've got to get to the office."

"Well, the story goes back to the 1890s. Virgil Nobel, a forefather of a member of the original group, bought up hundreds of acres along that west coast after the area had been lumbered. The land wasn't worth much after the trees had been cut and the area had been burned over to make it easy to get the logs out. He farmed part of the land away from the shore. Later he and his wife built a hotel north of Crescent Cove, it was the first summer resort in the area. There was still a big pier left over from the lumber days, and during the summer lake steamers would drop off passengers coming from Chicago for vacations. Fairly quickly some of the summer visitors wanted to have their own cottages, and Virgil started selling off some of his lakefront. At the same time he was buying up the property around the nearby inland lakes and turning it into resort property. Virgil was a real entrepreneur: built a general store, started a bank. But Crescent Cove and Round Island, he always held onto that. Late in life he built a grand cottage on Round Island, but that burned down during the winter a few years later, shortly after his death. Some of the old timers—this was years and years ago—told me the locals who were used to hunting deer on the island had torched the place in revenge for being told they couldn't hunt there any more."

Nora paused and poured some more coffee, adding cream and some honey to her cup. She held out the pot toward Ray, who covered his cup with his hand.

"Do you want to know about the Indian legend?" she asked.

"Sure," said Ray, resigned to the fact that Nora would get to the part of the history he was most interested in when she got to that part of the chronology.

"Well, the Indians always said the island was a land of evil spirits. I'm not sure why, but they usually had a good reason for their beliefs. Hugh thought it was perhaps because of the shoals that run along the west side of the island and the entrance to the cove."

"That makes sense," said Ray. "I've kayaked through that area many times. When there's a strong wind from the southwest, it's tricky just paddling a kayak through there without getting capsized. And when it's really blowing, the water moving up the coast gets funneled through. There's a strong and unexpected current."

"Some of the old-timers talked about drownings there, people swimming on the north side of the cove being pulled out into deep water. They'd talk about the awful undertow."

"When the conditions are right, there's probably a rip current," Ray observed. "Perhaps we're lucky that that stretch of beach hasn't been available to the general public for decades."

"And that leads us back to your initial question, I think. How did Boyd come into possession of Crescent Cove and Round Island?"

"Yes, how did that happen?" asked Ray, slightly amused at the way the conversation had suddenly shifted toward his original inquiry.

"Well, Virgil's son, Percy, went down to Ann Arbor and got a law degree. He moved on to Chicago, became a big time LaSalle Street lawyer. He had two sisters, Lucinda and Matilda. After the old folks died, the estate was divided in thirds. Percy wanted the land, and he had the cash to buy out his sisters. He developed the hunt club at Crescent Cove and sold memberships to his rich friends. For its time it was a very exclusive club. The first building was a massive log lodge. The main building had hotel-like suites, each with a bath. This is at a time when most of the people up here were still using outhouses. There was a large dining room where everyone ate. The members brought their servants with them, cooks and maids. They didn't employ locals. Behind the main lodge were stables with servants' quarters on the second floor.

"The place was open during June, July, and August; every member got so many weeks they could be at the lodge with their family. And then the club was open for deer season, but that was a strictly stag affair." Nora giggled. "Well, perhaps not strictly stag. There were lots of stories about the carrying-on during deer season. Let's put it this way, wives weren't included."

"So how did the Boyds...?"

"Hold your horses, I'm getting there. So most of the hunting was done over on Round Island. There were a lot of deer over there, more than that small island would support. Yet they had one of their caretakers feeding the herd all year long. I heard from people that those animals were almost tame. They had blinds set up for the members, a warming cottage where they served lunch. These guys were really roughing it.

"Eventually some of the older members died off." Nora took a long sip of her coffee before continuing. "As it was explained to me, the club was set up so when a member died, his estate would be paid the price of the original share and some modest interest. Percy's idea was that some of the offspring might not be acceptable members. And I think new members were recruited for a while, but then with the depression and the war, well the club got very small.

"Along the way, your predecessor, probably the longest serving sheriff in the history of this county—maybe the state, became sort of an honorary member of the club."

"How did that happen?" asked Ray.

"Well, old Orville just loved doing favors for rich people, whether it was fixing a ticket or driving a drunk home. During the late thirties or maybe during the war years there was some vandalism up at the club. I think some poaching, too. Orville worked out an arrangement that he'd provide special protection in exchange for hunting privileges and the occasional use of the lodge, when the place wasn't occupied by members. Orville's special deputies were included in this deal. Percy thought it was a great idea, and the arrangement lasted for decades."

"What does this have to do with…?"

"Just wait, I'm getting to that. Some time ago, in the 70s or early 80s there weren't many members left. By then Boyd was president of the club. And one year during deer season one of the older members, Talmadge Hawthorne, was shot and killed on Round Island. Orville and this group of young guys who ran the department investigated the incident. It was reported that Talmadge shot himself accidentally and bled to death before anyone found him.

"There was a lot of talk at the time because Talmadge was trying to stop Boyd from getting control of the club. There was some kind of settlement with Talmadge's family, it was all sort of hush, hush. Soon after that, Boyd managed to buy out the last few members. And as long as Orville lived, he and his special deputies continued to hunt there.

"That all changed when Boyd tore down the old buildings and built his own place. And you know he brought in an out-of-state firm to do the work. He didn't want the locals to know anything about the place. He's even got a landing place for a helicopter. Have you been there?"

"No," said Ray, "Not yet. I've just seen it from the water. It almost looks like an office complex. Lots of dark glass and metal. Do you know where their money comes from?"

"The old man owned a trucking company somewhere around Chicago that Boyd inherited. But I heard he liquidated that right away and used the money to start other businesses. One rumor was that Boyd was an international arms dealer. But I also heard that he's made most of his money in currency trading." Nora paused for a moment. "You know, dear sweet Hugh tried to explain that to me, currency trading, years ago. But I never quite understood it. Let's just say he's made millions, or tens of millions."

"So you mentioned the young deputies," said Ray. "Did you know who those people were?"

"Not really," Nora said. "I just heard that Orville had sort of lost it, and these young guys ran the department. They even helped him get reelected, which isn't too difficult to do around here with our one party system. Thing I could never understand is why one of them didn't run to replace Orville?"

Ray sat for a long moment without responding. "Interesting question, Nora. They probably didn't want the paperwork that goes with being the sheriff."

"You want some more coffee, Ray?"

"I've got to scoot," he responded. "Thanks for breakfast and the talk."

Nora followed him out of the house, the dogs circling in the yard. As he drove away, he imagined Nora was lighting up a Chesterfield as she took Prince Hal and Falstaff on their walk around the neighborhood. Ray thought about his conversation with Billy Coyle and what he had just learned from Nora. He felt like he was trying to fit together the pieces of an elaborate, multi-level puzzle.

24

As Ray parked his Jeep in the visitors' section of the sloping parking lot near the main entrance of the TV studio, he thought about the summer evenings when he was a teenager. He and his friends used to come by and watch the locally produced news at 11:00 p.m. In the station's first iteration, the offices and studios were all crowded into one cement block building, remnants of which he imagined were still present somewhere in the new glass and steel structure that stood before him.

In those days, back in the late sixties, on hot summer nights a large garage door that formed the back wall of the main studio would be open to provide some relief from the heat generated by the spotlights and equipment. At the time air conditioning would have been considered an unnecessary luxury in northern Michigan. Ray and his friends would park just beyond the garage door and watch the news. Two reporters shared all the duties of the 11:00 p.m. news, moving between the three sets: the News Center, Weather Center, and Sports Center. The reporters, both male, usually dressed in sports shirts and jeans or Bermuda shorts—camera angles were maintained to only show the head and chest—

would move to different parts of the studio during commercials, followed by one of the two cameras. The announcer would glue on a smile and be ready to read the news from folded sheets of paper pulled from the Associated Press, whenever the director, wearing a headset and dancing between the cameras, pointed at him.

Ray thought about the old days again when he entered the building, passing through two sets of glass doors. He was now confronted by elaborate security procedures. A receptionist, a pretty, young woman with a bleached-teeth smile and wearing a blazer with the station's logo embroidered on the pocket, asked him who he wished to see from behind the protection of a thick Plexiglas window. Ray said he had an appointment with the station manager. She glanced at the screen in front of her.

"Oh yes," she responded, her disembodied voice echoing in the empty reception area from a speaker above the window near the ceiling. "Mr. Plumb is expecting you. I'll buzz you in," she said, pointing to a steel door on his right. By the time Ray got through the door, the receptionist was in the hallway ready to guide him to a small conference room.

"Mr. Plumb will be with you in a few minutes," she said. "Would you like some coffee?"

"Please," Ray responded. She closed the door behind her, leaving him alone in an empty room. While he waited, he looked around. One wall was covered with glass and opened to a hillside that overlooked the bay and the edge of town. The other three walls were paneled in cherry and covered with awards and photos. He looked closely at the awards, most from the Michigan Association of Broadcasters, for excellence in various aspects of programming. Ray noted that all the certificates were from the last decade. He looked at the photos, most were of current station personalities standing with nationally-known broadcast figures. "There must be photo ops at national conventions," Ray thought to himself.

"Sheriff, good to see you," said Plumb as he entered. The receptionist was at his heels carrying a tray with a coffee decanter and mugs, the station's logo on them too. She quickly disappeared, leaving them in the closed room.

While Ray's interaction with the station's reporters happened on a regular basis, he hadn't seen Plumb in a number of years. Ray noted that he had become rather rotund.

"You've got a wonderful view here," Ray commented as Plumb passed him a mug of coffee.

"We do, don't we. I'm glad I insisted that we put the conference room in this position during our last rebuild of the station." He and Ray looked out at the vista, snow covering the open fields and woods, beyond the gray-blue water of the bay under a heavy overcast.

Finally Plumb broke the silence. "It looks like the view will be unchanged until I retire. For years I've worried that some developer will build a ton of overpriced view condos between here and the bay. Fortunately, it's never happened. But you're not here to talk about vista preservation or whatever they're calling it." He paused for a moment, sadness sweeping across his countenance. "I can't imagine those two beautiful little girls growing up without their mother."

Ray didn't respond. He too was thinking about the girls, thinking about the trauma that had already been inflicted upon them.

"And all we could get out of you last night was that the investigation was continuing. No clear suspects, no one in custody."

"That hasn't changed," said Ray. "And that's why I'm here. Lynne came to see me over a week ago with some letters she had received here at the station. She told me that you had insisted that she contact law enforcement."

"When I saw the letters, I wanted her to make sure you knew about them. Lynne did her best to say it was nothing, but if it was nothing why did she bother to show them to me." He paused and looked at Ray before he continued. "Even though the writer's approach seemed silly, I mean words and letters cut from papers, and then the whole thing Xeroxed. This person obviously watches too much television," he said with a short laugh, and then looked embarrassed by his joke.

"Have any of your other employees received this kind of mail?"

"Not like the ones Lynne got. Our on-air people get mail, mostly e-mail now. The vast majority of it is friendly. If a viewer is unhappy, I'm the one who gets the mail or phone calls."

"But you haven't received…?"

"Not like these. These were clearly directed at Lynne. The writer didn't like what she was saying, but the threats and sexual part, we don't get stuff like that. This was personal."

"The series that these letters reference, when did it air?"

"I think it was about three weeks ago. Lynne had been working on the series during the late summer and fall. Perhaps you remember that last spring there were two accidental shootings in our coverage area involving young children. In one case a six or seven-year-old shot himself with a loaded gun. In the second one—and this is the one that really struck home for Lynne—a toddler killed his twin brother with a handgun they found in their babysitter's bedroom. I think the woman was doing something else, like making lunch, and the boys found the gun, and it went off. And there was a third death last year involving middle school boys. Lynne covered all three stories and was really moved by the enormous tragedy suffered by these families. I know she took these personally, especially the one with the twins. At the time she mentioned that she and her husband had had words a number of times about the way he secured, or I should say didn't adequately secure, his gun. Late this summer she asked me if we could make this one of the topics for our fall news magazine."

"Let me ask something again. Before this series aired, she hadn't received any letters, e-mail, or phone calls of a threatening nature?"

"Not that I'm aware of."

"Ever?"

"Not since that incident with her old boyfriend years ago."

"Have any of your other employees received threatening letters, e-mails, or phone calls?"

"No, this is most unusual. Like I said, when viewers are unhappy with something, most complaints come to me, as station manager. And the complaints are usually about network programs, not things locally produced."

"Like what?"

"Sex, language. And then there's politics. A certain number of viewers are convinced that we're part of the mythical left-wing media." Plumb paused and chuckled. "Actually, now that I'm a few months from retirement, I'm finding it harder and harder to be nice to these assholes. I just want to tell them, 'Hey, all the networks and most of the stations are owned by corporate America. The whole network news structure provides a corporate view of the world. And maybe the corporate view is not as conservative as some doped-up wacko who broadcasts from a bunker in Florida thinks it should be, but it's hardly left of center.'"

"But none of your communications from unhappy viewers has ever looked like the mail Lynne received?" asked Ray, trying to keep Plumb on topic.

"I mostly get phone calls. Usually from old people who want to talk my ear off. Some of them are probably just lonely and need someone to listen to them. But why me? I don't want to listen to the newest conspiracy theories from talk radio. "

"How did Lynne get along with people here at the station?" Ray asked, needing to move the interview forward.

"No problems. She's just a good person. Everyone liked her: crew, colleagues. Everyone."

"If Lynne doesn't come back, is anyone's career advanced?"

Plumb considered the question, his gaze shifting out to the swirling snow and then coming back to Ray.

"We'll have to make changes. I'll try out some of the young reporters for that spot or look at the possibility of going outside. But there's nothing here worth killing for. We're a small station; we don't pay much. The kids who come through here look on this place as a stepping-stone to a major market. Their view of professional growth is tied to getting out of here as fast as possible, not moving up in our organization.

"Lynne's staying around was anomalous, if she hadn't married and had the twins, she would have been long gone: Chicago, New York, D.C., maybe California. She's smart, attractive, and very professional. All those traits would have quickly carried her to a big station or a network job. I've always felt that we were lucky to be able to hold onto her. But our good fortune might have been at her expense."

"So you don't think she has any real enemies here," asked Ray, trying to get a definite answer.

"No, I'm sure of it," Plumb answered emphatically.

"How about office romances?"

"Lynne involved with someone here at the station?" Plumb asked, his tone incredulous.

"Yes."

"Not here."

"You're sure?"

"Not possible."

"How about Lynne being involved in a romance somewhere else?" Ray continued.

"I don't think so. She's not that kind of person. And given her family obligations and all the time she spends here, I don't know how she'd schedule it. That said," he stopped and looked away.

"That said, what?" pressed Ray.

"Her husband, what an asshole. I can sort of understand how she might have gotten involved with him after that tragic incident, but I don't know why she married him. She deserves better than that."

"You don't like Dirk?"

"No. Do you?"

Ray avoided the question. "Why do you say she deserves better?"

"I just can't see her with that guy. What joy can he give her?"

"Do you know that she's unhappy in the relationship?"

"Lynne keeps things to herself. But remember, I'm a native. I've encountered Dirk lots of times over the years. And she's said things, albeit obliquely, that suggest it's not a happy marriage."

"Do you think there's any abuse?"

"Not physical, but I imagine he plays mind games with her, he does with everyone else. The guy's into power and control."

"Can you think of anyone who might want to harm her? Or anything that might give someone a motive to shoot her?"

"No, none. But, as you know, there are lots of wackos out there. And there seem to be more all the time."

"Do you know if Lynne has any close friends, and if so can you give me their names?"

"Here at the station we're all friends, but I don't think people spend much time together away from work. Away from here, I don't know. But if she's like my daughter, her women friends would be other young mothers."

Ray felt the buzzing in his pocket before the ring became audible. "Excuse me a second," he said to Plumb. He pushed the answer button after seeing that the call was coming from Sue Lawrence's cell.

"Yes."

"Ray, I've got Dirk, and we're on our way back. Any news on Lynne?" asked Sue, her voice starting to break up.

"Nothing has changed," he answered. "Where are you?"

Ray waited, but there was no response. "Hello," he said. He waited again, then hit the end button.

"I've got to run," he said to Plumb. "Things are happening that need my immediate attention."

"Can we get you on camera, just a short statement for our evening news?"

"I don't have the time right now," Ray said. "We'll have a press release out this afternoon."

"How about Lynne's husband, Dirk?"

"We will be talking to him and anyone else who might help us find the assailant."

"Is he, what's the police term, a person of interest?"

"We will be talking to anyone who might help us get the shooter," said Ray, knowing that he was doing a poor job deflecting Plumb's questions.

25

When Ray entered the interview room he found Dirk Lowther sprawled in one of the chairs. Ray offered his hand and said, "Hello."

Dirk looked up at him, his arms resting on the table. He did not immediately respond to Ray's greeting. Finally, he fixed Ray in his gaze for a few seconds, made a low guttural response of recognition, and looked down again.

Ray settled across from Dirk, "Would you like some coffee?"

Dirk looked up briefly, "Yeah."

Ray filled a worn ceramic mug and pushed it within Dirk's reach. As he poured himself a cup, Sue Lawrence entered the room and sat at the end of the table at Ray's right. They exchanged glances, Ray wishing that he and Sue might have had time to debrief before this interview.

"This all must be a horrible shock to you," said Ray. He looked across at Dirk, whose present demeanor and appearance contrasted greatly from his usual swagger and spit-and-polished look. Dirk's hair was uncombed and oily, his eyes bloodshot, his face unshaven. After taking a sip of coffee, Dirk unzipped and peeled back his parka, a woodsy camo design, exposing a frayed and soiled hooded sweatshirt. The stink of tobacco, perspiration, and hard drinking filled the room.

"Yeah, it's a shock," he responded without affect. He remained silent a long time, then asked in a hostile tone. "Am I a person of interest?"

"Do you know anyone who might want to harm your wife?" Ray asked, not responding to Dirk's question.

Dirk looked up at Ray and held him in an unsteady gaze. "Let's cut the shit," he responded. "We all know that I'm suspect number one. When a woman is killed, start with the husband or boyfriend and nine times out of ten you've got the assailant."

"Okay, Dirk, let's start with you," Ray said. "Where were you yesterday morning at 10:00 a.m.?"

"I was on the road heading toward the U.P." Dirk delivered his answer directly to Ray in a hostile tone, without showing any recognition that Sue was in the room. "And I got a witness to where I was in the U.P. and when I got there."

"So let's go through your story, Dirk. I want the complete chronology of your trip. According to your Away From Duty Form you were going to be gone for two weeks." Ray placed the form on the table in front of him. "And you were going to leave this area on Thursday and go to the U.P. Is that correct?"

"Yeah, just like I wrote."

"But today is Tuesday, not Thursday?"

"Yeah, well I was going to stay around till after Thanksgiving dinner, and then head up hunting, but things changed."

"What changed?"

"The bitch had me served."

"I'm not following," said Ray.

"Sunday night when I came on duty, well you know the routine. I took care of some stuff and was heading out towards my car when old Nat Peters came walking up. I stopped to talk with him and asked what the hell he was doing out in such bad weather. He says he's got a delivery to make, and he hands me this big envelope. I sure as hell knew what it was. And I don't know why she had to do it in that way, having me served. Shit. I told her I'd talk to the lawyer, and we'd work it out. But I guess I wasn't going fast enough for her."

"So you were served. Tell me what you were served with?"

"Are you listening or what?" said Dirk, angrily. He glared at Ray through bloodshot eyes.

"Dirk, we're going through this step by step. I'm going to ask for detail, and if I don't understand something, I'm going to have you provide some clarification. You were served with divorce papers, what did you do then?"

"I sat in my car and started to read them. Before I got through them I had to respond to an accident. And that's how the night ran. You can check my log. Bad driving conditions, fender benders, or single vehicle accidents—people running off the road. And I had to bring one drunk to jail. It was a busy night."

"It looks like you signed out early," said Ray, holding a time sheet in front of him.

"Yeah, I wanted to go by the house and get my hunting stuff before anyone was awake. Like I said, I'd planned to hang around till Thanksgiving, then go hunting. But after I had been served, I just thought the hell with it. I'm just going to get out of Dodge. Her and her family can go fuck themselves."

"The two of you had not discussed divorce?" asked Sue.

"We'd barely been speaking for months. Sometime in the summer we'd talked about going to see a lawyer, but it never happened. Obviously, she went ahead and did it on her own."

"So after you went off duty, what did you do?

"I drove home, loaded my stuff into the SUV, got the trailer with my four-wheeler out of the barn, hitched it up, and took off.

"Did you see anyone at the house?" Ray asked.

"Just that French girl; she was in the kitchen."

"You didn't see your wife or daughters?"

"No one else was up yet."

"The SUV, that's Lynne's vehicle?"

"Yes."

"Why didn't you take your truck?" Ray asked.

"I was having trouble with the wiring harness for the trailer. There was a short somewhere. I was going to get it fixed this week before I went hunting, but I didn't get a chance to do that."

"Was Lynne aware that you were taking her vehicle?"

"No, but like I cared. And I didn't want to be hauling the trailer to the U.P. with no lights in this kind of weather. I've done a lot for her over the last few years; she can do something for me while she's getting ready to boot my ass out."

"Okay," said Ray, "Then what did you do?"

"I started for the U.P. How much detail do you want?"

"I want it all, every stop." Ray pressed.

"I stopped in Grayling for gas, again at the rest area just before Gaylord, the toll booth on the north side of the bridge, and then I stopped in Munising to see an old friend."

"And…"

"We spent some time in a bar, had dinner, went to her house for the night."

"Your cell phone working?"

"I didn't take a cell phone. I left it right in that tray between the seats so Lynne would know that she couldn't call me."

"When did you hear your wife had been shot?" asked Sue

"This morning, one of the troopers told me after they took me into custody."

"This woman in Munising, does she have a name?" asked Sue.

"I don't want to get her involved in this."

"Well, she is involved. We will need to talk to her. What's her name?" Ray asked.

"Sheila Maddox."

"She was with you the whole time?"

"The whole time I was in Munising."

"So let's go through this again. What time did you leave the area?

"Like I said, a little after 6:00 in the morning."

"What time did you cross the bridge?"

"It was after eleven, I was creeping till I got to 75, then I was probably averaging about forty, sometimes less."

"And you stopped in Grayling and Gaylord. Anywhere else?"

"Oh yeah, I stopped in Cut River and got a whitefish sandwich and a beer."

"How long were you there, in Cut River?"

"Not long, forty minutes, maybe an hour. The waitress's name was Marge."

"You stop anywhere else?"

"I topped up the tank in Engadine."

"How long were you there?"

"Fifteen minutes."

"How did you pay for the gas?"

"Credit card."

"Grayling too?

"Yes.

"How about lunch?"

"I used a card there, too. All the receipts are in the car."

"And this woman in Munising," Sue looked down at her notes, "Sheila Maddox, did she know you were coming?"

"She was expecting me Thursday night. But I called her from a pay phone at Cut River to say I was going to be a few days early."

"Tell me about your marriage," said Ray.

"What do you want to know?"

"You're being sued for divorce; you indicated that you knew this was coming."

"Lynne told me she didn't think we had much of a marriage, then she got a bed for the room she used as her office and started sleeping in there. She said we needed to talk to a lawyer."

"When did that happen?"

"Late spring, early summer. I thought things might improve, that she was just going through one of her bitchy hormone things."

"Were you surprised by her assessment about not having much of a marriage?" asked Sue.

"No. I sort of agreed. Great sex in the beginning, but after the girls were born she lost interest in me. The divorce was just a matter of time."

"How do you feel about this?"

"What do you mean?"

"The end of your marriage, the pending divorce. Are you angry, sad, upset?" pressed Ray.

"Look, she used me; I used her. We both got what we wanted for a time. Now we're not. It's just the way things are."

"So you can walk away with no bitter feelings?" asked Ray, putting less than a subtle hint of incredulity in his voice.

"I've been down this road before. I get bored being with the same woman. They probably get bored being with me."

"How about your daughters?"

"How about what?" Dirk responded. "The truth is that I don't find little kids very interesting. And they were Lynne's little girls from the beginning. If she hadn't gotten pregnant, we'd never gotten married."

"Why did you marry her?" Ray asked.

"Like I just said, she was pregnant; she wanted to get married. I told her to get an abortion; she wouldn't hear of it. In the end I think I was flattered because a beautiful young woman wanted to marry me."

The three of them sat in silence for several minutes: Dirk, looking defeated, his body slouched forward onto the table; Sue and Ray exchanging glances, each wondering in what direction to move the interview.

"Did Lynne tell you about any threats she might have received?" Ray asked.

"Like I've said, we haven't been really talking for a long time."

"Might she have had an outside romantic interest?" asked Sue.

Dirk was slow to respond. "I didn't see or hear anything, but who knows. Maybe she was getting it on with that skinny-assed French girl," he said bitterly. "They seemed like quite the pair. Or maybe she had a thing for that old fart psychiatrist."

"Dirk, you've been in police work a long time. Arresting and putting people in jail, it's hard not to make some real enemies. Is there anyone you can think of who might shoot your wife as a way of getting at you?"

Dirk slowly moved his head from side to side. "Lots of people have been pissed at me over the years. I mean dozens of the assholes that I put away would be happy to put a bullet in me or flatten me with their pickup. It's part of the baggage that goes with the business. We all have to deal with it." He stopped and gave Ray a knowing look. "I can think of lots of people who'd like to get me, but I don't think anyone would do that to Lynne."

"What kind of financial arrangements do you and Lynne have? Does she have a life insurance policy that would help you with a mortgage on the house if something happened to her?"

"There is no mortgage. Her old man bought the land we built on and paid for the house," he answered with hostility. "The property is in a trust with a trustee who would manage Lynne's assets in the interests of her daughters. That was put in place when her father gave her the house."

"So there's no joint ownership there."

"No."

"Do you own anything together?"

"My truck is in my name, same with my property in the U.P. and some rentals down here."

"Do you have a will?"

"I'm going to die intestate and let the scavengers fight over my bones."

"So Lynne has an estate and trust established, but you have nothing in place?"

"Like I said before, I was the outsider, so I didn't play any of their games."

"Whose games?" asked Sue.

"Lynne's family's," he answered bitterly.

"How about your insurance with the county?" Sue asked. "Who are the beneficiaries on that policy?"

"Kids from another marriage. They're grown now."

They sat in silence again, until finally Dirk asked, "Am I a person of interest? Don't you want to know if I'm pissed enough at Lynne to hire someone to blow her away? Or maybe one of my girlfriends might want her dead. I'm a real catch," he said sarcastically.

"When are you planning to come back to work?" asked Ray.

"I got lots of vacation time. If you don't have any problem with it, I think I'll stay off for a few weeks."

"I think we can arrange that," Ray answered.

"Would one of you accompany me out to the house?" asked Dirk.

"What for?" asked Ray.

"I started moving out weeks ago. I want to get my old pickup and the rest of my possessions, and I want you to see what I'm taking. Then I will give you my keys to the place. I want my life completely separated from Lynne's, so I don't have to deal with her parents if she doesn't make it."

"I'll take you," answered Ray. "You have a place to move to?"

"I own a few rentals in the area. One of them came vacant last summer, and I started moving my stuff there months ago." After a long silence, Dirk said, "If you don't have anything else, can we get going? I'm dead tired and want to get this over."

"Okay," said Ray.

Dirk stood and left the room.

"Stick around, will you? I should be back fairly quickly, and we have a lot to discuss," Ray said to Sue.

"I'll be waiting," she responded.

26

S ue was arranging materials for Ray on his return. Two thirds of the long table in Ray's office was covered with her papers and diagrams. At the far end of the table were two bags and a thermos of hot water.

"What's that?" asked Ray, pointing at the bags.

"It's supper and a peace offering."

"Why the peace offering?" Ray asked.

"I thought you might be upset that I went out of county without talking to you first?"

Ray shrugged his shoulders and grimaced.

"I got you won ton soup, shrimp in garlic sauce, white rice— no MSG—and a fortune cookie. I thought I'd feed you before you fire me."

Ray made a sub-vocalization and moved his head from side to side.

"You know what I really like about you?" Sue asked.

Ray remained silent.

"Your capacity to control your rage."

"And you know what I like about you?" he shot back.

"My intelligence, work ethic, and skill at making cognitive leaps."

"All that and the idea you can buy me off with a container of garlic shrimp sans MSG."

"How did your trip to Dirk's house go?" Sue asked.

"It may have been all theater," Ray answered, "and I was the special audience. We went in, I followed him to the master bedroom. He packed his clothes in a couple of large duffels and got some toiletries from the bath. His closet and drawers were mainly empty, so he was telling us the truth when he said he had already moved most of his things. After we left the house and he got his old pickup from the barn, he handed me his keys to the place." Ray fished through a vest pocket and removed a small, green karabiner with two keys on it. He tossed the keys to Sue. "Those are to the house and barn. Let's get them locked up in the evidence room for safekeeping."

Ray and Sue settled into chairs and started unwrapping the food. "What are you having?" he asked.

"Sesame chicken, shrimp fried rice, hot and sour soup, an egg roll, and two almond cookies. Lots of fat and sugar, but I've more than burned off the calories in the last twelve hours."

"Sure," said Ray. "One of these days your metabolism is going to change."

There was a long silence as they both focused on their food, neither having eaten for most of the day. Finally Ray said, "Tell me about the trip. Just give me the highlights," he added, long aware of Sue's inability to summarize.

She was on her second almond cookie by the time she had provided him a full account of her day, from arriving at the office until they started the interview with Dirk. Ray, who ate only half as fast as Sue, had allowed her to give her report without interruption.

"I need to go over a few points," said Ray as he gingerly squeezed the remaining liquid from a tea bag he had just pulled from a thick white porcelain mug. "When you first encountered

Dirk at the State Police post in Mackinaw City, did he still appear to be intoxicated?" He paused for a minute as he calculated the time. "Let's see, that would have been close to four hours after they found him."

"Yes. His eyes were red, his speech was slurred, he was unsteady on his feet, and he stank of booze, cigarettes, and God knows what else."

"And you told him again that Lynne had been shot?"

"Yes."

"And his response?"

"He was angry, like why was I giving him old news. He had already been told that. Then he said that we must think he did the shooting, and he launched into an inarticulate and rambling denial. Finally he asked about his daughters. When I said they were safely ensconced with their grandparents, he went into a tirade about what rotten people the Boyds were."

"How was he on the trip back?"

"He didn't say much. He appeared to be brooding, some of the time he was sleeping. Which was okay with me because I didn't feel like talking with him." Sue paused, considering her next words. "He seemed angry at me, like I was interrupting his hunting trip."

"You're not over-reading the situation?"

"Perhaps, but when you have any history with this man, it's hard to be neutral."

"It is, but if he used a credit card like he said he did, he's going to have a pretty tight alibi," Ray observed.

"But he's got such a strong motive. His wife is dumping him. He's just been served, which is a rather indelicate way of letting him know. That's got to be awful hard on someone who is totally full of himself," said Sue.

"But this wasn't an act of passion after he got served. He didn't go home and shoot up the place. Dirk's rage was limited to taking Lynne's car without her permission. That's a very tame response."

"Like he said, he knew this was coming. Perhaps he got someone else to do the shooting, and it's just a coincidence that it happened the morning after he got served." Sue suggested.

"That's possible, but again, what's his motive? If he was telling the truth about their financial arrangement, he has nothing to gain by offing her before the divorce."

"How about custody of the girls?" she suggested

"I don't think Dirk would be particularly interested in taking over the care of two young children," said Ray.

"Yes, that's hard to imagine," Sue responded. "Okay, so maybe he arranged a hit because he's just an angry, vengeful man."

"Dirk is one hostile dude, but I almost believe his story that leaving town was a sudden decision, not something he had planned. And even if he's just giving us a line, it's hard to get away with a hit. Dirk's not stupid, he knows we'll start the investigation with him," Ray countered.

"But, how about his, what's your word?"

"Hubris," Ray suggested.

"He is so arrogant, perhaps if he's behind this he thinks we're too stupid to ever figure out how he pulled it off."

"Okay. Let's carefully follow up on Dirk: verify the times on his credit cards, and we can probably find him on surveillance tapes. Will you interview this Maddox woman?"

"Sure," Sue responded.

"But," continued Ray, "we must not lose focus of other possibilities. At this point I think he's a long shot." Ray looked over at Sue. "You're tired."

"The adrenalin has just run out," Sue responded.

"We can go over this in the early a.m.," said Ray gesturing toward Sue's carefully arranged stacks of data.

"There are several things...."

"Can it wait till morning?" Ray pressed.

"Yes."

"Go home and get some sleep. We'll hit it again about 7:00. I've got an interview scheduled with Lynne's friend at 9:00. See if you can reschedule the interview with Lynne's mother that you missed today for after that. We still need to see if her daughter might have shared anything with her."

"You talked with Lynne's father?"

"Yes, at the hospital last night. I didn't get much other than his dislike of Dirk. I would like to talk to him again. This morning I had breakfast with Nora Jennings. I got a short history of Crescent Cove and Round Island. I'll share that with you tomorrow."

"Tell me now."

"You're on your way home. That's an order. Let's see if you can follow it without being insubordinate. And thanks for the dinner, I'll clean things up. Get going."

"Thanks, Ray," said Sue, pulling herself to her feet. "I'll be in early."

27

Ray was on the way out of his office when the phone rang. He hesitated briefly, then walked back and lifted the receiver.

"Ray, this is Carol in dispatch. I have Jack Grochoski on the line. He's insisting on talking to you."

"What seems to be the problem?"

"Dirk Lowther is at the Last Chance. Jack say's he wants him to leave, but Dirk is too drunk to drive."

"Just dispatch a car to the scene," Ray said.

"Jack didn't want that. He wants you to personally handle the situation."

"Did this call come in on the 911 line?"

"On the regular department number."

"Okay," Ray responded. "Tell Jack I'm on my way. Who is in the central sector right now?"

"Ben Reilly."

"Good, have him meet me there, but ask him to wait in the parking lot if he gets there before me."

"Will do," came the response.

In the few minutes it took to drive to the Last Chance, Ray thought about Ben Reilly and Dirk Lowther, two officers he had inherited from the previous sheriff. Ben was smart, reliable, and honest, the kind of person who gives stability and strength to an organization.

As he pulled into the parking lot, Ben Reilly was already out of his car and waiting for Ray. They found Dirk sitting at a table near the back of the bar. Ray noticed that Donna Bateman was sitting at the table, talking to Dirk.

Ray and Ben settled on stools at the other end of the bar. Jack set a mug in front of each of them and poured coffee from a freshly made pot.

"I think everything has settled down now," said Jack, motioning with his head in the direction of Dirk. Once Donna came in and started talking to him, he sort of quieted down."

"What happened?" asked Ray.

"Dirk came in about an hour ago, maybe a little more. He ordered a shell and a shot at the bar then settled over at that table. He was looking worse for wear, but I served him anyway. I told him how sorry I was about his wife, and he says something like, 'Yeah, whatever.' I thought that was awfully damn strange, so I just left him alone. He sat there and nursed the first beer a long time. He looked like he was waiting for someone. Eventually he ordered another beer that I brought to him. Then a couple of hunters come in. They have a couple of shots at the bar and take a pitcher over to a table near Dirk's."

"These men, do you know who they are?" asked Ben.

"Don't think I've ever seen them before."

"So what happened?" asked Ray.

"After a bit I could hear something starting. Didn't know what was being said, but you could tell by the tone it wasn't good. That's when I called you, Ray. I thought you'd want to come over here and deal with this before it became a real problem.

"Then suddenly Dirk was on his feet, and so were these two guys. I was heading over there to tell them to take it outside when Donna came in. Well, she's so damn good at handling men. Whatever was going to happen, she headed it off. The two guys left, and she got Dirk settled down. She's supposed to take over the bar at 6:00, but I told her I'd look after the bar till you came, and we figured out what to do with Dirk.

"Okay," said Ray. They picked up their coffee mugs and joined Donna and Dirk. Donna excused herself as soon as they seated themselves.

Ray looked across the table. Dirk was wearing the same clothes and looked in the same condition as when Ray last saw him.

"Didn't make it home yet," said Ray.

"Ain't got no home," said Dirk, his speech sloppy and slurred.

"You told me you had a place, that you'd moved most things there. You sure didn't have much at the house you shared with Lynne," Ray added.

Dirk remained silent, his mind slowed by exhaustion and alcohol. "Yeah, I got a place. Didn't get there yet. Thought I'd stop for a beer on the way."

"Jack says you had words with a couple of men."

Again the response was slow in coming, "Yeah, a couple of assholes from somewhere around Grand Rapids."

"Did you know them?"

"Not really. But I guess I busted one of them for a DUI sometime. He was making some kind of smart-assed remarks. He wanted to know how tough I was when I wasn't wearing a badge."

"Let's get you home," said Ray.

"I don't wanna go home. I'm perfectly happy here."

"Your drinking is over for the evening," Ray said slowly. "I'm going to drive you home in your truck. Ben will follow."

Dirk fumbled with a zipper on the breast pocket of his soiled jacket and retrieved a pack of cigarettes. He extracted a cigarette from the pack and lit it with a battered Zippo lighter. After he inhaled deeply, he responded. "Okay, let's go home."

He struggled to pull himself to his feet and then followed Ben toward the door, Ray bringing up the rear. Dirk paused at the door, turned back toward the bar, and gave Donna an awkward wave before leaving. Ray escorted him to the passenger side of his truck and held the door open. Dirk picked up the duffle bags and tossed them behind the seat.

Ray pulled out the seatbelt and told Dirk to put it on before closing the door. As he was coming around the back of the truck, he noticed two men in camo leaning against the back of a red Dodge truck, watching the process.

"Key," said Ray, sliding into the driver's seat.

"It's in the ignition."

"Where we going?" Ray asked, as he searched for the switch to the headlights.

Other than providing occasional directions, Dirk said nothing during the fifteen-mile trip over snow-covered back roads to his house. At Dirk's direction, Ray turned onto a recently plowed drive and followed it several hundred yards to a house that was secluded from the road by a large stand of pine. He helped Dirk carry his things in and looked around briefly. The house was large, neat, and nicely furnished, hardly what Ray had expected for a "rental."

"It's cold in here," Ray noted.

"Yeah, just need to turn up the thermostat."

"Everything else working?"

"Yes."

"How about a phone?"

"I'm okay. Just leave me alone so I can go to bed."

Ray nodded, pulled the door shut, and walked to Ben's waiting car.

"I'm so absent-minded, I pocketed Dirk's truck key," Ray said handing the key to Ben. "Take this in at the end of your shift. Arrange to have someone drop it by tomorrow morning."

"Will do." Ben chuckled as he dropped the key in the interior pocket of his heavy winter jacket.

"Did you know Dirk was getting divorced?" Ray asked

"Sue briefed me about what was going on."

"Dirk told me he was moving to a rental he owned. Doesn't look like a modular, does it?"

"No," agreed Ben, "but then nothing about Dirk was ever ordinary."

28

~~~~

It was after 9:00 p.m. when Ray turned off the road and slowly climbed the steep, curved driveway to his house. The drive had been plowed some time during the day, only an inch or two of snow covered the surface. Ray noted tracks in the snow and found Sarah James's small Subaru SUV parked near the front. Lights were on in the kitchen and living room. He reached up and hit the garage door remote.

Ray found Sarah curled up on the couch reading a book. She rose to greet him.

"Hope you don't mind my dropping by," she said, after they embraced. "I was hoping to surprise you. But you weren't here, only the man from the well company, he let me in."

"Billy Coyle."

"Yes, Billy, he gave me his name. He was just leaving, said to tell you he replaced some parts and everything should work."

Sarah slid into his arms again.

"I thought you were going to New York to spend Thanksgiving with your son."

"I am," said Sarah. "I'm on the first flight out of Traverse City at 7:00 a.m. tomorrow morning, which means I should be at the airport close to 6:00. How would you like to have a house guest that you have to get up and push into the shower about 4:30?"

"I would love that," Ray replied.

Sarah moved around the counter and poured two glasses of white wine from a tall, elegantly shaped bottle. She handed a glass to Ray and picked up the second glass, gently clinking it against Ray's before she took a sip.

Ray swirled the wine, inhaled the bouquet, and carefully tasted it. "Very nice," he said. "Very nice, indeed."

"And if it weren't?" she quizzed playfully. "Would you send me away?"

"Absolutely," responded Ray. "Straight into the teeth of a furious winter gale."

"I just needed to see you," Sarah said. "And I know you've been incredibly busy. So I took a chance that I could see you tonight. Cheeky of me."

She refilled their glasses and they settled on the couch.

"You look tired," she said.

Ray nodded.

"Most of the time since we met, you've been totally absorbed with a murder case."

Ray nodded, then took a sip of wine.

"The other Ray, the one that's not completely focused on his work, what's he like? Would I find him attractive, too?"

Ray thought about her question. "He's a lot like the guy you know. When all his energy isn't needed by his job, he's passionate about other things. He spends time in his kayak, listens to music, reads, experiments with recipes. His mother used to tell him she thought he was sort of boring because he was always so busy doing things."

"How is that boring?"

"She liked to do different things. Things that required lots of sitting, something I can't do."

"Like what?"

"Like going to movies; Mom didn't miss many. Or going out for breakfast or lunch and chatting over coffee for hours."

"And you can't do that?"

"Maybe if you fill me with Ritalin...."

"So you probably spent a lot of time in the principal's office when you were a kid."

"Actually I didn't. I was in a one-room school for the first six years—two teachers and about forty kids in six grades. I loved learning and was a good student. And those two women kept me busy with projects or teaching the younger kids. I think I was lucky to have been in the last one-room school in the county."

"Where was it?" Sarah asked.

"The building is still there. As the crow flies, it's about five miles from where you work. It's on a back road in the National Park, one of the buildings they're preserving. During the lumbering days a small village surrounded the school. Everything but the foundations of the homes were gone by the time I was a kid."

"I'd like to see it,"

"I'll take you there," said Ray.

"Anyway," said Sarah, "I like your kind of boring. I think I'm sort of boring in the same way: too job oriented and not able to kick back and party, at least that's what my ex-husband used to say.

"When you were investigating Ashleigh's death, well, I don't know how to explain it. I was watching you and trying to figure out what was going on in your head. You seemed to be in your own world much of the time."

Ray remained silent as he thought about Sarah's observation.

"Maybe you don't want to talk about it," she finally said. "And I understand completely."

"It's not that. It's just that I've never tried to explain the process I use in working through a complicated case. I've been doing it so long, it's sort of automatic. There are some basic principles, the things you study in college and professional workshops, and then there are guidelines you have to follow to protect the rights of possible suspects. And those things are sort of automatic. For me, much of the investigation does take place in my head. I have to be the victim and try to see the world through their eyes. I also have to be the assailant. I have to try to understand their drives, motives, anger, and even their craziness. It's a kind of theatre of the mind. I think about these characters when I'm driving or have a few free minutes in the office. At night I dream about them. And I'm totally absorbed with the case until it's solved." Ray stopped for a minute, then added, "While all this is going on, I'm probably not much of a companion."

Sarah snuggled in close to Ray. "I like you," she said. "My approach to getting things done is not too dissimilar from yours. But my world is less dramatic—well, usually less dramatic, like before I met you."

Sarah pulled herself from under Ray's arm, retrieving his wine glass as she rose to her feet. She rinsed the glasses and put them in the dishwasher. Ray corked the wine and slid it into the refrigerator.

She slipped back into his arms briefly. "I think you should take this woman to bed. 4:30 is going to be here far too soon."

29

By the time Sue Lawrence arrived at the office, Ray had already worked through the pile of requisitions and other forms that required his attention. During his tenure as Cedar County Sheriff he had modernized and streamlined the department's operation, but he was still struggling to reduce the amount of paper generated by a small police agency.

"You look happy this morning," Sue offered as she entered his office.

"I am," said Ray. "It looks like you've benefited from a good night's sleep, as well."

"I did. I followed your advice and went home, took a hot bath, and went straight to bed. Didn't even try to read; I just wanted to sleep. And I could have slept in this morning."

Sue set her large, wide-based stainless steel coffee mug on the desk and looked over the assemblage of notes and data she had laid out the previous afternoon.

"What's the news on Lynne?"

"No change during the night. She's still in critical condition," Ray answered. His answer was followed by several minutes of silence.

"You know what?" Sue asked.

"What?" responded Ray, looking up from the pile of requisitions he was signing.

"I know I mentioned this yesterday," she started, "I mean, I think I did. Everything was such a whirl of activities and emotions. And this was bugging me all day long…."

"Your point, Sue," Ray urged. "What's your point?"

"Dirk," she began, "all the time I was with him, from the moment I first saw him until we got here, and then during our interview, not once did he voice any concern for Lynne. Not once. There wasn't the slightest hint of compassion, or even the suggestion that he cared whether she lived or died. He was totally indifferent. Totally indifferent."

"Well, you can't accuse him of making an insincere show of…."

"True," Sue responded. "But this woman gave birth to two of his children; she was his wife for four or five years. Ray, Dirk's not a whole person. He didn't show any emotion, no sadness or anger. He's damaged in some profound way. The archetypal sociopath."

"He may be," agreed Ray, "but that doesn't automatically make him the prime suspect." He neatened up the pile of requisitions and returned them to the appropriate folder and placed it in the out tray on the left side of his desk. "That said, we need to check his alibis and look at the possibility that Dirk might have enticed someone else to do this shooting."

"A pro?"

"I don't think so. My guess would be that he'd lean on someone who owes him a favor. Maybe someone he let off the hook, but that he could still nail if he wanted to."

"How about a girlfriend who wanted to make Dirk a free man?"

"Possible," said Ray. "Listen to us, sitting here spinning our wheels because we have no clear direction to take the investigation. Let's get to work," he gestured toward Sue's carefully arranged materials, "Show me what you have."

"Okay, we'll start here." Sue went to her first stack. "Here are the diagrams of the crime scene. They're not to scale yet; I'll do that later. I've got most of the measurements. As you know, we found two possible locations for the shooter, here and here. Given the heavy snow and the mess made by the plow, we might have missed the real location. But here are the best possibilities." She placed a diagram in the center of the table, and using a pencil as a pointer, indicated the two areas. "If the shooter were in this first location, they might have parked a vehicle somewhere along here off the main road. We found tire tracks where someone pulled off to the side here. Not good ones, but perhaps good enough if we could find the vehicle. I've got photographs and casts."

"Is there a path between that location and where the shooter might have set up?" Ray traced a straight line with his finger as he asked the question.

"No, it's a swamp, I don't think the shooter could have waded through there. My theory is he pulled off the main road so his truck wouldn't be visible, then he walked back along the road and found a position behind a downed tree that gave him a view of the front of Lynne's house."

"Could someone driving down the road have seen the shooter in position?"

"Not easily. There is a utility easement that parallels the road on the east side. A lot of small pines and cedars have gown up near the road, but there aren't any trees or brush across from the victim's home. The shooter could have set up here directly across the road," Sue pointed to a location, "and had an unobstructed view of the end of the drive and the mailbox."

"This area, what's the distance?" Ray asked.

Sue looked down at her notes. "About fifty yards."

"Other than a possible path in the snow and a place where a shooter might set up, did you find any physical evidence at this site?"

"No. By the time we did the search and found this area—remember we were wading through deep snow—things were drifted over. I carefully worked down to the packed area, but didn't find anything. Then we used a metal detector. One very rusty beer can, but no shell casings. And the path, it could have been an animal or just a figment of my imagination. Wanting to make something out of nothing."

"How about the second site?" Ray asked.

"It's right here," again she indicated the place on the diagram using her pencil. "It's at the top of this rather steep hill along a ridgeline that overlooks the whole area. It appears that the woods on this side was partially lumbered a few years back. From this location you can also see the front of Lynne's house. The site also overlooks a little valley on the north that runs down to Mud Lake. There were tracks in the snow up from the two-track...."

"This is the same road you mentioned before?"

"Same road. You can see it on this Geological Survey Map," Sue opened a well-used map of the area, "there are a series of little roads that run through this whole area, and there's been snowmobile and ATV traffic on most of them."

"And how far is this?" asked Ray, running his finger from the top of the hill to the road near Lynne's home.

"I used an optical range finder. It's slightly less than 300 yards."

"Any brass?" Ray asked.

Sue placed a plastic bag in the center of the table. Ray pulled it close and peered at a collection of brass casings of different gauges, with one exception all tarnished and corroded.

"One recent 30-06 casing, the rest have been around awhile. Looks like you found a good place to hunt deer from."

"That one might have come from the gun of our shooter or just been fired at a deer in the last few days. I'll send it off to the State Police lab. Maybe there's a fingerprint or something else we can use down the road."

Sue traced her route on the map. "I walked around from this direction. Someone has been baiting in that valley. I found piles of apples and carrots."

"But you found no clear evidence the shooter was up there."

"Other than the one piece of brass, no."

"And given the weather..." said Ray.

Sue pulled a sheet of paper from another folder. "I called NOAA, and they provided these numbers. At the approximate time of the shooting the winds were 22 miles an hour, gusting to 35 miles with blowing and drifting snow. We were getting both system snow and lake effect snow."

"How about visibility?"

"Not very good."

"You're talking about an almost impossible shot," said Ray.

"Yes," Sue agreed. "And we both know that Dirk is qualified as a sniper, and that he trains SWAT team members for other police agencies."

"Yes, but he has a solid alibi."

"I hate to rule him out," Sue argued. "You know, he probably trained some very competent marksmen over the years."

"Interesting thought. But I think we have to be careful not to allow our mutual dislike of the man distract us from other possibilities. And if it was a hit, we need to start looking for who else might want Lynne dead." Ray paused for a moment. "Let's finish our discussion of the scene. You seem to be assuming that the assailant came in a car or truck."

"Yes, but...."

"But it's just as possible they used a snowmobile or ATV to get to the area, stashed it in the woods and walked in."

Sue nodded her agreement.

"And this time of year no one thinks twice about seeing someone walking down the road carrying a rifle with a big scope on it or even riding a snowmobile with a gun strapped around them." Ray stood and slowly twisted from one side to the other, stretching his back. Leaning against his desk and looking across the table at Sue he asked, "How much time passed between the first 911 call and the time we closed off the roads to the crime scene?"

"I don't have that, but I ..."

"Just a rough guess?" asked Ray.

"Thirty, forty minutes, perhaps more," Sue speculated.

"And in that time our hardworking colleagues from the road commission ran a plow through there in both directions at high speed to get the snow off the road and the shoulders. So we have no physical evidence other than one piece of brass. And that may not be connected to this crime in any way."

"True."

"This is a long shot, but take the people who were on the roads in that area. See if they saw anything unusual. You've got the postman, the plow driver, maybe a FedEx or UPS driver. And then there are the people who live in the neighborhood. Maybe you could assign Brett this task. It would give him an opportunity to learn more about the area."

"Good idea. I'll do that," said Sue.

"We've got things to pursue, and you know how an investigation starts to grow once you get into it. It would have been good if we had found some physical evidence that would have quickly led us to the shooter. It didn't happen, but you gave it your best shot."

"I know. I'm just frustrated," said Sue as she carefully ordered and gathered up her materials. "I'll check with the State Police lab and see if they've gotten any results from the letters Lynne received."

30

~~~~~~

Sue Lawrence was chatting with an attractive woman when Ray entered the conference room a few minutes after 9:00. Although they had never been introduced, Ray recognized Elise Lovell immediately. He had seen her around the village at the grocery store, farmers' market, and perhaps the hardware store—usually in the company of two towheaded children. He could not have helped but notice them; they were always such a happy, energetic trio. And both the mother and children were always dressed in bright colors: reds, yellows, and blues—their coats and hats made of materials with lots of texture. He remembered thinking the woman was probably a weaver, perhaps a spinner, too.

"Sheriff Elkins, this is Elise Lovell." Sue made the introductions as Ray settled in the chair next to Elise.

"Thank you for coming in," said Ray. "I imagine Sue has told you that Lynne Boyd's au pair, Marie, identified you as one of Lynne's closest friends?"

"We were just chatting about that," Elise responded. "And Sheriff, I'm very happy to help in any way, but this whole thing is just beyond my comprehension. And…" she reached for a tissue from a box at the center of the table.

"I understand how difficult this must be for you." Ray stopped and waited for her to regain her composure. "We were hoping that you might be able to tell us about Lynne. I hope you could give us a sense of what was going on in her life. Did she share with you anything that you think might help us in this investigation?

"But perhaps we should start at the beginning. How long have you known Lynne, how did you meet?"

"I met her when I was pregnant with Justin, he's my second. We actually met in the waiting room of our OB/GYN. We started talking and hit it off right away. In the beginning we'd occasionally meet for coffee, and then after her twins were born we sort of lost contact, just occasional phone conversations for about six months. I did visit her a couple of times at her home. Justin was born about two months after her girls, so I wasn't getting out much, either."

"But since then, I gather you did start spending time together."

"Yes and no," Elise answered. "She was new to the area and in the process of making friends. I thought she was a natural fit for our circle of friends. My husband and I tried to include them, Lynne and her husband and the girls at social gatherings, but that didn't quite work out."

"How so?" asked Sue.

"Let me set the stage a little. You know how people gather, especially people like us with young kids and little money. We do potlucks, drink wine, share food, and let the kids play. We invited them a couple of times to potlucks we were hosting. It was a disaster."

"Because?"

"Her husband, Dirk. He's older than us, fifteen or twenty years. And we've all been to college; we pretty much have shared values and similar politics. Dirk, he's from another planet—superior, condescending. You don't have a conversation with him; you're an audience as he tells you the truth about whatever the topic is.

"In fairness, we might have been, I don't know what word to use. Intimidating was floating around in my head, but we're hardly intimidating. But perhaps because we were younger and more educated, we triggered something in him to cause him to act this way. All I know is that everyone was uncomfortable, and we didn't include them anymore."

"But you remained in contact with Lynne?"

"I like her a lot. And we've found ways to meet on a fairly regular basis, usually something that involves the kids where we can talk and they can play."

"When was the last time you saw her?"

"Monday morning at the children's yoga class; I gather from what I've seen on the news the shooting happened not too long after that."

"Did you talk, have a conversation?"

"It was barely more than, 'How are you?' We were late getting there and the kids had a dentist appointment later in the morning."

"How did she seem?"

"Just the same, glad to be with her girls. Lynne was her happy self. And those girls, they're so special. I can't imagine the effect of this trauma. And if she doesn't make it." Elise collapsed in tears. She worked to regain control, finally saying, "You were asking about?"

"I was just trying to establish how much time you spent together, and what you might know about her private life. We're trying to find what prompted this attack, and who might have a motive to do something like this."

"Your first question. How much time did we spend together? Or did I know her well enough that she might have talked about things other than the merits of different brands of disposable diapers?"

"Yes," answered Ray.

"I did see her on a regular basis. She knew about my background and realized that she needed to talk to someone."

"Your background?" prodded Sue.

"I'm a psychiatric social worker by training. I did that before we moved here and had a second child."

"What did Lynne need to talk about?" asked Sue.

"In the beginning it was kid stuff, and that's before I met Dirk. There were just a lot of things she didn't know about, what should I call it, the care and feeding of babies. I had a few more years experience, my daughter was two, and I was happy to share what I knew. But then things got a little more involved. She had what probably would be termed as postpartum depression. We spent a lot of time on the phone for several months."

"Would you tell us what those conversations were about?" asked Sue.

"Am I violating any confidentialities?" she asked. Her question seemed to be as much inner-directed as addressed to Sue and Ray.

"Your conversations were part of a friendship, not a professional relationship. Your cooperation in this investigation might help us quickly find the person responsible for the crime," said Sue.

"From the outset," Elise began, after taking a few moments to formulate her answer, "Lynne was just thrilled with those little girls, but then I think she realized that her life was going a whole different direction. For years her ambition was to become a network news personality, and she had really planned on accomplishing that by sometime in her early thirties. All at once her life had been changed: first by that tragic shooting of her ex-boyfriend, and then by the marriage and the birth of her children. She's a very ambitious person; she was having difficulty refocusing her life."

"And there were other issues as time went by?" probed Sue.

"I think she slowly realized how impossible her marriage was," Elise said. "I mean it was obvious the first time you saw them together. But she didn't seem to get it. And she's a very optimistic, determined woman. She was going to make the marriage work somehow."

"Would she talk about her unhappiness, her frustration…"

"Her frustration with Dirk? She wasn't ready to say she was unhappy. And most things in her life were good, and she focused on them: the girls, her work, and the house she designed. She acted as her own contractor. I think her dad helped some, but she did most of the work. Dirk didn't want to be involved."

"Was there any violence in the marriage?" asked Sue.

"I'm very sensitive to that issue; it came up a lot in my practice. I think I can say with rather great certainty that there was not physical abuse. I'm sure Dirk played mind games, but Lynne's a strong person. He would have met his match."

"Would you say that they were loyal to one another?" Ray asked.

Elise looked at Ray. "That question was gently put. Did Lynne think Dirk had other lovers and did Lynne have a secret someone? I can't really answer your question. We never talked about that possibility. I've heard Dirk was a bit of a rake. I don't know if that is true, but this is a small town and people talk.

"As for Lynne, if something was going on, she never mentioned it to me, and I saw no indications that she might be having an affair. That said, she's a beautiful, accomplished woman, and I wish she were sharing her days with a loving companion. Life's too short and happiness is sometimes fleeting."

"So, as far you know, she had no outside love interest?" Sue asked.

"No."

"Did she ever say anything to suggest that she was in danger or threatened?"

"Nothing."

"Did she tell you about receiving some threatening letters?" asked Ray.

"Letters?"

"Letters. Something she might have received at the station."

"No."

"Divorce or separation, did that topic ever come up?" asked Ray.

"Not directly," she responded after clearly taking a moment to think about her response. "A couple of months ago she asked me if I knew anyone who did family law, she said that she wanted to establish a legal guardian for the twins. I wondered at the time if there wasn't something more going on."

"Did you give her a name?"

"Martha Grey. We've had her do a number of things for us, including establishing guardianships. She's real good."

"But the subject of divorce never came up."

"Not directly."

"Just a couple of background things, Elise," said Ray. "How long have you been in the area?"

"Five years this past summer."

"And what brought you to this neck of the woods?"

"We were looking around. My husband had been teaching at Northern Illinois. When he didn't get tenure, we decided to think about other things we could do with our lives. I was working at the student health services at the time. His family has had a place up here for generations, and we were invited to spend the summer here. His sister's husband is a contractor and asked him if he wanted learn how to do trim carpentry. Bob wasn't sure, but he didn't have anything else going so he gave it a shot. Turns out he loves carpentry; he's finding it very rewarding. We both think we're so lucky to be here, and it's such a special place to rear children.

"Can you tell me anything new about Lynne. The report I heard on the early news did not say much."

"You probably know what we know. She's very seriously injured," responded Sue.

"Thank you, again, for coming in," said Ray.

"I can't imagine I told you anything useful," Elise said.

"You helped us get a sense of the person, maybe it will help us connect the dots."

Ray got up and opened the door. After Elise had left the room, he closed the door again and settled back into his chair. "What did we learn?"

"More of the same about Dirk. I don't know what else," Sue said.

"Think she's reliable, or might she cover for a friend?"

"Not under these circumstances. I think she's credible, but there could be things about Lynne she doesn't know," Sue observed. "Women don't always tell all like you guys seem to do."

"Touché," Ray responded with a smile. "I'm sure I'd remember if this had happened, but would you check and see if we ever had a domestic violence call...."

"It's one of the first things I looked at," Sue responded. "No, there's not a record, not with Lynne, anyway. And Ray, I would have remembered it, too. I'm less than neutral when it comes to that man."

31

Sue Lawrence, after first knocking on the doorjamb to get his attention, escorted a woman into Ray's office.

"Sheriff, this is Mrs. Guerski, Rachael Guerski. She has come in with some information that she feels might have some bearing on the Boyd shooting. She's shared her story with me, and I want you to hear it."

Ray rose to greet the woman. He took the hand she extended to him and held it for a long moment. He noted that she was tall and very thin, almost anorexic looking. He guessed her to be in her late thirties, but her fragile physique and the way she carried her body gave her the appearance of a much older woman. Her delicate blond hair was teased into an elaborate hairdo. Soft blue eyeliner and a delicate peach lipstick provide the only hints of color on her pale continence. She was dressed in a dark blue suit with a ruffled white blouse. Ray found her costume curiously formal and somewhat dated. And he noticed that her cloying perfume did little to cover the smell of cigarette smoke that hung to her.

"Please have a seat," Ray offered, moving to the small conference table in his office. Can we get you some coffee, water, or perhaps a soft drink?"

"I'm fine, thank you."

"Mrs. Guerski, would you tell the sheriff what you just told me?" Sue asked after they were seated.

"Rachael, please call me Rachael," the women requested.

"Rachael," Sue repeated.

"My husband works at the TV station with Lynne Boyd," she started, her gaze down at the table. "He's the sports caster, Biff Guerski."

"Yes," said Ray.

"Well, I know that he and Lynne are friends, but lately I've found out that he's been having an affair with her."

"How do you know this?" asked Ray.

"I discovered it accidentally. I was taking some of his clothes to the cleaners, and as I was going through his pockets I found a credit card slip from a motel in Grayling. I thought that was really strange. I went into his office; Biff has a home office. I never go in there; it's his private space. But I went in there and looked through the bills that were stacked up in a basket on his desk." She hesitated a moment and then explained, "Biff, he pays all the bills; I don't have anything to do with that. Biff has done that from the time we were married. It will be nineteen years this June." She paused and wiped a tear away with her long, carefully painted nails.

"And you found something?" Ray asked

"I found an American Express bill with four charges to the same motel," she said, looking up. "Charges to a motel sixty miles away, on Wednesdays. That morning I drove over to Grayling, I didn't know what else to do. I went to the motel. I needed to see the place."

"And?"

"You don't know my husband?" she said looking at Ray.

"No, I don't. I've seen him on air, but I've never met him."

"Well," she said, her mood shifting from sadness to anger. "Biff likes the good life. This isn't the kind of place he would stay. It's a mom and pop operation. He wouldn't be caught dead there unless…" her voice trailed off.

"Unless…," Ray repeated.

"It's a no-tell motel. He and Lynne were meeting there. A place far enough away that no one would probably notice them."

"So how did you find out that it was Lynne?" Ray asked.

"The day after I found the American Express bill, after the kids were on the school bus, I confronted him. He was sitting at the breakfast table, and I handed him the bill and asked him why was he renting a motel room in Grayling on Wednesdays. He always comes home at night, this must have been in the morning or afternoon."

"And his response?"

"First he got really angry at me, he was shouting at me for going through his office. Then he calmed down a bit and said one of his friends was having an affair, and he was letting the guy charge the room to his account so his wife wouldn't find out. So I asked him why didn't his friend use cash, he couldn't answer that. Then I confronted him with the charge slip I found in his suit pocket."

With a bitter smile she continued. "He knew then I had him. So he confessed. He said Lynne had been going through some bad times in her marriage, and he was spending time with her so she could talk things out. He gave me this incredible story about how nothing was really going on, and I just kept pushing until he confessed, but even then it wasn't his fault. He was an innocent in the whole thing. He told me that he had been seduced by a determined woman."

"Do you know how long this affair has been going on?" Ray asked.

"Biff said a month or two. But, Sheriff, he doesn't seem capable of telling the truth, not about this. It's just one story after another," her eyes fell back to the table, and she appeared to collapse into herself.

"I know this must be very difficult for you," Ray said. "Did you discover this before or after Lynne Boyd had been shot?"

"A couple of weeks ago."

"Do you think there is any connection between the shooting and this alleged affair?"

"Sheriff, it's not an alleged affair. And I don't know if there is any connection. But I just want it out there. I want everything out. If Biff is involved in any way, I want to know. I'm not going to protect him."

"Have you asked him if he is?"

"Yes."

"And his response?"

"Biff, he says that he has no connection, that he can't imagine anyone would want to kill Lynne."

"Do you believe him?"

"I don't know what to believe anymore. We've been married all these years, and now I think I'm living with a complete stranger. I don't know who he is, and I don't trust anything he says."

"Is your husband a hunter; does he have a deer rifle?"

"Sheriff, Biff owns every kind of sports equipment there is: hockey sticks, footballs, skis, baseball gloves..."

"Does he own a rifle or other guns?"

"I'm sure he does. He hasn't gone deer hunting in recent years, but I know he's got one. In fact it came up in one of our arguments." Her face went crimson as her anger swelled. "He asked me if I had shot Lynne," she spit out, and then she collapsed in tears.

Ray retrieved a box of tissue from his desk and placed it before her. They waited for her to regain her composure.

"I don't understand it," she continued. "He doesn't seem that upset about her. And he's angry with me. Like I'm somehow responsible for everything that's wrong."

Ray allowed her last statement to hang a long moment, then he said. "Rachael, I do have to ask you if you shot Lynne Boyd. By your own admission, you clearly have a motive."

"I do," she responded, some strength flowing back into her voice. "I have wished her dead, both of them, actually. But I had nothing to do with it. I will take a lie detector test."

"What kind of work do you do?" Ray asked.

"I look after our kids and work part-time for a real-estate broker."

"Tell me about your kids?"

"We have a ninth grader and a senior, two girls. Laura is going to be going to college next year. She hopes to go to Michigan State like her dad. And now I just don't know what's going to happen. I may be a single parent before long."

"Is there anything else you want us to know?" Sue asked.

"I think that's everything. And I'm not telling you that I think he had anything to do with the shooting, but I needed to tell someone about this, and you should know what I know."

"Do you think you are in any danger from your husband?"

The answer was long in coming. "He's never touched me or the girls."

"We will need to have a conversation with your husband, and he will quickly know that you've talked to us. We don't want your personal safety in jeopardy."

"If it happens, it happens. Perhaps it will bring clarity to this whole incredibly awful situation."

"If you feel threatened in any way, please call 911. One of our dispatchers will immediately get you the assistance you need."

The conversation was over, and they all rose at the same time.

"Thank you for coming in," said Ray. "I know this has been very difficult."

"Thank you for listening," She responded. "I hope Biff isn't involved, but if he is I need to know."

They shook hands again, and Sue escorted her out of the office and returned a few minutes later.

"What do you think?" she asked.

"I think we should talk to him as soon as possible. See if you can get him in here later this afternoon. And after you get that set up, would you check and see if Lynne's mother is still available. I want us to drive up to Crescent Cove to talk to her. While you're doing that, I'll call the hospital and see if I can get a medical update. If only we could question her."

"Will do," said Sue, and she hurried out of Ray's office.

32

S ue had pulled her vehicle next to the rear entrance and was waiting as Ray emerged from the building. He opened the door on the passenger side and asked, "Going my way?"

"Get in," she responded. After she pulled onto to the highway, she said, "It's interesting being your chauffeur."

"How's that?" asked Ray.

"Before you were injured..." she looked over at him, wondering if she should have opened this topic.

"Go ahead," said Ray.

"When we were traveling in the same car, you always drove. We were like an old married couple. Now you seem to prefer the right hand seat."

Ray thought about what she had said, then responded, "Well, I never knew what I was missing before. I've been behind the wheel since I was sixteen, never in the passenger's seat. I've never had the opportunity to relax and look around. My eyes were always focused on the road. Since you've been driving me, I've seen all kinds of thing I've never noticed before. And these are roads I've traveled hundreds of times."

"Are you going to ask the county board for a permanent driver?" she teased.

"Sure, that will be my top request for the next fiscal year."

"Anything new on Boyd's condition?"

"She's stable, and they consider that a good sign. How are you feeling?" Ray asked, changing the subject.

"I assume you're talking about the case?" Sue responded.

"Yes."

"Probably the way you are, frustrated. I've never worked a crime scene before where I didn't find something useful."

"No one will ever fault you for not doing a thorough job," Ray responded. After a brief pause he continued, "Assuming that this wasn't a random event, and nothing about this appears to be random, let's focus on other strands."

"So we switch to motive, the "Ls" again," said Sue.

"Would that have worked in the Leiston case?" Ray asked playfully.

"I think so, to a degree," Sue answered. "Love and lust were part of it, perhaps loathing, too. They seemed to loathe the rest of humanity. But lucre was not. The two of them had enough lucre between them to get along. Maybe we have to add codependence to the list. And lunatics, too. I guess that's not too politically correct," Sue looked across at Ray.

"Lovers and madmen have such seething brains, such shaping fantasies, that apprehend more than cool reason ever comprehends."

"Do you know how much better I've gotten at Jeopardy since I've started hanging with you? Shakespeare, right."

"Now give me the play and the speaker of those lines?" he quizzed.

"Hey, Ray, that's enough proof of my cultural literacy for today. Don't push it," cautioned Sue with feigned gravity. "How about wrapping that mind of yours around this again."

"I've been doing that. After Dirk, we've got to look at friends and family. And even with what appears to be a fairly airtight alibi, there still is a hell of a lot more I want to know about him."

"Like what?"

"Like he might have known Lynne's parents, at least her father, long before he entered her life."

"Well, that's an intriguing bit of information. Where did you get that?"

Ray told her about his conversation with Nora Jennings. How there was a fatal hunting accident on Round Island during deer season. Sheriff Orville Hentzner, Ray's predecessor, deemed the shooting accidental, and according to Nora's story, by this time Orville had more or less turned the day to day operations over to three younger offices, Dirk being one of them.

"That's amazing," Sue responded.

"So there's that," said Ray, "but back to friends and family. As I told you, Lynne's father doesn't look too healthy. Does she have siblings who are out there waiting for him to die? Could there be a brother or sister trying to limit the number of inheritors? And we may have had an impossible crime scene, but if there's a shooter who planned to kill Lynne and hoped her husband would be suspect number one, well Dirk's credit card receipts are an unexpected twist."

"So you want to know about the family? If a brother or sister might have some motive to off Lynne. Fratricide," said Sue.

"Sororicide," Ray retorted.

"Touché."

"I want to know about the family, siblings or anyone else who might want Lynne dead. I also would like to know more about her father. Might he have enemies who would strike at his children as a way of getting to him?"

Sue turned onto the private road that ran into Crescent Cove and came to a stop at the bright orange steel beam that blocked the road horizontally. A young man in the uniform of a private security company got out of a large white SUV and approached her vehicle.

"We're expected," Sue said after opening the window.

The man looked down at a clipboard. "You're Detective Lawrence?"

"Yes," she responded.

"And who are you, sir?" he asked, looking toward Ray.

"That is the sheriff of this county," Sue answered.

The man peered over at Ray, studied his face and uniform, and then carefully inspected the contents in the rear of the vehicle.

"Okay," he said, then he walked to side of the road and easily lifted the heavily counterbalanced bar.

Sue slowly accelerated.

"Tell me I'm in Oz," said Ray.

"The gate was open, and there was no security person here on Monday," said Sue. "But this is really strange. What just happened?

"Check your rearview mirror. See if one of those little black helicopters is tailing us," Ray quipped.

33

~~~

Ray had seen the main house of the estate from his kayak the past summer and thought he had a sense of the size of the place, but when Sue turned onto the large circular drive that ran to the main entrance of the building, he was surprised by the enormity of the building.

"Like I told you," said Sue, noting his reaction, "quite a joint."

"Yes," he agreed.

Before they got to the entrance one of the double doors swung open, and Harry Hawkins greeted them.

"Sheriff and Ms. Lawrence I believe," he said, momentarily holding Sue in his gaze.

"Yes," said Ray. "This is Harry Hawkins, Mr. Boyd's personal assistant and lawyer."

"Let me give you a more complete description of what I do. Actually, I work for an international law firm headquartered in Chicago. I've been assigned to the Boyds' corporation, and I look after the day-to-day needs of Mr. Boyd and the family."

"Mrs. Boyd is expecting you. If you would follow me, please," Hawkins directed, after shaking hands with the two of them.

They were led down a large staircase into the atrium area. A wall of windows faced west, providing a view of Lake Michigan and Round Island. Ray paused briefly and looked at the waves breaking on the shoal at the south end of the island. He wished that he were out there in his kayak paddling into the swell and then turning and surfing back to shore—directly experiencing the power of nature.

"Strong winds from the south today," Hawkins observed, as he paused, waiting for Ray.

They followed Hawkins across the atrium, Ray inspecting the elaborate pattern of the parquet floor, noting that he saw no native woods.

At the south end of the room, double doors stood open. Hawkins led them into a large paneled room. Two ample couches in a rich, port-colored leather faced one another in the middle of the room, separated by a rectangular coffee table. Several chairs were positioned near the couches. An elaborate silver tea service and delicate china cups and saucers were arranged at the center of the table. Lights high in the ceiling brightly illuminated the sitting area. Ray observed that the room was lit like a theater stage and wondered if they were about to be participants in a play.

"We have coffee and tea set out, but if you wish to have anything else…," Hawkins inquired, after he indicated they should sit on one of the coaches. He looked first at Ray, then at Sue.

"Coffee would be fine," Ray responded.

Hawkins picked up a cup and saucer and poured a steaming stream of mahogany-colored liquid from the silver coffee pot.

"And you?" he asked, looking in Sue's direction. When she didn't instantly respond, he asked, "Would you like something else, perhaps a Diet Coke?"

"Yes," Sue answered. "A Diet Coke."

"I'll get that for you," Hawkins said. "And Mrs. Boyd will be with you in a few minutes."

After Hawkins left the room, Sue said, "What do you think?"

Before Ray could respond, Amanda and Breanne came running into the room, followed by Marie and their grandmother. After a noisy greeting, the girls hugging both Sue and Ray, Marie herded them away, saying that Ray and Sue needed to speak to their grandmother. But before the children were escorted from the library, Sue promised to visit their bedroom before she left. Then Sue formally introduced Ray to Mrs. Boyd.

Hawkins reappeared carrying a silver tray with a Diet Coke and two glasses, one with ice, one without. He placed the tray on the table in front of Sue. Without asking as to a preference, he poured a cup of tea for Mrs. Boyd. Then he poured himself a cup of coffee, and seated himself in a chair at her right.

"This has been an extremely difficult time for you," said Ray.

"Yes. It is almost beyond comprehension. But I've had to remain strong and optimistic for the girls. And finally this morning we got some encouraging news on Lynne's condition. It's like this horrible nightmare might be coming to an end." She paused and looked directly at Ray, her eyes locking on his. "Has Dirk been arrested?"

"We have interviewed him," Ray said. "At this point there is insufficient evidence to place Dirk or anyone else under arrest." As he focused on Dorothy Boyd, he noticed how beautiful Lynne's mother was. Her hair, blond and to her shoulders, was less luxuriant than her daughter's, and her skin was softer and more delicate. He remembered Sue's comments about Dorothy's appearance; she was slender and fit, clearly working hard at keeping the ravages of time at bay.

"Sheriff, he is an evil man; I can't believe he's not under arrest," she said slowly, carefully enunciating each word.

Ray weighed his words before he responded. "We are vigorously pursuing every lead. And at this point we need your assistance."

"How may I be of help?"

"Did your daughter say anything to you in the last few months that suggested that she was apprehensive? Did she tell you of any threats she received?"

"No, she didn't tell me anything."

"Do you have the kind of relationship where she would share this type of information?"

She looked startled by the question and carefully weighed her reply. "My daughter and I are very close. However, Lynne is fiercely independent. She didn't have the need to tell me everything that is going on in her life."

"Did she share with you what was happening in her marriage?" Ray asked.

"Yes and no," Dorothy responded.

"Would you elaborate, please?" Ray pressed.

"I knew intuitively that things were not okay. They are such an unnatural couple; it's a marriage that should not have been." Dorothy looked at Ray and then at Sue. "Lynne was always one to make the best of everything, but I think by this summer she had finally given up."

"So she told you she was filing for divorce?"

"Yes, several weeks ago on the phone. I suggested one of our lawyers should be involved. But Lynne had retained a woman up here in whom she had great confidence."

"Was your daughter worried about how Dirk might react?"

"Sheriff, I asked her about that because I was worried. She told me there would be no problems. Dirk had already starting moving his things to a house he owned; it's the one they lived in before they built the new place. Lynne said she thought he seemed relieved that the marriage was over."

"Do you know if there was ever any violence in this marriage?"

"Physical violence, like Dirk hitting Lynne?"

"Yes."

"She would not have allowed it."

"How about verbal and psychological abuse."

"Did Dirk play games? Of course," Dorothy responded. "But Lynne was able to take care of herself. This was not a good marriage for Lynne; it was not a healthy relationship. But the marriage did produce two beautiful children, and Lynne has proven to be a wonderful mother. I'm so proud of the woman she has become the last few years."

"When people leave a failed marriage," Ray started, carefully, "there is often something that precipitates the decision. Might Lynne have…?"

"Are you trying to ask if there's a new love in her life?"

"Yes," Ray responded.

"As I've told you, we are close, but Lynne doesn't share everything."

Ray let her answer hang. Finally, she filled the silence. "Since she was a teenager, Lynne has always had some love interest. But I don't think at this point there is anyone new. She's too busy with her girls and career. I believe that she would complete the divorce before she would become involved with someone new."

"Did you know Dirk before he and Lynne became a couple?"

"What do you mean?" Dorothy asked.

"You and your husband have been property owners in this region for a long time. And Dirk has worked for the sheriff's department for more than thirty years. Did you ever meet him over the years?"

"Not to my memory."

"And you're sure?"

"Quite. I think I met him for the first time when Lynne brought him home after that unfortunate incident with her ex-boyfriend. We never anticipated they would marry." She stopped, looking slightly abashed at what she had shared.

"How about the former sheriff, Orville Hentzner? It's my understanding that he and some of his deputies once had permission to hunt on this land."

"Oh, yes. I remember him. He was quite a character, real up north. Orville was a friend of Prescott's father. I think he was sort of an honorary member of the club. Most members of that group were heavy drinkers, and Orville seemed to fit in. But to be quite frank, Sheriff, the man seemed to be a caricature of a police officer. Maybe something created by Gilbert and Sullivan," Dorothy chuckled. "And that big red nose with the bulging blood vessels, you just don't see that anymore."

"So Orville drank with the members. Did he hunt with them?"

She glanced over at Hawkins before continuing. "I'm sure he did; he was one of the boys."

"Did Orville keep a watchful eye on this property in exchange for hunting privileges?"

"I don't know that," Dorothy responded. "I was a young bride during the last days of the hunting lodge. Those old men, they were a bunch of characters. I wouldn't be surprised at anything."

"What does any of this have to do with your investigation of Lynne's shooting?" Hawkins asked.

"I'm collecting background information," Ray answered, then returned his focus to Dorothy Boyd. "So this originally was a hunting lodge?" Ray asked.

"Yes, the club went back more than a hundred years. People had memberships; it was very much like a country club."

"How did you and your husband end up owning the property?"

"It's a long story," she answered cautiously.

"Would you give me a synopsis?"

"As I understand it, the club was established by a group of businessmen from Chicago. In the beginning it was a place where they came to hunt, no women allowed. Later it also became a summer resort, too. As original members died off, the remaining members bought their shares in the place. That's the way it was set up legally; the remaining members could keep offspring of deceased members they didn't like from inheriting shares in the club. The shares would be then offered to individuals that the remaining members found acceptable. The intent was to maintain the membership at a level where the club would be viable. But at some point things came apart, the lodge fell into total disrepair, and even the property taxes were in arrears. My husband arranged to buy the club from the few remaining shareholders. We've spent years redeveloping the property. But it's only been since Lynne had the twins that we've expanded the house and have spent so much time here."

"Well, you've done a wonderful job," said Ray. He sensed this highly sanitized history was all he was going to get. "Do you have other children?"

"We have a son and a younger daughter. They are both here now. In fact, they are at the hospital allowing Prescott to get some rest."

"What do your children do?"

"Our younger daughter is currently living in Paris. She's working on an advanced degree in art history, and our son is a graduate student in history at Harvard. He wants to be a college professor."

"Are they married?"

"No, both are still single, and they seem very focused on school and careers at this point. It's wonderful to have them here right now for support, and the twins adore them."

Looking over at Sue, he said, "Perhaps this would be a good time for you to visit with the girls."

Dorothy stood, appearing rather relieved that the interview was over. "I'll take you to them."

"I'm going to stay here with Mr. Hawkins for a few minutes. I have a few questions for him." Ray watched with interest as Hawkins and Dorothy exchanged glances. Then Dorothy guided Sue out of the room.

34

Ray had come to his feet when the women left the room. He was still standing. "Do you mind if I walk around a bit. I get uncomfortable if I sit too long."

"Of course not," Hawkins answered, following Ray as he walked to the large floor-to-ceiling window.

"Quite a blow out there today," observed Ray. "In the early days of shipping on the Great Lakes more than a few boats were destroyed on those shoals."

"Really," responded Hawkins, his tone flat. "I don't know much about local history."

"Yes," continued Ray, glancing over at Hawkins, "November was always the most dangerous month. If you got caught in open water by a fast-moving storm, you were in a lot of trouble. Dozens of ships went down between here and Point Betsie. And the Manitou Passage can be an especially treacherous piece of water."

"You have questions for me?" Hawkins asked impatiently.

"Yes," answered Ray, still gazing out at the tempestuous seas. "I know little about the Boyds and their business. We are trying to find out what might motivate someone to commit this crime. We were wondering if someone might have attacked Lynne as a way of getting at her parents."

"Shouldn't her husband, Dirk, be your number one suspect?"

"He's a person of interest. But many investigations fail by focusing too early on only one suspect. Now tell me, Mr. Hawkins, what type of business are the Boyds in? I couldn't help notice the high level of security around the estate."

"Really," responded Hawkins.

"Let's not play games. The property is gated, the entrance secured by an armed guard. There are security cameras on the road leading in, on the perimeter of this building, and even in here. I suspect our conversation is being recorded. What do the Boyds do that requires this level of protection?"

Hawkins was slow in responding. "Well, it is actually not quite what it seems. The corporation tests new systems here before they install them in the homes and offices of clients."

"So the Boyds have a security company?"

"Well, not exactly."

"Well, what exactly?" probed Ray.

"It's quite complex."

"Try me," said Ray. "I'm reasonably bright. I might be able to figure it out. Let's start with a name. Does the company have a name?"

"It's not publicly traded, you won't find it anywhere."

"But it does have a name?" Ray pressed.

"Yes, Magnus Conservus. It's a corporation."

"Registered in the U.S.?"

"Well, no. U.S. corporate laws are too restrictive in the international business climate."

"And what's the business of Magnus Conservus?"

"Whatever the clients want."

"I'm not following," responded Ray, his voice with more than a hint of irritation. "Let's try this again; what's the business of Magnus Conservus?"

"Let me explain by providing some background. As a young man, Mr. Boyd inherited a large trucking company from his father. And he did quite well in the business for a number of years. Then he started to branch out. He has told me that the idea for his current business venture came to him when he was in residence here one summer in the early 70s. He wanted to surprise his houseguests with a New England seafood boil that included fresh lobster. He had them flown in on a private jet the day of the party, something that was quite extraordinary at the time. His guests were very impressed. Soon he was getting requests from people of means for similar logistical feats. He leased one Lear jet and launched a high-end concierge service. It started with food, then people wanted the chefs and a serving staff as well. Then some of his clients asked for transportation services so they wouldn't have to travel commercial. Later they wanted other services, like access to the world's best physicians and medical centers, private guards, even fire protection if they were dissatisfied with what was available in the public sector."

"So for a price Magnus will provide...."

"That's just the point, with their clients, money isn't an issue. There has been an explosion of wealth in the last decade here, in Europe, South America, and the Middle East. They try to provide any service the clients request, anywhere in the world."

"And the customers are?"

"Like I said, most are people of means, but Magnus also contracts with corporations and, in a few cases, with governments. They have a large staff of highly-trained personnel as well as a variety of specialists on retainer."

"And is this corporate headquarters?"

"No, the main operations center is west of Chicago, but when the Boyds are in residence here, many of the key staff members accompany them." Hawkins paused briefly, then continued in a condescending tone. "Mr. Boyd has been very patient with you, Sheriff. He could easily bring the best investigative minds in the world in to solve this crime, but he's decided to wait and see if you're up to the task."

Ray didn't respond. He went back to looking out the window for several minutes, breathing deeply, trying to control his rage. Then he turned to Hawkins again. "So going back to an earlier question, could the Boyds have enemies who might go after their daughter as a way of getting at them? Perhaps a business competitor, a disgruntled employee, or maybe someone whose family once had an interest in this property?"

"I couldn't say," Hawkins responded.

"You don't know or you don't want to talk about it?"

"You cannot attain a position of power and wealth without some people being envious of your accomplishments. That said, I am not aware of the Boyds having any enemies who would inflict injury on them or their offspring."

Ray held Hawkins in his gaze. "If the man knows something, he clearly isn't going to share it," he thought.

Ray walked beyond the window to a wall covered with photos. There appeared to be several such areas spaced on the perimeter of the room. Small spotlights in the ceiling illuminated a collection of moments from Dorothy Boyd's past. There were shots of her as a young girl, many posed with a collection of wirehaired terriers, the poses and backgrounds suggesting that they were taken at dog shows. There were also shots of her as a young woman playing polo and standing next to ribbon-bedecked horses. And then were photos of her standing with members of a college rifle team, carrying a rifle across her back as she skied, and firing at a target on a snow-covered range. And finally, there was a collection of photos from various marathons showing Dorothy crossing the finish line.

"It looks like Mrs. Boyd is quite the athlete," Ray observed, allowing his gaze to come back to the biathlon photos.

"She is the consummate athlete," Hawkins said. "She participated in the winter Olympics after college."

"Does she still shoot?" Ray asked.

"Not that I know of, not since I've been with them."

"And how long has that been, Mr. Hawkins?"

"It will be one year in January."

"And would you explain to me again what your role is?"

"I'm Mr. Boyd's personal lawyer and his administrative assistant. Because of the nature of his business, I provide guidance on possible legal or taxation problems. I also serve as a gateway to my law firm when Boyd needs expert consultation in specialized areas."

"Like what?"

"Since Magnus Conservus has clients worldwide, they need to be sensitive to the laws of the countries in which they operate."

"Does sensitive mean obeying the law of those countries?"

"Not always. At times when civil authority has broken down, Magnus has to take extraordinary measures to protect its clients and their property. But given the chaos of these situations, there are seldom any legal problems."

"And what's your training, Mr. Hawkins?"

"I was an undergraduate at the University of Virginia and have a law degree from American University. Both my parents are lawyers."

"Do they practice law?"

"After a fashion; they both work for the same Washington think tank."

Before Ray could ask a follow-up question, Sue returned with the twins, Dorothy, and Marie. After kneeling and greeting the girls again, Ray stood, reaching out to Sue for a steadying hand, his recently wounded leg still not at full strength or flexibility.

He called Sue's attention to the wall of photos, "Mrs. Boyd was once an Olympian."

Dorothy joined them looking at the black-and-white pictures. "Not an Olympian, they weren't ready for women yet, but I did show up for the trials. And I almost made the team competing against men. That was so long ago," she said wistfully. "I wish I were still in that shape. Age…"

Before anyone could comment, the girls were dragging their grandmother out of the room. Ray and Sue followed, Hawkins at their heels. Farewells were said and Hawkins walked Ray and Sue to the door.

After they were back in the Jeep rolling on the ribbon of carefully cleared blacktop, Sue said, "So mother was on a college rifle team and showed up for the Olympic trials in biathlon. She must have been a very plucky young woman. Perfect training for someone intending to do a winter hit."

"I was watching her closely as we were standing there. She didn't show the slightest hint of concern in our knowing that. And why would she want to shoot her own daughter?" questioned Ray.

"Families and madness," rattled Sue flippantly.

"You're stealing my lines again."

"Tell me about Hawkins; he's sort of cute."

"I was having a flashback," said Ray.

"Flashback to what?" asked Sue.

"Those days when I was in the hospital on heavy drugs and everything was surreal," said Ray.

"Why am I'm not following your conversation?"

"My talk with Hawkins was that strange. I felt like I was part of a vintage James Bond film. It's like Lynne's father runs Spectre, only he's given it the pompous name of Magnus Conservus."

Before they reached the gate, Ray had given Sue a brief summary of his conversation with Harry Hawkins, including the Maine lobster roots of Magnus Conservus and Hawkins's comment about Boyd being patient and not bringing in his own experts to solve this crime. After they turned on the highway she asked, "Does Hawkins think their people can take over the investigation?"

"Hawkins knows better; he's a lawyer. He was just blowing smoke. That said, a lot of these companies are cowboy operations. In parts of the world where civil authority is lacking, they're often left to their own devices."

A long silence followed. Finally Sue asked, "Are you just irritated, or is something else going on?"

"I was thinking about medieval Europe, where the rich and powerful surrounded themselves with their private armies."

"Well I hate to pull you away from your musings, but we need to talk about our interview with Biff Guerski. We're running late for it."

"So I would like to know more about Magnus Conservus and whether their personnel have the necessary licenses and permits to operate in Michigan. This will be a challenge because it's a privately-held corporation."

"Biff Guerski," Sue repeated.

"I'm also curious about the target distances in the biathlon."

"You think that her mother...?"

"No, not impossible, but no."

"I'll start on this as soon as we've interviewed Guerski," Sue responded.

35

If Biff Guerski was nervous in any way about being interviewed by the police, Ray could find no hint of it in his manner or appearance. Sue Lawrence introduced Biff to Ray just before they entered the interview room. As they shook hands, Ray noted Guerski's physiognomy: features softened by excessive flesh, sagging jowls, thinning blond hair, and faded blue eyes. Biff's large shoulders and a bulging mid-section filled his blue blazer. His gray gabardine trousers were skintight and the cuffs were a bit too high above a pair of polished, tasseled black loafers. Ray thought Biff looked far better on the eleven o'clock news than he looked in person.

"Thank you for coming in," said Ray as they were settling on opposite sides of the conference table, Sue between them at the head of the table.

"My pleasure, Sheriff, my pleasure. I'm happy to help law enforcement get to the bottom of this awful crime. You can't believe the effect it's had on both me and the entire News Six family. We are just devastated by what happened to poor Lynne."

"Do you know anyone who might have wanted to harm Lynne Boyd?"

"I wish I could help you, but I don't have a clue."

"Did she say anything to you recently that suggested that she thought she was in any danger?"

"Nothing, Sheriff, nothing at all."

"So tell me, Mr. Guerski, how long have you known Lynne Boyd?" Ray shot in his question as Guerski paused for a breath.

"From the first day she came to the station, what's it been, five years, maybe a little more."

"And how well do you know her?" Ray asked.

Guerski seemed to consider the question. "What do you mean, Sheriff, how well?"

"Are you just professional colleagues, do you just see her at the office? Perhaps your families get together, maybe the two of you have lunch occasionally."

"I'd say these days we're mostly work friends," Guerski answered.

"So there was a time your friendship was different?"

"Yes, especially in the beginning. She had a lot of trouble that first year."

"You're referring to her ex-boyfriend?"

"Yeah. I'm a pretty big guy, and at times I escorted her places and went out of my way to look after her. It was sort of a big brother, little sister kind of relationship. But after that all came to a head, and she got married, I really didn't see much of her anymore."

"Have you been seeing her recently?"

"At work," Guerski responded, perspiration forming on his florid countenance.

"And outside of work?"

"Never."

"And you're sure of that?"

"Of course I'm sure of that," Guerski answered, his geniality being replaced by an undertone of hostility.

"You travel around the region quite extensively, don't you Mr. Guerski?"

"I do, Sheriff, I do. I try to keep close to the high school sports, especially football and basketball."

"So occasionally you do stories from some smaller high schools in places like Harbor Springs, or perhaps Gaylord, or Petoskey."

"Yeah, I know them all," responded Guerski, warming to the topic. "High school sports is really important to our viewers. We need to be showing their kids on TV, and they need to see us walking the sidelines with a cameraman."

"Been in Grayling lately?"

"Not this season. But someone from our sports team was there for at least one home game. And that's what we try to do. Make sure we're in almost every small town in the region once during football and basketball seasons."

"You ever get to Grayling?"

"Drive through occasionally when I'm heading for the U.P."

"You're probably wondering why I keep asking about Grayling?" said Ray.

Guerski didn't respond.

"We've heard you've been spending Wednesday afternoons there. We did some checking, and you have been renting the same room in the same motel for several months. It's a room in the back of the building, the kind that would allow one to come and go fairly discreetly."

Guerski remained silent.

"The owner can identify you, but says she never saw who you were meeting. I was wondering who that might have been."

"Sheriff, what I was doing might not have been right, but I wasn't breaking any laws." Guerski said after a long pause. "Oh, I think I get it. Bet some little birdie flew in and told you I was having an affair with Lynne."

Ray and Sue remained silent.

"It's not what you think, Sheriff."

"What should I think, Mr. Guerski?"

"Well, it's like this. My wife found a credit card bill. She confronted me. I told her I was involved with Lynne."

"And?" prodded Sue.

"I just told her that."

"It's not true?" Sue continued.

"Not the Lynne part."

"Why did you tell her that?"

"It was an easy way out."

"Out of what?" asked Sue.

"Well it's hard to explain," said Guerski.

"Try us."

"The wife and I, we haven't had much of a marriage for years. I've just been hanging in there. The kids, you know. I've just been waiting until they're off to college. And all these years I've been faithful. But recently, well, I got involved with one of Rachael's friends. I mean Rachael's best friend. When she confronted me, I just couldn't tell her. It's bad enough that I was unfaithful, but to have to tell her she had been betrayed by her best friend. Well I just couldn't do that. I told her it was Lynne. I mean that's the first person who came to my mind."

"And you will give us the name of the other woman so we can verify your story."

"Do I have to?"

"Yes," Ray responded; his eyes fixed on Guerski.

Guerski settled back in his chair and exhaled loudly. "Sure," he said, in a tone of resignation. "I'll give you her name. You won't tell my wife?"

"You get to figure that one out," said Ray. "We just want to make sure you are in no way connected with this crime."

"I'm not, Sheriff, absolutely not."

36

~~~~~~

fter the Guerski interview, Ray wandered off to his office. As he worked his way though a new pile of forms and memos, he felt tired. He struggled to attend to the work in front of him, but all he really wanted to do was fold his arms on the desk and put his head down. He woke with a start. Sue was standing in front of his desk.

"Sorry to disturb you," she said.

"I don't know what happened," he said in an embarrassed voice.

"Ray, you're exhausted. You're still in recovery mode, and you've been pushing yourself nonstop. I think I should drive you home; you've put in a full day already."

"You know I wouldn't normally ask you to do this, but would you get me a mug of coffee?"

"You need rest, not more coffee."

"Please," implored Ray.

"Martian," said Sue as she headed down the hall. In a few minutes she returned with a mug of coffee and set it on Ray's desk. "Careful. It's from a fresh pot, and it's very hot."

She settled in a chair across from him and opened a manila folder, "I've got some information on private military companies that I think you will find interesting."

"What?" asked Ray, after carefully taking a sip of the steaming brew.

"You asked me to do some research. Magnus Conservus. I googled them. Couldn't find a website for Magnus Conservus, but I did find them on several sites that listed private military forces, security forces, or armies. Let me read their description from one of the sites:

Magnus Conservus provides security services to corporations, governments, NGOs, and private individuals. MC employs a team of highly-trained professionals to meet every contingency including: security/military, medical, logistical, and communications. Security personnel are recruited from the elite military forces worldwide.

"I should add, Ray, that this description is fairly typical of all the companies listed on the website. I was just astounded. I knew that there are soldiers of fortune working in far off places, and our government has hired some of these companies in recent years, but I had no idea it was this extensive or this organized."

"Did they mention bringing in fresh Maine lobsters for beach parties?" Ray asked sarcastically.

"No. That's probably not part of the business plan anymore," said Sue.

"Or in contemporary business parlance, not part of the brand," Ray added. "And what else did you discover?"

"Magnus Conservus is listed as the owner of the Crescent Cove/Round Island property. All of it, including Round Island, is taxed as commercial property. And as far as I can tell in a fast and superficial search, the company seems to be in compliance with state laws."

"Good."

"There's something even more interesting. I was just curious to see if they owned any other property in the county...."

"And?"

"The Boyd/Lowther home, or at least what we thought was their home, belongs to Magnus Conservus."

"Interesting," responded Ray.

"As for the biathlon, according to Wikipedia, the shooting distance is 50 meters or 164 feet. The target size in the prone position is 1.7 inches, 4.5 inches in the standing position."

"And the contestant is sucking wind from skiing just before they set up to shoot."

"Yes," agreed Sue.

"So at the scene of the shooting, what's the terrain like 50 meters out? We've assumed that the assailant was carefully concealed and positioned and shooting from a far greater distance. Where did that idea come from?"

"The deer hunter paradigm," Sue responded. "It's in the air right now."

"So could someone have just skied in, popped up at the right moment, taken a shot, and been on their way, probably before Marie had Lynne back in the car?"

"Possible, but we have to look at the scene again. But given all the fresh snow and the boggy terrain, I don't think anyone would have moved in and out of there very quickly. The high ground would still be an advantage."

"Let's go look," said Ray, "before it's completely dark."

Twenty minutes later they were at the scene of the shooting. Sue pulled her Jeep into the drive of the Boyd/Lowther home, and they climbed out, Sue reaching back in to retrieve a flashlight before they walked to the far side of the road and looked over the scene in the half-light of a gray late November afternoon.

"Should have brought some boots," said Ray.

"You wouldn't have gotten far," said Sue. "It's mostly muck. You can only get across there by finding stumps and logs that will hold your weight. And remember on Monday we had close to two feet of fresh snow covering everything. It's collapsed a bit, but it's too deep for skis. You would have needed snow shoes, and we would have seen the tracks, even with all the blowing and drifting."

Ray nodded his agreement. "I'm just trying to make something appear out of nothing."

"Aren't you the one who is always telling me to be patient, especially during the early stages of the investigation. I think Hawkins really got to you."

"If we had more resources, would we be doing things differently?" Ray asked.

"I don't think so, we'd be able to spread the work around, and your involvement would be more administrative than hands-on. But I don't think you'd like that very much."

"So," said Ray, not responding to Sue's answer, "the shooter had to be very familiar with Lynne's schedule. He, or perhaps she, had to know that they went to yoga on Monday, so they had either been observing her actions for a period of time or…"

"Someone familiar with her routine, like her soon to be ex-husband," Sue continued, picking up the thought, "either used the knowledge, or more likely passed it on to the shooter."

"And Marie doesn't remember anyone lurking about. That said, it would be easy enough to keep tabs on Lynne for a week or two without causing suspicion."

"If we could only question Lynne," said Sue.

"Not in the near future, anyway."

In the few minutes they stood at the side of the road chatting, the last vestiges of daylight had slipped away. They turned and walked toward their parked car, both startled by the sudden perception of a large man standing in the darkness near the back bumper.

"Who's there?" asked Ray, feeling suddenly uneasy.

"Private security," came the answer.

"Can I see some identification," asked Sue. She lifted the Maglite to shoulder height and switched it on, training its beam into the eyes of the figure. She reached for her weapon with her right hand.

The uniformed man had lifted both arms, showing gloved hands. He pulled a plastic ID tag from his jacket. Ray walked forward and took the ID while Sue held her position.

"What are you doing here?" Ray asked.

"Routine security."

Ray looked at the picture ID. "You're with Magnus Conservus?"

"Yes, sir,"

"Ex-military?" asked Ray.

"Yes, sir."

"And it says here you are Gary Johnson. Is that correct?"

"Yes, sir."

"Are you armed?"

"I have a tactical baton, nothing more."

"No side arms, no knives?"

"No, sir."

"Would you face the car please and put your hands on the vehicle."

"I don't understand?"

"Now," yelled Ray, his voice filled with anger. Ray quickly patted him down, finding nothing. He stepped back and said, "You can turn around now."

"Was that necessary?" Johnson asked.

"Absolutely," said Ray. "We don't know who you are, why you are here, and whether your firm is in compliance with Michigan law. Do you have a Michigan driver's license?"

"Yes, sir? Do you want me to get it out for you?"

"Yes," said Ray.

Johnson pulled a wallet from an inside jacket pocket.

"Would you remove the license from your wallet, please?" Ray instructed. He took it from the young man's hand and passed it to Sue. "Would you run this, please?"

He turned back to Johnson, "What are you doing here?"

"We are securing the exterior of this home and the other buildings on the property against break-ins and vandalism."

"By whose order?"

"Sir, I am an employee. I am only doing what I've been instructed to do. If you wish to speak to my supervisor, I will get him on the phone."

"Do you have a vehicle here, Johnson?"

"Yes, sir. I'm parked next to the barn. When I saw your headlights, I came down to investigate."

"This is what I want you to do, Johnson. Call your supervisor. Tell him that the man who has been living here is a deputy sheriff and probably doesn't know that an outside security service is on this property. I don't want anyone hurt or killed. Will you do that?"

"Yes, sir."

Sue returned with the license and handed it back to Johnson. "He's clean," she said to Ray.

"Go about your business, Johnson," said Ray.

They climbed back into the Jeep. After starting the engine, she switched on the headlights, and they watched Johnson disappear at the top of the snow-covered drive. They sat in silence for several moments. Then Ray said, "When the going gets weird, the weird turn pro."

"Who are you quoting now?"

"Hunter Thompson, I think. I'm embarrassed that I lost it there."

"I've never heard you use that tone of voice before," Sue observed. "But I was feeling the same way. We need to both chill a bit. And tomorrow you are to stay away and not think about this case. I've got every shift adequately covered. And there are instructions that no one is to call you. I am the filter; they are to call me if there is some crisis."

"You're not heading downstate to spend Thanksgiving with your parents?"

"I called home yesterday and just told my parents I was too busy. I think it would be better if I stayed around."

"So you're not on duty, but you are staying in the area."

"I'll work in the morning, take the afternoon off. I'm looking forward to a quiet day."

"Do you want to come to dinner? There will be lots of good food."

"I thought you might be spending the day with your friend, Sarah."

"She's out of town, visiting her son. It's going to be Marc and Lisa, Nora and the dogs, and me."

"I'd love to join you and your friends," said Sue. "The one thing I was dreading was that Banquet turkey dinner."

37

Billy Coyle struggled to get his Ford van down the heavily rutted road. He could see that it hadn't been plowed since the snow had started, just packed down through repeated use. As he made the last turn toward the beach the old cottage came into view, a shake-sided Victorian, one of the oldest summer homes in the county.

Billy could remember coming to this place with his father when he was a kid in elementary school. In those days his father still looked after the water systems in some of the older seasonal cottages, priming and starting the pumps in the spring and draining the plumbing and pumps in the fall. Billy would travel with his father on Saturdays, and his size when he was eight or ten made him very useful. He could easily maneuver into crawl spaces to open hard-to-reach drain plugs, removing them in the fall and replacing them in the spring.

At the end of the drive near the house he maneuvered the van around, getting briefly stuck in the process, rocking the vehicle free, and finally backing in next to the snow-covered Bronco.

He walked to the back of the truck and opened the rear doors. He looked at the collection of wrenches in a white drywall bucket, then added a propane torch and a couple of Channellocks. He hefted the bucket with his right hand and trudged toward the house, pausing briefly, noticing the state of decay the exterior of the building had fallen into in recent years.

Following the path through the snow to the rear porch, Billy climbed the three steps and set the heavy bucket down before knocking. He looked through the window in the door and peered into the kitchen. Waiting in the winter silence, Billy listened for movement in the house. After a long moment he banged on the door again, this time his rap was louder and more sustained.

Finally he heard someone moving inside, and Gavin Mendicot came into view. Billy waited as several deadbolts were withdrawn and the door finally opened.

"I thought you were going to be here yesterday," Gavin slurred in an accusatorial tone.

"Check your voice mail. I got your message and called back saying I couldn't make it until this afternoon."

"It's the same fucking problem again. Everything is fine, and then suddenly the water isn't working."

"Gavin, we go through this every year. How many times have I told you the system was never designed for winter use?" Billy looked around the large kitchen and into the adjoining living room. He remembered how magical the place had appeared to him when he was a boy—the antique filled rooms, the elegant wicker furniture, the neatly arranged bookcases, and ornate pump organ standing near the French doors that opened onto the screen porch that faced Lake Michigan. Then everything was in its place and the whole building smelled of cedar and Murphy's Soap. Now the space was cluttered, dirty clothes heaped on the furniture, discarded and broken furniture pushed off to the sides of the room. The kitchen was stacked with empty food and beverage containers. The sink was heaped with glasses, mugs, and a few dishes. The one oasis from the overwhelming clutter was the sturdy oak dining table that stood at the center of the kitchen. A collection of rifles and pistols covered the tabletop, many in pieces, carefully arranged for reassembly. Boxes of bullets, like a collection of children's blocks, were neatly stacked near each weapon.

"Getting ready for a war?" asked Billy motioning toward the table.

"Just get the goddam water going," Gavin hissed.

"Don't imagine you shoveled around the pump house?" said Billy.

"I thought you'd want to do that," Gavin responded.

"Get a shovel," ordered Billy. "We'll start there and work our way back until we find the problem."

38

As Ray pulled into his drive, he saw the package leaning against the front entrance to his house. After parking his car, he walked through the house from the garage. He opened the front door, brushed the snow off the box and brought it to the kitchen counter. Using a utility knife, he cut the packaging tape at the sides, then across the top, and pulled the cardboard flaps open, and inhaled a tantalizing hint of the contents.

On top was a gift card with the Zingerman's logo. Ray unfolded the note that listed the contents of the package along with a message from the senders.

We are so thankful that we can break bread with you tomorrow.

Mark, Lisa, and Nora

Ray lifted the carefully wrapped pieces of cheese from the container and arranged them on the counter, perusing the labels that identified the contents. At the bottom he found two loaves of Pain de Montagne, a thick-crusted peasant bread, and a bottle of artisanal olive oil from Provence.

After putting the cheese and the Pain de Montagne away, he put on the teakettle. Then Ray set out the ingredients for his supper: a petite baguette he had picked up on the way home, some Vermont cheddar, a small piece of less-than-heroic Stilton, and two apples—yellow-skinned with reddish tones. He opened the new bottle of olive oil and poured some into a ramekin. He held the container under one of the spotlights positioned over the stove and examined the oil. He cut some bread and dipped a piece into the oil, studying its gold-green color before he tasted it, slowly chewing the bread, alert to the delicate flavors.

He moved the cutting board with the bread, cheese, apples, and olive oil to the kitchen table. Then he carried over a large mug of ginger and green tea. Ray ate slowly, looking through the day's mail as he consumed his supper. Occasionally he watched the network news with his dinner, but this evening he was far too late.

After he cleared away the dishes and neatened the kitchen, Ray moved packages of fish and venison, the basic ingredients for the two dishes he was making for the Thanksgiving dinner, from the freezer to the refrigerator, so they would be partially thawed by morning.

Ray went to his writing desk and retrieved his journal from under the hinged desktop and paged through to his last entry from earlier in the week.

For the next hour he methodically filled lines and pages with carefully constructed sentences and paragraphs. This evening he recorded his reaction to his encounter with Dorothy Boyd and Harry Hawkins. As he wrote, he tried to put himself back into the scene—to hear their voices again, to see their eyes, and watch their body language. He wondered what was real and what was theater.

He next moved on to listing the facts of the case, what was known and what was not. Ray used bulleted columns on opposing pages. After he completed the lists, he studied the graphic, hoping to see a connection that had been missed earlier or something that would provide new directions in the investigation.

With Ray's growing sense of frustration at the lack of progress, the energy that had enabled him to stand and write so long seemed to vanish. Suddenly he was very tired, struggling to stay awake. He looked once more at the diagram, hoping something would leap off the page, then closed the journal, replaced the cap of the pen, and returned them to their place in the desk.

As he prepared for bed, he thought about the things he would have to do in the morning to complete his part of the Thanksgiving dinner by the time guests arrived.

Ray climbed into bed and started reading a long profile in a current New Yorker. He woke at three, his bedside reading lamp still on, the magazine on his chest. He turned the light off and fell back into a heavy slumber.

39

It was already well past 7:00 when Ray awakened, but it wasn't the dull light of the winter dawn that pulled him from his slumber. A persistent knocking that he couldn't ignore got him up, and after retrieving and donning a long black fleece monk's robe that his friend Lisa had made him during his recovery, he moved toward the front door.

He found Nora, accompanied by her two dogs, Prince Hal and Falstaff, waiting for him.

"I didn't wake you," she said as she walked by him, placing a large wicker basket on the food preparation counter next to the stove. Once the load was out of her hands, she looked around and then back at Ray, noting how he was attired.

"Joining a religious order? I hope it's not one that practices celibacy. That could be dreadfully tedious."

"Yes," he agreed with a smile.

"And you haven't even made coffee yet," she said incredulously. "Ray, I've never known you to sleep in before."

"What are you doing here so early?" he asked. "We were going to gather sometime this afternoon and begin cooking."

"Well, Dotty's kitchen is so small, and the temperature control on her oven is not dependable. It's just so much easier to make pies here. I'll get them put together and baked, and then I'll disappear for a bit. I brought you some fresh banana bread for breakfast, and here's today's Free Press and yesterday's Times."

"Pies," said Ray, "there are only going to be five of us, how many are you making?"

"Just three, pumpkin, cherry, and pecan. People have different traditions, I want to be sure everyone gets a choice."

"Our tradition was crème brûlée," said Ray.

"Crème brûlée! Sure, Ray Elkins," said Nora, with a breathy laugh. "Your mother was a good cook. Baked wonderful pies and bread, but none of us had tasted crème brûlée back in the old days. Now get some coffee made and go read the paper, I need to get to work."

Ray put a kettle on the stove and measured the dark, shiny beans into the grinder. As he started turning the crank, Nora asked, "Why aren't you using the electric mill?"

"It makes too much noise in the morning," he responded. Ray emptied the drawer of finely-ground coffee into a glass carafe and scanned the headlines as he waited for the water to come to a boil. He allowed it to cool for a few minutes and then poured it over the coffee. After allowing three minutes for the infusion to take place, he pushed the grounds to the bottom with the finely-screened plunger.

Ray placed a mug of steaming coffee at Nora's side and settled at his dining table with the papers, the banana bread, butter, and coffee. The dogs, one on each side, accepted small donations until it was clear Ray was finished eating, then they wandered off to find a place for their morning nap. Falstaff curled up in a pool of sunshine on an oriental rug. Prince Hal settled on a couch, his head elevated on a pillow.

Ray luxuriated in having the leisure to sip coffee and read the paper, occasionally glancing out at the snow-covered landscape—the shadows changing as the morning sun moved across the horizon. Nora, the dogs in tow, was on her way out before he had finished scanning the Times.

"The pies are done and cooling, and I hope you will note the kitchen is back to what it was when I arrived, with a few improvements, of course. What time should I come back?"

"People are coming about 3:00 to get started. Then we were planning on hiking on the Lake Michigan shore before dinner. Perhaps starting hors d'oeurves between five and six and dinner when we get to it."

"Well, I will be here at three. The boys will love the walk. They really miss not living near the beach," Nora said. "And stay out of those pies," she admonished as she moved toward the door.

Before showering, Ray put in a call to the hospital and had a brief conversation with Hanna Jeffers, Lynne Boyd's attending physician, the plucky surgeon credited with saving her life. Ray learned that Lynne's condition, while still critical, had continued to improve and that Lynne would probably be moved to Cleveland Clinic, perhaps by the beginning of the next week, for further evaluation. Jeffers opined that Lynne would require weeks of hospitalization, followed by months of limited activity during her recovery.

By 3:00 in the afternoon Ray completed preparations for his two entrees, tenderloins of venison in a butter and thimbleberry sauce and steelhead filets poached in white wine. Marc would be preparing medallions of duck breast. Ray knew Marc would arrive with crusty baguettes just out of the oven. And Lisa would prepare a collection of greens for a salad after the entrees.

Nora and the boys marched in on the hour, Marc and Lisa fifteen or twenty minutes later, and finally Sue Lawrence, still in uniform, carrying a bottle of wine in a brown paper bag, a backpack slung over her right shoulder.

"Everything okay?" Ray asked, accepting the wine.

"As usual, it's a very slow day," she responded. "And we are more than adequately staffed. And short of the end of the world or the sky falling, Ben knows you are not to be called." Sue disappeared for a few minutes and returned to the kitchen in mufti, black velour jeans and a soft, blue sweater that set off her aquamarine eyes and long, red hair. Ray was startled by her appearance. He had never seen her dressed and groomed in such a feminine manner.

The whole group, including the dogs, crowded into Marc's vintage van. After a short ride to the Lake Michigan shore and a long walk at the base of the dunes under clear skies and waning sunshine, they returned to Ray's home in high spirits to start the final preparations for dinner. Ray was busy sautéing the venison when he was startled by a large pop. He turned to see Nora with a newly-opened magnum of champagne.

"My family tradition," she said with a smile, showing Ray the Dom Perignon label on the bottle.

"A good tradition," said Ray.

The cooking and conversation continued, livened by Nora's assiduous attention to keeping all the glasses full.

After the frenzy of preparation, they settled into a leisurely meal with the appropriate wine served with each entree: a Chateauneuf du Pape with the poached steelhead, a Shiraz to accompany the venison, and a Pinot Noir partnered with the duck. The main courses ended with Lisa's salad, then the dishes were cleared away, and coffee and pie were served.

As they lingered over their coffee, Lisa asked, "Anything new on the Boyd shooting?

Marc looked across the table at Lisa and said, "She promised me this morning that she wouldn't mention the subject today."

"The day's almost over," she sheepishly offered in her defense.

"I wish we had the shooter," said Sue.

"How about Lynne? How's she doing?" asked Lisa.

"I think there's growing optimism," said Ray. He shared what he had recently learned from Dr. Jeffers.

"That's something to be thankful for," said Nora. "Those beautiful little girls should have their mother."

"Nora," Ray paused, thinking about what he wanted to ask, "the shooting up at Crescent Cove, the one you told me about...."

"When was this?" interrupted Lisa.

"Oh, years ago," Nora explained.

"The person involved, the man who died, what was his name?" asked Ray.

"That was Talmadge Hawthorne," she answered.

"And I think you said something about a settlement with his family. What was that all about?"

"As I remember, it was about Talmadge's membership. His heir was unhappy with the buyout arrangement. He argued that the share should have been much larger."

"This was a son of Talmadge Hawthorne?" asked Ray.

"No, it was a stepson, the child of Talmadge's second wife. Beautiful woman she was, too, about thirty years his junior. Looked a lot like Grace Kelly, wonderful hair, beautiful eyes. Her death, what a tragedy."

"What happened to her?" Ray asked.

"She drowned. She was out swimming alone, I think it was in August, got carried out into the big lake by that current. At first, no one noticed she was missing. The next day they found her body washed up on the shore up the coast a few miles. Some people said she had a drinking problem; I don't know."

"And her son, do you remember his name?"

"Oh yes. You know he was gone for years, but I've seen him around the last year or two."

"His name, Nora."

"Yes, his name, rather unusual. Let me think. The first name was like a screen actor. Hollywood sounding. Gavin, yes that's it." She paused for a minute. "Gavin Mendicot. That's his name. Thank God things are still connected up in my head."

"Oh, Gavin," said Lisa, coming back into the conversation.

"What do you know about him?" asked Ray, turning his attention to Lisa.

"Not much. He's a couple of years older than me and was around in the summer when I was in high school and college. He was an Adonis. Lots of blond hair, great definition, a real six-pack. If he had only had a brain."

"Brain?"

"He was real political, far right wing. And he drank a lot and was into drugs. He went to one of those colleges that cater to dim-witted children of car dealers," Lisa explained.

"Is she always this hostile?" asked Ray, laughingly.

"You don't know the half of it," responded Marc. "Fortunately, I'm a calming influence."

"Anything more about Gavin?" Ray asked Lisa.

"I heard he joined the military, Special Forces. I think he was in Iraq. Someone told me he was eventually mustered out of the service with severe emotional problems. I ran into him at the hardware last spring. He knew me by name; I didn't recognize him; he had changed so dramatically."

"How so?" asked Ray.

"He'd ballooned up, gone mostly bald, and had this vacant, confused look about him. And when blond guys go to seed they just look like hell."

"Wasn't he the man Donna Bateman was living with?" asked Sue, looking at Ray. "The source of the...."

"Yes," Ray answered, exchanging glances. He looked back at Lisa. "Anything else?"

" I think that's about all I remember."

"Nora, anything more you can add?"

"Let me think. It seems to me that he was around when his stepfather had that accident. Ray, that was a while ago, and what I heard was mostly gossip. I don't remember anything else." Before she could say anything, Prince Hal interrupted with a sharp, command bark. "The boys need walking, I think they want to go home."

"It is getting late," said Marc. "We need to get things cleaned up and out of here so Ray can get some sleep."

A flurry of activity followed and finally the kitchen was in order and everything put away. And then the final hugs as Marc, Lisa, and Nora said their good-byes. Sue was last, retrieving her backpack. She gave Ray a parting hug, and to his surprise it turned into a passionate embrace. She pulled his head to hers, their lips met, and Ray felt her tongue slide slowly back and forth across his lips. They embraced a second time, this time Ray responding to her passion. Then Sue suddenly pulled back.

"I'd better go," she said.

Ray desperately wanted to reach for her, but he restrained himself. He remained silent as she quickly slipped out the door.

40

~~~~~~~~

Ray was awakened by the sound of his cell phone sitting on the nightstand at the side of the bed. He turned on the light and pressed the answer button.

"Ray, it's Ben. Sorry to wake you so early when you're suppose to be off, but I think you'd like to know this."

"What's happening?" Ray asked.

"Dispatch just took a call from a department in the U.P. wanting us to do a notification of death. I called them back and verified the information. It's Dirk's brother, Ray. He died in a snowmobile accident."

Ray did not respond. He let the information seep in.

"I'm happy to make this run alone, but I thought you might want to be involved."

"Yes," he responded.

"Want me to pick you up?" asked Ben.

"Sure," said Ray, "give me about twenty minutes."

Ray was waiting just inside the front door when Ben pulled his patrol car in close. Ray slid into the passenger's seat, moving his insulated coffee mug to his left hand so he could pull the door closed.

"Have a good Thanksgiving?" Ben asked as he carefully maneuvered his patrol car down Ray's snow-covered drive.

"Yes," Ray answered, the rather surprising events of the previous evening flashing through his brain. "Spending time cooking and eating with old friends," Ray continued, needing to fill the silence, "was very special this year."

"I know Sue was excited to be invited," said Ben. "She's told me when you and your friend Marc get together the food is amazing. I bet she enjoyed herself."

"Seemed to," Ray responded. "How about yours?" he asked, needing to move away from the topic.

"Everything was ready when I got home, and fortunately it was a quiet night, nothing to pull me back in. The kids were home from college. Jamie brought her fiancé, and Maureen was worried about the sleeping arrangements."

"How did it work out?"

"Well, you know when they were small we built on that wing for them with bedrooms and a family room of their own. We had dinner and sat around and talked over dessert. Then we got things cleaned up and went off to bed. Maureen finally stopped worrying. She said the kids would figure it out. No one did bed checks. You've avoided these crises by not having children."

"True," said Ray, remaining silent for a few moments as he thought about how he might have reacted if he had been confronted with this situation.

"Tell me about the early days, Ben. When you were first in the department. What was it like with Dirk and his brother?"

Ben didn't respond immediately.

"It was a culture shock in the beginning. I was young, just a few years out of college with a degree in criminal justice. I spent a year in Detroit before getting a job with the Birmingham department. We had sort of settled in to our life down there. Maureen had a teaching job in Royal Oak; we had a real nice apartment and were starting to look for a house. Then Maureen's father got lung cancer; we had only been married about a year. We were driving up here every weekend or two to help out. This city boy had to learn about fruit farming. The sicker her dad got, the more they needed our help. Orville was a friend of the family and offered me a job. It was the last thing in the world I wanted to do, but Maureen was very close to her dad and felt needed. Our original plan was to be here for a year or two and then go back to the city, but we sort of settled in. Maureen got a teaching job and then got pregnant. It was just sort of natural the way we ended up here."

"How about your job?" asked Ray.

"It was awful. I was trying to figure out how I could pick up a teaching degree or do something else."

"What was going on?" Ray asked.

"I don't think we've ever talked about it, but I know you've heard a lot of stories over the years. Even though Orville had sort of gone into retirement while still on the job, he got re-elected every four years. Dirk, his brother Danny, and Kenny Obermeyer ran the department. They were all ex-military and started in the force when they came out of the service. They weren't happy when Orville hired me, and they did their best to isolate me and make me feel unwanted. I think they were hoping I would quit."

"But you didn't," said Ray.

"I ended up working nights, so I didn't have to deal with them."

"So what was going on in the department?" Ray asked

"I can't say that my knowledge is first hand. Like I said, they isolated me. They seemed to figure out right from the outset that I was a straight arrow."

"How were things organized?"

"There was Orville, and then those three were the undersheriffs. They gave themselves the rank of captain. And like I said, I didn't see anything, but ...."

"I'd be interested in hearing your take on things," pressed Ray. "What do you think was happening?"

"Well, roughing up people at traffic stops and arrests, womanizing, entrapment, drugs—you name it. And then there was that thing with Kenny Obermeyer getting shot."

"What did you hear about that?"

"It was in the summer, late July as I remember it. I wasn't on; it was a weekend. The story Orville put out, the one fed to him by Dirk and his brother, was that Kenny was shot during a routine traffic stop. I heard they picked up the body in a field way off the road, and Kenny was not in uniform. Some traffic stop."

"So what do you think happened?"

"I'm not sure, there were so many stories. I just know the three of them were spending a lot of money, many times their salary. Right after the shooting, Orville took back the day-to-day operation of the department and cleaned house. He turned out to be a lot more with it than I thought.

"Danny supposedly quit; he moved his family north, and Dirk disappeared for a while, and when he came back he was on road patrol. Orville made sure the investigation of Kenny's death didn't go anywhere. Today you couldn't get away with that, but things were a lot looser then."

"Tell me about Danny?"

"He's Dirk's kid brother, cut from the same mold, only much bigger and tougher. He was a violent person who loved to fight. I can remember a couple of instances that first year where he stopped bar brawls; his technique was to go in and beat the hell out of combatants and then drag them to jail."

"So Danny was this tough guy, but when Kenny got killed, he wasted no time getting out of town."

"They had gotten into something really bad. And the people they were involved with didn't hesitate to blow one of them away to make a point. I was glad to see Danny go. He was dirt."

"You said they had a lot of money then?"

"For a few years they had all the toys: new cars, trucks, and snowmobiles. They were living high on the hog. Danny and Kenny seemed to blow it all. Dirk was better at hanging onto some of it.

I don't understand how he's done it. I mean, he's gone through a couple of divorces, he's got kids from previous marriages he's had to support, but he always seems to be in the chips."

"Any ideas?"

"I know he's got some rentals, he owned a pizzeria early on, and he's been doing some moonlighting."

"I've heard about the moonlighting," said Ray, "but I've never been able to figure out exactly what he does. And he will never take any overtime."

"He's told me he does consulting. When I've pushed him on it, he's said something about designing security systems."

"Interesting," said Ray. "Ben, over the years has Dirk ever been involved in domestic violence?"

"Like Dirk as the perpetrator?"

"Yes."

"I'm not sure I can give you a good answer. When I first moved here, the three of them really covered for one another. And all of them were pretty good at slapping people around. Whether that extended to Dirk's wives and girlfriends, I don't know. Now Danny, on the other hand, was pretty physical with his girlfriends. But like I said, they covered for one another."

They sat in silence as Ben drove through the snow-covered landscape. Ray looked out at the neat rows of fruit trees in the orchards, gray and dormant against the gently rolling blanket of fresh snow. He absorbed the beauty of the moment before allowing his focus to come back to the bleak business at hand.

41

~~~~~

"Looks like Dirk hasn't been out yet," observed Ben as he turned off the highway. An unblemished dusting of powdery lake-effect snow covered the surface of the long drive.

"Not this morning," agreed Ray.

As they came around the corner at the top of the drive, they saw a second pickup parked on the apron in front of the garage next to Dirk's truck.

"That truck looks familiar," said Ray.

"It's Donna Bateman's. Seems like she's not spending every night at home supervising young Clay. Perhaps Dirk's going to replace Gavin Mendicot as the homme du jour."

"What do you know about Gavin?" asked Ray.

"He's had a few run-ins with law enforcement over the years," Ben said.

"Remember to tell me about him when we're heading back. I've become sort of curious about him," explained Ray.

"Will do. You're going to do the talking when we get inside?" asked Ben.

"Yes," answered Ray.

"Good," said Ben as he started to unfold his tall frame out of the car.

After ringing the bell and hearing the Westminster-like chime from the interior, they stood for thirty or forty seconds before Ray pushed the button a second time. After a second interval, he pushed the bell a third time. Finally they could hear a voice, followed by the sound of the deadbolt being withdrawn. The door opened to the length of the chain, with Dirk peering out.

"What do you guys want?" he asked.

"We need to talk to you," answered Ray. "Let us in."

"Did Lynne…."

"No, Dirk. But we need to talk to you," said Ray.

The door closed and they could hear the chain being released. Dirk opened the door and they followed him into the living room. He was wearing a heavy terrycloth bathrobe and, it appeared, little more. Ray saw Dirk set the revolver he had been holding in his right hand when he opened the door on the fireplace mantle. He motioned them to sit; he remained standing with his back to the fireplace.

"If nothing happened to Lynne, what's so important that you have to come barging in here so early in the morning," Dirk asked, putting an unlit cigarette in his mouth.

"It's your brother, Danny."

"What about him?"

"We had a call early this morning from the sheriff's department up there. He was killed in a snowmobile accident."

Dirk pulled a kitchen match out of the pocket in his robe and lit it with the flick of his thumb. He inhaled deeply, tossed the remains of the match on the cold coals in the fireplace, looked over their heads, and slowly exhaled.

"What else?"

"That's all I know, Dirk." Ray looked over at Ben.

"They said the cause of the accident is still under investigation," added Ben. "It happened during the night. They were going to do a more thorough investigation this morning. The body has been sent to Marquette for an autopsy."

"Dumb bastard," Dirk said, his gaze still way above their head. "I told him he shouldn't be riding all the time."

"I don't understand," said Ray.

"Danny owns this bar. In the winter he rides his sled to and from work almost every day. It's the going home after he closes that I was worried about. Most nights he's real tired and probably had too much to drink. Fifteen, twenty miles of back roads and two-tracks—a breakdown, an accident, or even running out of gas—you'd fucking freeze to death before anyone found you."

"Danny got a wife?" Ray asked.

"Yeah, but he's been living with a girlfriend. That's why he was traveling so far. He's got a house just down the road from the bar."

"Anything we can do?"

"No. But you asked me to stay around town. When I know about the funeral, I'd like to go up there for a day or two."

"We'll work something out," said Ray

"I need to be alone, now," said Dirk, finally looking directly at Ray. "Thank you for, ah, coming to tell me."

Ben and Ray let themselves out of the house. Once they were settled back in the car and Ben was starting to maneuver out of the drive, he observed, "Over thirty some years I've done a fair number of death notifications. I think this was the most unusual."

"How so?" asked Ray, wondering if Ben's response was similar to his own.

"No affect," he paused. "That's not quite right. There was some emotion, but it seemed more irritation than anything else. Maybe we interrupted some good lovemaking?"

"Were Dirk and Danny close, back in the old days?"

"I think so, but I always got the impression it was a really strange, violent family."

"I'm surprised they didn't make your life so miserable that you quit," said Ray.

"They gave it their best shot," Ben said as he pulled onto the snow-covered county road. "One night during my first summer in the department they lured me up to this place near Bass Lake; it was an old farm that Kenny had bought at a tax sale. I could see that they had all been drinking heavily. They told me they wanted to show me something in the barn, and as soon we got into this empty old building, Kenny says something like, 'College boy, we're going to show you a few things you didn't learn in school.' Then he takes this real clumsy swing at me."

"What did you do?"

"Well Ray, you know I'm an old-line Detroiter. My grandfather—who spent his working years in the steel mill at the Rouge—was a semi-pro fighter, my father was a Golden Gloves champ, later a coach. I boxed until I was in tenth grade, when I made the Fordson High basketball team. You should have seen me back then; I was so tall and skinny."

"You're still tall," Ray joked.

"Yeah, it's the other dimension that I struggle with."

"Did you play basketball in college?"

"I didn't get a scholarship, but I was going to try to make the team. Then I met this exotic woman, she was a fencer, and I followed her to practice. The coach, this really incredible old Hungarian, looked at me, told me to hold out my arm, and said I was born for the epee. So I fenced for four years. My hoop dreams were replaced with a sword."

"What happened to the exotic woman?"

"She was an art major. Did one of those junior years abroad in Paris. I went to visit her once at Christmas break. By spring she had fallen madly in love with a painter. She stayed over there. Last I heard she was living in Spain."

"Were you crushed?"

"Truth be told, I had met someone also."

"So back to the barn," said Ray. "What happened?"

"So Kenny and Danny started after me. I knew I couldn't take on both of them, so I said something like, 'Don't you guys have enough balls to fight me one at a time?' I took off my gun belt and handed it to Dirk who was just standing there watching. Danny came after me first. He was big and strong and tough. But he was also drunk and clumsy and didn't know how to box; he was strictly a brawler. With my reach he was never able to get close. And luckily for me, he had a glass jaw; I put him away fast. Kenny was a bit more challenging. I had to close one of his eyes and push in his nose before he decided he wasn't having much fun."

"How about Dirk?" asked Ray.

"He stood on the sidelines. Finally he asked Danny and Kenny if they had had enough. Then he gave me my gun back and walked me to my car. Before I left he said something to the effect that it would be best if I didn't mention what had happened to anyone."

"Did you?"

"From that point on they left me alone. I had decided I would hold onto the job until I could find something else to do with my life. But before I found a new position Kenny was dead and Danny was gone."

"What did Maureen say?"

"I never told her. It would have really frightened her."

"So you never told anyone?"

"I didn't see the point in it," said Ben. "Before we went in you said you wanted to know about Gavin Mendicot."

"Yes."

"Well, like I started to tell you. He's been picked up on a couple of DUIs in recent years. Back in the '80s he was a wild kid, came from a family with lots of money. He had piles of speeding tickets. He might have been one of the kids the musketeers roughed up in their local behavior modification program. Then he was in the military, a couple of tours in Iraq, I think. When he came back he was pretty screwed up. But, who knows, he might have been pretty screwed up before he went. And I think he and Donna have been a couple on and off the last year or two, but it looks like she's found a new man, at least for the moment."

"Anything else about Gavin?"

"No, that's about it. He's just one of those people on the edge. He needs mental health services, but when things go to hell, we're the agency that ends up dealing with these characters."

"We do," agreed Ray.

"Do you want me to take you home to get your car or just go into the office?"

"Let's go to the office; I'll catch a ride home at the end of the day."

42

~~~~

Ray had barely settled into his desk chair when Sue arrived. "Think I had a bit too much champagne last night," she said, looking rather abashed.

"We all did," Ray responded. "What's up?" he asked, not wanting to dwell on the events of the previous evening.

"I just had a conversation with the Luce County Sheriff; he wanted to verify that Dirk had been informed of his brother's death."

"What did he think, we wouldn't do it?" asked Ray.

"When they called early this morning, they were talking about an accidental death. The guy on road patrol was responding to a call about a badly damaged sled and a body, something that's not too unusual during the winter. The deputy identified Danny by sight, and asked the dispatcher to send someone to his home. The State Police got that duty, and it turns out Danny wasn't living with his wife at the moment. Danny's wife told them to contact Dirk; he would have to make the funeral arrangements. She wasn't going to do it."

"Sounds like one angry woman," commented Ray.

"That's just the half of it. The deputy had the EMTs bag and remove the body, and he taped off the accident scene before he responded to another call." Sue paused for a moment. "The sheriff told me the price of gas is killing them, and they can only afford one road patrol on duty from eleven to seven. The plan was to have people from the day shift complete the investigation. But now it doesn't look like an accident any more."

"Because?"

"Because they got a call from the medical examiner—seems Danny has a bullet hole in him that no one quite noticed in the darkness and cold. He says the State Police are helping them investigate the crime scene. The sheriff was wondering if we'd share this information with Dirk before he hears it from the media."

"Does he have any suspects?" Ray asked.

"Exactly my question."

"And?"

"The sheriff says there will be no shortage of suspects. Danny was one mean son-of-a-bitch, his words. Danny's bar was a favorite of local tough guys, renegade snowmobilers, and a gathering place for passing motorcycle gangs during the summer. Danny loved knocking heads. The sheriff also said Danny was a real womanizer; there were a lot of husbands and boyfriends around that would probably like to see him dead." Sue paused briefly. "Did you know the family, the people, who produced Dirk and Danny?"

"I asked him once where he grew up during one of our few conversations. He said he was an army brat, but the family had roots near Brethren. He and his brother got jobs here after they got out of the service. He told me once they were shirttail relatives of Orville. Where were you going with the question?"

"I just wondered if all the males in the family were lowlifes and rounders."

"What are you betting on, environment or genes?"

"Both, want some fresh coffee?" Sue asked.

"Wait a minute," said Ray, not responding to her question.

"What?"

"Lynne. We've always assumed the shooter was trying to take her out. What if they thought Lynne was Dirk?" Ray asked.

"How did you get there, Dirk being the intended victim?"

"I thought about that possibility early on, but rejected it. But let's go with it for a few minutes. Lynne, Marie, and the girls were in Dirk's truck. They were following Dirk's pattern—completing his shift, having breakfast, and coming home. I bet that he would get the mail on his way up to the house." He paused and looked at Sue. "You think there's a good possibility that the shooter was several hundred yards out. We know it was near blizzard conditions at the time."

"But Lynne isn't Dirk."

"Yes, but they are about the same height. The shooter would have been concentrating on putting a shot into the center of the chest. Remember, the shooter had to have been watching Dirk for a while, becoming familiar with his patterns. And the day of the shooting they wouldn't have been checking the face before they pulled the trigger. They knew who they were shooting at. We need to get Marie in here."

"Why so?"

"I want to make sure Dirk's daily routine was similar to the one they followed Monday morning. I want to know what Lynne was wearing."

"I've got her jacket in the evidence room. It was left behind at the fire station; everything else went with her to the hospital."

"Would you get it, please?"

"Be back in a few," said Sue, as she headed out the door.

While she was gone Ray pulled up his notes from their conversations with Marie Guttard. In his rapid scan of the material, he could not find any reference to what Lynne was wearing.

"Here's the coat," said Sue, setting a clear plastic bag containing the garment on the conference table. Ray came to her side. They both peered at the canvas barn coat. Looking at the label, Ray read,

"Men's large. Do you think Lynne would buy one that size? She's very slim."

"And the jacket has a hood," noted Sue. "I wonder if she had it pulled up."

"See if you can round up Marie and bring her to the office."

"Couldn't I do this on the phone?"

"I want her here without anyone listening in." Ray said emphatically.

"I will see if I can get hold of her, and I'll run out and bring her in if she's available."

"Keep me posted," said Ray, as he started thinking about who might want Dirk dead.

43

An hour later Sue return with Marie Guttard.

"Good morning, Sheriff," said Marie, offering her hand and shaking Ray's enthusiastically. "Did you have a pleasant Thanksgiving?" she asked politely.

"Very nice, thank you," he responded.

"We have a couple of things we'd like you to clear up," said Ray. He pointed to the barn coat in the plastic bag still on the conference table. "That's the coat Lynne was wearing when she was shot."

Marie went over and inspected the garment, then turned to Ray and explained, "She grabbed it from a peg in the mud room that morning. We were running late. And the white ski jacket she usually wears, she had taken it to the cleaners. This one was handy."

"So she didn't usually wear this jacket."

"Oh no, it was Dirk's. He's been using it since the weather changed. I've never seen her wearing it."

"Why wasn't Dirk in it on Monday?"

Marie took a few seconds to respond, "He was wearing a hunting jacket that day, he left this one," she pointed to the heavy canvas coat in the plastic bag.

"I want to check one more thing. We've talked about this before. You've told us that when Dirk gets off work he goes to breakfast, and you mentioned the Cottage Inn. Then what?"

"He comes home and takes a shower and sleeps for awhile."

"How about the mail?" asked Ray.

"Yes. He always picks up the mail on his way to the house. He sorts through it and leaves most of it on the kitchen counter."

"But on Monday," said Ray, focusing her response.

"Yes, Monday. As we were coming up the road we could see the tracks left by the postman. When we arrived at the house, Lynne said she would get the mail since Dirk was out of town."

"I notice there's a hood on the jacket. Any chance Lynne had it up when she got out of the car?"

"Yes, she joked about needing it; it was snowing and blowing so hard. She pulled the hood up just before she got out."

"We've asked you about this before, but you've now had a few days to reflect on it. Did you see anyone around in the days before the shooting who might have been watching the house, or did Lynne mention to you anything like that?"

"No. I remembered your question, and I searched my mind. I do not recall seeing anyone suspicious."

"Thank you, Marie. This has been very helpful," said Ray. "How are things with the girls?"

"They are in good spirits considering everything that has happened. Of course, they are very anxious about their mother and want to see her. I keep them very busy, and their grandmother is with me most of the time. She is so much like Lynne and so good with the girls."

"Is it difficult being in that new environment, the big house, the security and all?" asked Sue.

"It is very different, but everyone is very nice. They are all doing their best to help look after the children."

"And what do you hear about their mother?" asked Ray.

"I'm sure you know what I do. Things are better. They say there is guarded optimism. I think they are planning to take her to Cleveland Clinic in a few days."

"I heard that," said Ray. "Again," said Ray, "thank you for coming in." He caught Marie's extended hand and her strong grip.

"I'll arrange transportation for Marie," said Sue, and the two women disappeared through the door.

Ray settled into his desk chair. He was lost in thought when Sue reappeared. She dropped into a chair on the other side of the desk.

"It all fits, doesn't it? Lynne's driving Dirk's truck, wearing his coat, picking up the mail at about the time he usually does," said Sue.

"I should have considered that more seriously at the beginning," Ray responded.

"Oh, come on Ray. We've only been at this a few days." Sue paused for a moment, "So who wants Dirk dead, and is it the same person who wanted Danny dead?"

"I think we need to have a conversation with Dirk. Do you want to drive?"

"Sure."

"I'll give him a call and tell him we're coming," said Ray.

44

~~~~

Ray relaxed in the passenger's seat and looked out at the snow-covered landscape as Sue maneuvered the slippery roads.

"Did you ever talk to her psychiatrist? What's his name?"

"Ruskin," Ray answered. "Yes, I had a brief phone conversation with him. He confirmed that she was a patient, noting that he had only seen her a few times. I asked if anything came up during those appointments that might lead us to Lynne's assailant."

"And?"

"Ruskin said nothing was discussed that would suggest that Lynne felt she was in danger. His answer was very carefully worded; he told me what I needed to know without divulging any personal information about his patient."

They rode on in silence for several minutes, finally Ray said, "Did I tell you that Donna Bateman's truck was parked at Dirk's house this morning when we came by to tell him about his brother? It looked like she spent the night."

"Did you see her?"

"Just Dirk. He was in a bathrobe; we got him out of bed."

"It doesn't look like she's interrupting her social life to look after Clay," Sue observed. "And Dirk doesn't waste any time finding female companionship."

"True," he agreed.

"Tell me about Donna," said Sue

"Don't know much about her. Until this incident with Clay, I don't think we've ever had any official dealings with her. Maggie Engle told me Donna is a savior type. Collects lost souls as boyfriends. Been doing it since high school."

"You probably meet a lot of them tending bar," Sue observed.

"Three deer up on the left," Ray warned.

"I see them," said Sue slowing down. After she passed the animals standing near the side of the road she said, "Wonder why they're in the open during daylight. They should be hiding."

"I imagine they're moving around looking for food. This deep snow is tough on them."

"What are we going to tell Dirk?" asked Sue.

"I made a few notes," he answered, pulling a small notebook from his shirt pocket and opening it. "First we have to tell him about Danny being shot. And then we say that we suspect that last Monday the shooter was probably gunning for him rather than Lynne. Perhaps we can get something out of him that might help us find the shooter."

"You optimistic about that happening?" asked Sue.

"What do you think?"

"No."

"So much we don't know about him. There's a whole history that we can't lay our hands on. And as Ben was pointing out to me this morning, Dirk has always seemed to have a lot of money. I'd like to know the source."

"Maybe he's thrifty and a skilled investor," Sue quipped, a wry smile spreading across her face.

"Sure," said Ray. "Dirk is a day trader, that's why he likes working nights."

"There's something else that's bothering you," said Sue. "What's going on?"

"I was thinking about Harry Hawkins, his very condescending tone, the suggestion that Boyd might have to bring in some experts to solve the case. Then I thought about Boyd and the things he could make happen with his money and connections.

"And," said Sue, knowing that there would be more.

"What if Boyd wanted to get rid of Dirk?" Ray asked.

"For what reason? His daughter is divorcing the guy. He's finally getting Dirk out of the family. This is a cause for celebration, not a reason to bump the guy off."

"Yes, but maybe that's a problem. In the old days Dirk was one of the deputies who provided security for Round Island and Crescent cove in exchange for hunting privileges. Ben Reilly commented on Dirk always having a lot of money."

"Where are you going with this?" Sue asked.

"Well, maybe if Dirk was married to his daughter, Boyd had some control over him. But with the divorce he would lose that. And remember, Boyd bought out the remaining members of the old hunt club after one of the members who had resisted his takeover accidently shot himself during deer season. I imagine Dirk was one of the people who investigated that tragic death."

"So what are you thinking? Maybe Dirk got hush money along the way. Danny might have been part of it, too."

"Something like that. So what if Boyd wanted them both dead," Ray continued. "Look at the resources he has available. He could bring in one of his mercenaries. They have their own private transportation system; they have access to sophisticated weapons. They could fly a guy in from Europe, or Asia, anywhere on the planet, do a hit, and get them out of here. A piece of cake for them and almost impossible for us to trace. Can't you see them laughing about a couple of up north county Mounties. Look at the assets they have available compared to ours."

"But the hit wasn't completely successful."

"True, but I wouldn't bet on Dirk's longevity." Ray made a pointing motion with his right hand, "His drive is coming up on the left."

Sue turned into the drive, and Ray remained silent as she wound her way up the drive to the house.

"Looks like Donna left," he said, noting the absence of her truck.

The door was opened before they reached it. Dirk was dressed in a fresh denim shirt and jeans, the careful pressing on each indicating they were just back from the laundry.

Dirk led them in, only this time he took them to the kitchen, a large room near the front door. They sat at a rustic, pine table in chairs made from cut down whiskey barrels covered with black leather cushions. A coffee pot and mugs were at the center of the table. Dirk filled a mug and passed it to Ray. "You want some?" he asked Sue.

"No, thank you."

"You said you had something important to talk about," Dirk's focus was on Ray, his tone hostile.

"It's about Danny."

"What about him?"

"When they first called us, they thought his death was accidental. Seems it wasn't quite an accident. When they were getting the body ready for the autopsy, they found he had been shot."

"How could they...."

"The sheriff said Danny had crashed at a very high speed. The sled was wrapped around a tree, and it was after two a.m. and snowing hard. It just looked like an accident," Ray explained.

Dirk pulled a cigarette from a pack on the table and lit it. "I just don't fucking believe this. What else did they miss?"

Ray and Sue didn't respond.

"Is that all you got to tell me? If so, I'd be happy to have you go away and leave me alone."

"There is something else, Dirk. We think that the shooter who wounded Lynne might have mistaken her for you."

"What? Give me a break. We hardly look alike," he growled.

"But that morning she was driving your truck; she stopped to get the mail about the time you do, and she was wearing your barn coat with the hood pulled up."

"And the shooter was trying to get a kill in less than perfect conditions," added Sue.

Ray sat and watched Dirk absorb the information. He observed Dirk's tough exterior soften, he could see perspiration form on his forehead, and he could smell fear in the air.

"What does that have to do with me?" Dirk uttered, trying to wish away the obvious.

"Everything, Dirk. Your brother's dead, your wife almost died." Ray paused and let the information sink in. Then he continued, "Someone is trying to kill you, Dirk. Next time they probably won't miss."

"What do you want from me?"

"I want to know why. We might be able to help you if you help us. What's going on? Who wants you dead, Dirk?"

"How the fuck should I know," he responded, grinding the half-smoked cigarette in the ashtray and lighting another.

"Could it be something from the old days, like the thing that got Kenny dead?" Ray asked.

"Look, I don't need to talk to you about this. It's none of your fucking business. Just leave me alone. And you can take my job and stuff it, too."

"What are you saying?" asked Ray.

"I resign, I quit. Now get the fuck out of here. Leave me alone."

"Dirk, we can help you," said Ray.

"I don't want any help. I just want you to get out of my face."

They sat in silence for several minutes, and then Ray and Sue slowly stood and walked toward the front door. Ray stopped and turned, "If you want out, put it in writing. Until I get your letter, you're still a member of the department."

45

"Probably an Uzi or a weapon of that type," Sue blurted as she sailed into Ray's office through the open doorway.

"An Uzi," repeated Ray, not giving her his full attention, his eyes still focused on the screen in front of him. "Let me finish this paragraph before I lose the thought."

Sue dropped into a chair and waited, her impatience evident by her rocking as she waited.

"Okay," said Ray, looking in her direction, "tell me about the Uzi."

"I just talked to the lead investigator on the Danny Lowther murder," Sue began. "The guy's name is Bergman, Floyd Bergman. He said they estimate Danny was probably going more than seventy miles an hour when he lost control of his sled and smashed into the tree. The machine was completely destroyed, the plastic parts splintered and smashed, the frame wrapped around the trunk. But in the daylight they could see evidence that it had been sprayed with automatic fire. And at one side of the trail they found the brass, 9 millimeter, 20 spent cartridges. His guess is that the shooter emptied the magazine in Danny's direction. They are sending the brass to the State Police lab."

Ray closed his eyes for a few seconds. He could see the whole scene: the scream of the snowmobile engine, the ripping blast from the Uzi, the concussion as metal, plastic, and flesh deformed against the tree, and then the silence of a winter night and the smell of gun powder.

"Bergman said the shooter was obviously familiar with Danny's habits: the time he left the bar each evening, the route he took to his girlfriend's house. He said the shooter picked an isolated spot where there are no occupied dwellings in the area in the winter."

"But the body was found last night?"

"Yes, Bergman said that was sort of a fluke. A group of late night riders came through, probably not long after it happened, found the wreckage, and called 911. The EMS crew was at the scene before a deputy. There was massive damage to the victim's neck and head. It just looked like Danny was thrown head first into the tree. And given the hour and weather, that's the way it was treated."

"Any suspects?"

"Not yet. They're just getting started."

"Anything else?" Ray asked.

"Gavin Mendicot. I did some checking. A few speeding tickets, public drunkenness, and a DUI. His legal address is a piece of land on the shore south of Crescent Cove. I checked the tax records. The property is in his name, but the tax bills are sent to a law office in Chicago."

"Do you think this might have started as part of a love triangle—Donna, Gavin, and Dirk?" asked Ray.

"Possible. But how about Danny?"

"We don't know if there's a connection. It might just be a bizarre coincidence. But I'd like to have a conversation with Gavin as soon as possible," said Ray, using the desk to help pull himself to his feet.

Thirty minutes later, they were at the side of a snow-covered road, looking at a drifted-over two-track that disappeared into a low swampy area as it meandered toward Lake Michigan.

"I don't know if we can get through," commented Sue.

"Give it a try," said Ray. "We'll hike in with snowshoes if we get stuck."

Sue locked the Jeep in four-wheel drive and started down the two-track. He could hear the vehicle bottom out as they plowed through the snow and noted that Sue kept the speed up to have the momentum to break through the deep drifts. As Sue came around a tight curve, she suddenly jerked the Jeep to the right and barely missed a snow-covered Bronco blocking the two-track, her vehicle sliding to a stop off the road.

Sue attempted to back out, only to find that the vehicle was stuck. Then she attempted to rock the Jeep, but that only seemed to make it sink deeper into the snow and mud.

"Do you want to try?" she asked, looking over at Ray.

"No," he said. He keyed the radio, gave their location, and requested a tow truck.

They climbed out of the jeep and worked their way to solid ground and approached the dented and rusting black Blazer. Ray brushed some snow from the passenger side window and looked in. "Don't like that," he said.

Sue scrutinized the two loaded magazines and boxes of cartridges lying on the seat. "Nine millimeter," she said, a wariness coming into her voice.

"Get the prosecutor's office on your cell and request a search warrant," Ray said. He worked around to the driver's side as Sue made the call.

"Probably ten or fifteen minutes, they have to locate the judge," Sue said to Ray as she slid her phone back into a breast pocket.

They walked back and inspected the Jeep.

"I've got a shovel in the back," Sue offered.

"Waste of time, it's buried to the axles. But if you get the snowshoes, we can see if we can find Gavin's place."

They started up the road toward the lake, following a set of partially filled tracks. A large Victorian cabin stood in the center of a small clearing; a thin wisp of smoke curled out of a brick chimney.

Ray moved forward and looked in several windows, finally knocking at the rear door that faced the drive. Sue stood off to the side, weapon hand at the ready. When there was no response, he started circling the building, cautiously peering through windows as he went. After checking the front of the cottage on the lakeside, he motioned Sue to join him. He directed her attention to a set of fresh footprints in the snow that started at the front of the cottage and ran toward the shore. They followed the prints, Ray in the lead, Sue ten yards behind, looking for cover in case it was needed. They stopped on the bluff overlooking the beach. Far below they could see a man struggling to push an aluminum boat into the rolling surf. He jumped in and started to row, pulling hard on a pair of oars until he got beyond the breaking waves. Then they heard the whine of the starter and saw a plume of grayish-blue smoke as the engine coughed and finally started. They stood in silence and watched the small boat plow straight into the icy surge for several hundred yards before it turned north and started up the coast.

"Where do you think he's going?" asked Sue.

"I wonder," Ray responded.

As they retraced their steps on the snowshoe-flattened path back toward the Blazer, Sue took the call from the prosecutor verifying that the request for the search warrant had been granted. "We're legal," she called to Ray. Ray pulled on the latex gloves Sue had handed him and opened the door. He picked up one of the magazines and examined it closely, turning it over. Pointing out a small star near the base, he observed, "Military issue, the real thing. Wonder if he is carrying the Uzi?"

Sue reached in and picked up a credit card receipt. "He bought some gas this morning."

"Where?" asked Ray.

"On the other side of the bridge, Newberry. I think we might be about to provide a solid suspect for the Danny Lowther murder."

Sue opened the glove box. "Looks like we've got the village apothecary here."

"Quite an assortment," said Ray as he looked though the contents, "papers, weed, this is probably coke." Then he held up a prescription bottle, "And some Oxycontin."

"Maybe he medicates on the road when he's listening to Rush," offered Sue.

"Share the joy," Ray responded. "Seems to wash things down with schnapps or Hot Damn," he noted, pointing out the collection of pint bottles on the passenger side floor.

"He's not a neat," said Sue. "Let's check the back."

They moved to the back of the vehicle, opened the tailgate, and started looking through the chaos of soiled clothing, empty food containers, beer cans, and liquor bottles. Sue pulled a rifle case from the bottom of the debris and partially opened the zipper, exposing a high-powered rifle and scope. "Some deer rifle," said Sue sarcastically. She opened the bolt. The gun was empty.

"I wonder if there's a match between that and the casing you found," said Ray. "Let's put together a greeting party, if and when Gavin comes back. Also, request a search warrant for the house."

"Will do."

The sound of the diesel engine brought their attention to the large tow truck backing up the road in their direction.

"As soon as we get pulled out and are on the road, we'll have him tow this to the impound yard so you can do a thorough search and cataloguing."

46

It took only a few minutes to winch the Jeep out of the bog. The driver of the tow truck, Ronnie Toole, waited as Sue backed down the road and pulled on the highway, then he went after the Blazer.

"Let's sit for a few minutes and sort out what we should do," said Ray, pulling a small notebook from his coat pocket.

"Sheriff, this is central," the radio came alive.

"Go ahead, central."

"I have a Harry Hawkins on the phone. He insists that he must speak with you. Says it's an emergency."

"Give him my cell number," said Ray. They sat in silence for a few moments waiting for the call.

Ray pushed the answer key as the phone started emitting its tinny tone.

Sue listened to one side of the conversation.

"When did this happen?"

"Why is he out there alone?" he asked.

"Why don't your people handle it?"

"We will be there."

"Let's go," said Ray.

"Where to?"

"Crescent Cove," he answered. "As fast as you can without getting us maimed or killed."

"What's going on?"

"Let me get things started, and then I'll explain," said Ray.

As Sue drove toward Crescent Cove with lights and siren on, Ray called Ben Reilly, asking him to the bring the Zodiac, dry suits, body armor and additional weapons. He also told Reilly what they had found in Gavin Mendicot's truck, that Mendicot was the probable assailant in the Danny Lowther killing, and that they just saw him launch a boat, adding that he might be heading toward Round Island.

When he completed his call, Ray turned to Sue. "This is the situation. Boyd told Hawkins he needed to be alone for a while, and he was going over to Round Island to think things over. Boyd took the only boat they have operational; everything else is in dry dock for the winter."

"So what's the big deal?"

"Two things. Boyd said he'd be back by early afternoon, but he hasn't returned. Hawkins says Boyd is in failing health, and he's over on the island without his necessary medications. But the real big deal is Hawkins walked in on Boyd and overheard him having an angry conversation with someone on the phone this morning. After he got off the phone, Boyd told Hawkins that it was Dirk.

"You know how they have surveillance cameras all over; they've got them on the perimeter of the island, too. Hawkins was notified that a boat has landed on the west side of the island. He said he went and reviewed the surveillance video. The intruder is Dirk Lowther, and he's armed with a rifle. Hawkins says the two men hate each other, and he's worried about Boyd's safety."

"Does Boyd know?"

"Hawkins says Boyd must have his phone turned off, something he does when he wants to be alone."

"What's wrong with the private army?" Sue asked.

"Hawkins says this is a police matter. He doesn't want company personnel involved."

The gate was up when they got to Crescent Cove. The young, uniformed guard waved them through. Harry Hawkins was in the road waiting, directing them toward the beach. Most of the docking had been removed for winter and was carefully stacked far up the shore, away from the destructive force of lake ice.

Hawkins, carrying a map, came to Ray's side as he emerged from the vehicle.

"There's been another development since we talked."

"What's that?" asked Ray.

"A second boat has landed on the island at the south end. The person monitoring our cameras says the man was carrying a weapon.

"What kind of weapon?"

"He said it looked like an Uzi."

Ray look over at Sue. He wondered if he should request the regional SWAT team. He quickly rejected the idea, knowing that it would take hours to get everything in place, especially in this weather.

"I thought this might help," continued Hawkins, opening the map on the hood of the jeep. Ray peered at a detailed topographic image in the gray, flat light of the rapidly approaching dusk.

"Mr. Boyd is probably here at the old warming house, it's on the east side of the island, less than a mile from the dock. He likes to go over there unescorted, says he does his best thinking there." Hawkins paused briefly, his tone changed. "Mr. Boyd has a very bad heart. I tried to dissuade him from going over there alone. But he's a very stubborn man, and he's in control of his own life. I would hope you could get him back here as quickly as possible."

"Is he armed?"

"He has a deer rifle, probably has a pistol, too. Mr. Boyd collects guns. There are several bait piles of corn and carrots near the warming house. He said he hoped to get a shot at a deer." Hawkins brought Ray's attention back to the map. "There's a path through the woods to the warming cabin. After Mr. Boyd said he wanted to do some hunting, I had the cabin restocked with food and fuel this morning. You'll have no trouble following the trail through the snow."

The Suburban used by the department's marine patrol rolled in and turned, backing the trailer carrying a Zodiac close to the water's edge. Ben Reilly came to Ray's side, joined by Brett Carty, one of the deputies who coordinated the marine patrol. Brett and Ben were already dressed in cold-water survival suits. Ben pulled thick fleece coveralls and dry suits from the back hatch of the vehicle and handed them to Ray and Sue.

"Is there a place we can change into these?" Ray asked Hawkins.

"Follow me," Hawkins responded, leading them toward the house.

When Ray returned to the shore, Ben and Brett were still packing gear in waterproof bags and boxes and securing them on the interior of the boat. He walked to the water's edge and peered out at the small island a few thousand yards off shore. The wind had picked up and shifted to the southwest since he had watched Gavin Mendicot launch straight out into the surf; the dark gray water was being funneled between the island and mainland in confused patterns with reflecting waves and a rolling surf. He gathered the three deputies and explained the mission. Then he asked, "Sue, should you stay here and coordinate things as they develop?"

"Ray, if this turns into a crime scene, I'd like to be there early on."

Ray felt a flash of anger, but Sue was right. Ray knew he was trying to keep her out of harm's way.

"What kind of boat did Boyd take over?" Ray asked Hawkins, pulling things back into focus.

"It's a twin-engine Zodiac much like yours. There's a protected inlet just across from us at the south end of the island, and the dock is still in place. You will have no trouble tying up there."

"How far is the warming house?"

"Less than a mile."

"Brett, I want you to ferry people across as needed," directed Ray. "Get us over and stay with the boat. Also, request a couple of EMT units. Better to have them on the scene if we need them."

Ray, Sue, Ben, and Brett quickly struggled into life preservers and neoprene gloves and hoods. Hawkins directed his men to get the Zodiac off the trailer and into the water. Brett and Ben loaded weapons and snowshoes, and they pushed the boat out until only the stern was still on the sand. Once the other three were in, Brett pushed the boat out into the chop and scrambled over the low transom. Ray and Sue used canoe paddles to propel the boat into deeper water.

Ray turned toward Brett and pointed in the direction of the breaking waves near their destination. "There's a shoal there; watch out for the surf."

Brett nodded his understanding as he started the engines and headed toward open water. The Zodiac bounced along the large waves, rising on the crests and then slamming into the troughs. Ray could feel the sting of the icy spray on his face. As they approached the island, he could see that a narrow fringe of delicate shelf ice had formed at the water's edge.

Brett, spotting the cove, suddenly made an abrupt turn toward the shore, rising on the lip of a rogue wave just as it was starting to break. Ray grabbed onto a rope at the gunwale and held on with all his might, gravity pulling him toward the icy water. The boat stood sideways on the wave, the powerful grasp of the rolling surf holding it briefly at the edge of its tipping point before the hull crashed down into the trough and starting rising with the next swell, the crest of the breaking wave smashing into and over the left gunwale. He looked across at Sue and could see the fear in her eyes.

Brett pulled back the throttles and continued cautiously along the shore of the island, holding the bow into the waves and moving obliquely toward the shore.

Ray exchanged glances with Brett who appeared shaken by the near capsize.

Reaching the small cove, Brett piloted the craft into the narrow opening and guided it to the dock, the other side occupied by Boyd's boat. Ray, Sue, and Ben scrambled onto the dock and secured the boat. Brett passed weapons, body armor, and snowshoes up to them.

They traded their life preservers for the body armor and parkas, then buckled snowshoes to their boots. Ray pulled the map from his jacket as Sue and Ben huddled around him.

"It looks like a straight shot to the warming cabin. At this point we want to get Boyd off the island as quickly as possible. Then we'll try to sort out what else might be going on. Dirk and Mendicot are also out there and armed. Let's hope they are bogged down in the heavy snow. Stay about twenty yards apart and work alternate sides of the trail."

Ray took the lead, Sue followed, with Ben in the rear. The trail wound through a dense hardwood forest. Less than a mile up the road, the terrain rose and the woods opened to a treeless plateau. A dark structure stood in the center of the clearing, its somber form silhouetted by the golden glow of the setting sun that had broken through the thick gray clouds.

Ray found a protected position and waved the other two to join him. He was winded from trudging though the deep drifts in snowshoes. "I only want one of us out in the open at a time. When I get there and check things out, I'll radio what we should do next."

Ray became increasingly wary as he circled north and followed a ravine to stay below the horizon. Before he had made much progress, he heard the sharp crack of a high-powered rifle. He dropped into the snow and waited, taking time to carefully survey the area. The memory of being wounded earlier in the fall flashed through his consciousness, feeling again the searing pain when the bullet smashed into his leg. Ray pushed the specter back, focusing on the bleak terrain in front of him.

Just as he was about to come to his feet, the roar of a fully automatic rifle echoed through the woods, somewhere off to his left. Ten seconds later, two more bursts. The contrasting roar of the first weapon came again. A few seconds later another blast. Then silence, only the sound of his breathing and the blood pounding in his head. He keyed the mic on his radio. "Hold your positions," he instructed.

Ray waited, letting the minutes tick by. Eventually, he scrambled to his feet and moved forward, using a ravine for cover as he approached the building from the rear. He started around the building to the front. At the front corner he paused, released the straps and slid out of his snowshoes, and surveyed the long, covered porch that ran along the west-facing wall. Then he saw Dirk, sprinting toward the building, a rifle in his hands. Just as Dirk approached the front steps, Ray came around corner, his weapon at the ready. "Drop it," he commanded.

Dirk, still running, fired wildly from the waist without aiming. Ray ducked back behind the corner. He heard Dirk smash into the door, then several more shots, followed by silence.

Ray stood still; he could hear the sound of the wind in the leafless trees and the waves crashing into the distant shore. He climbed onto the porch, cautiously moved to the door, and peered into the room. Boyd was sitting at a table, a kerosene lamp at one corner, a pistol in his right hand, and a tumbler of brown liquor in front of him, a whiskey bottle near by. Dirk's body was sprawled on the floor just inside the door. His lifeless right hand was still clutching a rifle.

"Come on in, Sheriff," Boyd said, setting the automatic on the table.

47

Holding Boyd in his gaze, Ray knelt at Dirk's side and palpated his carotid artery, searching for a pulse. Then he stood and walked toward Boyd.

"Want a drink, Sheriff?

Ray didn't answer.

"Your predecessor appreciated good whiskey. I always trust a man I can drink with."

"What's happened here?" Ray asked.

"I came out here to have some peace and quiet; to think things over. Suddenly the door was kicked in by Dirk brandishing a rifle. I got him first. Self-defense."

"How did he know you would be here?"

"Lucky guess on his part?" said Boyd. He picked up the tumbler and sipped some of the liquor.

"Why would he want to shoot you?"

"He's a crazy man. Always was. He thinks I'm responsible for my daughter divorcing him." Boyd held Ray in his gaze a long moment. "I would like to go to the mainland now, I'm not feeling well. I'd appreciate it if you get me back."

"How about the other shots?" asked Ray, gesturing toward the outside.

"Someone should investigate that," said Boyd. "Wouldn't be the first time poachers sneaked onto the island."

Ray keyed his radio, "Boyd and Dirk accounted for. Come up, be cautious." He turned his attention back to Boyd. "Can you walk back to the beach?"

"I'd rather not, I'm having chest pains. Maybe you can have my people bring a sled."

"We'll get you out of here," said Ray.

Ray could hear Ben and Sue on the porch. Sue knelt at Dirk's side, Ben standing above.

"He's dead," she said.

"Yes," said Ray.

They stood for a long moment and took in the scene: the pistol on the table, the glass of whiskey, and Boyd, calmly staring back at them.

"Self-defense," said Boyd in a firm voice. "Dirk kicked down the door. I shot him before he shot me. Now, Sheriff, I need my medicine. You need to get me back to the mainland."

Ray turned to Ben. "Get some EMTs over here to check on Boyd before we move him. Then secure the area. There is another shooter out there." Motioning toward Sue, "We'll see if we can find him."

Ray and Sue, back in their snowshoes, followed Dirk's tracks back off the plateau and headed toward the western shore of the island. Near the edge of woods they found a pile of logs, the tracks in the snow suggesting that Dirk had taken cover behind them. Staying in the shadows of the forest, they worked their way forward, finding Mendicot in an open area less than 100 yards beyond the log pile, face down, an Uzi at his side, almost completely buried in the soft snow.

They carefully rolled him over, and Sue checked for a pulse.

"Anything?" Ray asked.

"Not much," said Sue as she extracted a small flashlight from her belt. Starting at the head, they quickly scanned his body.

"Big bleed here," he said, pointing at the left leg. Ray cut Gavin's jeans open with a serrated knife from the boot to above the knee, Sue illuminating Ray's work area with a small flashlight.

"Part of his leg is blown away. Let's get a tourniquet above the wound; maybe we can stop the bleeding. Call for a chopper, we need to get him out of here fast."

Sue talked to the dispatcher as she pulled off her backpack and retrieved a piece of rope and a headlamp, which she switched on and pulled in place.

Ray slit the pant leg farther, then carefully positioned the rope on the bare flesh well above the wound. He pulled the cord tight and made a knot. "I need a stick or something," he said looking around. "Give me the flashlight." He slid the small aluminum cylinder under the cord, then twisted it several times to increase the band's compression on Gavin's leg. He tied it in place with the ends of the cord.

"That should stop the bleeding," said Ray, "if there's anything left. Is he still with us?"

"Just barely. Very shallow respiration. He's in deep shock."

Ray stayed at Gavin's side while Sue moved into the clearing above them and marked the corners of a possible landing area with four flares. By the time she had scrambled back to Ray's side, they could hear the slapping sound of the incoming chopper.

Within minutes the chopper had lifted off again, the roar of the jet engine quickly receding as the blinking lights of the craft disappeared into the gray-blue dusk. They stood for a long moment, the sounds of wind and water gradually coming to the foreground again.

By the time they made it back to the warming house, Ben Reilly was alone, waiting for them.

"What's happened with Boyd?" Ray asked.

"It didn't take too long to get the EMTs here, a couple of young guys. As soon as they put him on oxygen he got a whole lot more comfortable. The chopper was on the way to pick him up, but you got first priority. Rather than waiting, they took him out on a sled that Boyd's people had brought over. I don't think he liked giving up his chopper ride to someone else." Ben motioned toward Lowther's body. "The ME is on his way."

"I'll get the scene photographed, do some evidence collecting, and stay here till the ME is finished and the body is removed," said Sue. She looked at Ben, "I think our friend Ray should be given a ride back to town. I don't think this quite fits the description for limited activities."

"I'm all right," said Ray, but now that the adrenalin was wearing off he felt exhausted and his leg throbbed. He wasn't looking forward to tramping back to the dock in snowshoes.

Hours later, after returning to his office and fortifying himself with coffee and some sandwiches he and Ben had picked up on the way back, Ray sat at his keyboard and sketched out the major elements of the afternoon's events. He called the medical center to check on Mendicot and Boyd. Hanna Jeffers, the surgeon who had saved Lynne Boyd's life, came on the line. She explained that Boyd had been admitted for observation and that Mendicot was in critical condition, but expected to live. Her tone was brisk, there was little elaboration, and then she was gone. No time for questions.

48

By the time Ben Reilly dropped him off at his house, Ray was completely exhausted. In fact, they had made the ride in almost complete silence, both men physically and emotionally drained by the events on Round Island.

"Quite a day," said Ben as he stopped near Ray's front entrance.

"Yes," said Ray as he swung the door open. "Thanks for the ride."

When he got into the house, he put a kettle of water on for tea and collapsed into his favorite chair. Rubbing the skin on his face, Ray noticed for the first time the effects of the wind, snow, and icy spray. He yawned and closed his eyes, waking suddenly when he was gently shaken.

"Ray, what kind of tea do you want?"

He didn't answer immediately. It took him several seconds to come back from deep sleep. Finally he said, "When did you get here?"

"Just a few minutes ago. And lucky I did. Your tea kettle was running low on water."

Ray pulled himself to his feet and joined Sarah at the counter.

"Remember, I was going to come by and see you when I got home."

Ray stood there trying to remember. It had been only a few days since he had last seen Sarah, but somehow it seemed like weeks had gone by.

"You didn't respond to my e-mails," said Sarah. "But as I look at you, I can see you've had some very difficult days."

"It has been an interesting time," Ray responded.

"How about chamomile, ginger, and mint," she asked, holding three tea bags in her hand. When she didn't get an immediate answer, she dropped the three bags in a brown, china teapot and poured in the steaming water. "Interesting time, you say. Like the fabled curse?"

"Yes, exactly" Ray responded. "And how was New York?" he asked, wanting to hear about Sarah's trip, rather than talk about the last few days.

"It was good. Not quite what I had expected, but good."

"Not what you expected? How so?"

"Well, when Eric asked me to come out for Thanksgiving, it was like the two of us were going to spend a couple of days doing the town."

"Well, didn't you?"

"We did. But what he hadn't told me is there's this other person now, a girl, Lori—this smart, sweet, beautiful young woman. I was feeling like the fifth wheel. They were doing their best to be gracious hosts, but they are just totally in love. They can't keep their eyes off one another; they were always reaching out to touch. And I was staying in his apartment, and you know how small New York apartments are. One look around and it was clear she's been living there. She obviously moved out for my visit.

"So how do you feel, Mom?"

"Well, good doctor, why didn't Erik Erikson write about this? Perhaps we need a book on the stages of motherhood, one of the later ones being Mom as baggage."

"I still don't know how you're feeling?"

"I just know things have changed, and I did enjoy seeing the two of them so happy. It's one of those special moments in life. I hope it lasts a long time." She looked over at Ray. "So I'm rattling on. And as I look at you, I feel guilty because you've been obviously dealing with some very difficult things."

"I'm tired and a bit dispirited, but I'm okay."

"Are you sure?"

"A lot has happened in a few days. I haven't had a chance to really process it yet. And I'm happy that you're here."

"My kid," said Sarah, "I didn't tell him about us. I'm not sure how he'd deal with it. For so many years the two of us were sort of a couple. Funny, isn't it. He and I are both dealing with the same thing. We have to separate so we can establish other relationships. Perfectly natural, but it just seems strange."

Ray didn't respond immediately, and then asked, "Do you think the kid would approve of your seeing me?"

"Yes," she answered without hesitation. "He has an innate sense of people. He would like you." She paused for a long moment. "But he probably wouldn't be comfortable with the fact that I might be sleeping with you. I am his mother, you know."

"Does this mean you're spending the night?"

"Only if you promise to get me up at six. I have to be back at the office by 8:00 when classes begin."

"Fortunately, I'm an early riser," said Ray.

"And if you weren't?"

"I'd set an alarm," he replied, taking her into his arms.

49

Ray actually met surgeon Hanna Jeffers in person for the first time the next morning outside the medical center's intensive care unit. "Sheriff Elkins, right?" she asked, holding out her right hand.

Ray took her hand and introduced her to Sue Lawrence. He looked at Jeffers closely as the two women shook hands. Jeffers was a tiny woman with a shock of wild, curly black hair—her movements and voice displayed energy and intelligence. He could see that the young physician and Sue had almost instant rapport.

Turning toward Ray, she said in a playfully sarcastic tone. "When I left the war zone, a friend enticed me to come up here. He said it was a paradise." She paused briefly, and then continued, lifting her eyebrows, "Given the carnage I've seen in the last few days, if it weren't for the snow, I might think I was back in Baghdad."

"This is quite anomalous," Ray replied. "How's the patient?"

"Which one?"

"Mendicot, for starters."

"I'm surprised we were able to salvage him. He had lost so much blood." Then she added, "That was a nice trick with the bungee cord and flashlight. I've never seen a windlass made with a mini Maglite. It did the job."

"You use what you've got," Ray said. "Can you tell us about the injury?"

"There was a lot of tissue destruction. We were able to quickly tie off the major arteries and get some blood in him. The bullet hit the femur straight on right above the knee. The bone is shattered. I don't know what the orthopedists will be able to do. But there's another problem we have to deal with that complicates everything."

"What's that?"

"The guy is a walking pharmacy. He's coming down from long-term alcohol and drug abuse. And, of course, now we're pumping him full of morphine. But what can you do, he's in enormous pain."

"So there was only one wound?"

"Yes, one wound, but he was hit a second time. And if he hadn't been wearing plated body armor, that one would have been fatal. He's got a big hematoma mid-sternum; the body armor saved his life."

"Is he awake?"

"He's pretty doped up and not making much sense."

"How about Boyd?"

"He's an interesting case; he has a long history of coronary artery disease. When he was admitted last evening, he was displaying the symptoms of unstable angina."

"What's the prognosis?" Ray asked.

"He has a very damaged heart. Each one of these episodes brings further deterioration. If you're asking about his long term prognosis…."

"Yes," said Ray.

"Not very good. A year to two, probably at best. He wants to go to Cleveland Clinic. From a medical point of view, I think that's a good idea. He's been seeing a cardiologist there for years. I don't know what legal problems he has, but he must be expecting you; his lawyer is already with him."

"So we can talk to him?"

"You can put in an appearance, but nothing more. I don't want him agitated for any reason. And I will be in the room with you, ready to run you out if necessary."

"When can we interview him?" Ray asked.

"When I think he's medically stable," she responded. Jeffers led the way through two sets of automated double doors into the ICU. A nursing station with scores of monitors was in the center of the room, a dozen or more women and men—clad in blue scrubs with boots and hats—were looking at screens, writing reports, or scurrying in and out of the individual patient rooms circled on the perimeter.

Prescott Boyd, looking far frailer than when Ray had last seen him the day before, was propped up in a hospital bed. High above his shoulder tracings in different colors marched across a video screen, with digital readouts for each tracing in the same color glowing on the right side of the screen. An IV tube ran from his left arm to a bag suspended above the bed. Oxygen was being administered through a nose tube.

Dorothy Boyd was on the right side of the bed, and Harry Hawkins stood at the left side. Their attention shifted from Prescott to the visitors.

"Good morning, Sheriff," Dorothy Boyd said, holding Ray in her vision.

Before Ray could respond, Dr. Jeffers quickly said, "The sheriff and Ms. Lawrence will only be here for a few minutes, and then they are moving on."

"Good morning," said Ray, catching the three of them with his eyes. He and Sue stood at the foot of the bed for a long, clumsy moment. "It looks like you're in the best of hands," said Ray, looking at Boyd.

"The people here have been wonderful," said Dorothy.

"Good," said Ray. "We'll be on our way."

He and Sue slipped out of the room headed toward the double steel doors. They were already into a main corridor when Harry Hawkins caught up with them.

"Sheriff, could I have a word?"

"Yes, of course."

"Perhaps we could talk over coffee."

Ray agreed and the three of them took the elevator down to the ground floor and walked to the cafeteria. After getting coffee, they settled at a table in an unoccupied corner of the room.

"Mrs. Boyd would like to move her husband to Cleveland Clinic as soon as Dr. Jeffers thinks he's up for the trip. Lynne is going to be moved, also; perhaps they could go in the same plane. Would you have any objections?"

"Mr. Hawkins, it's not whether I have objections. I haven't had an opportunity to discuss this case with the prosecutor yet. It's really his call."

"But given Mr. Boyd's condition and…"

"I will present the case to him, including a recommendation from Dr. Jeffers. And, of course, you can represent your client's situation to him yourself. The prosecutor likes to review all available information before he makes a decision. But like I said, I will get the process started at our end. Now I've got some questions for you."

"Yes," responded Hawkins, his tone becoming very guarded.

"When you reached me on the cell phone yesterday, you said you had overheard Mr. Boyd on the phone, and he was having an argument with Dirk Lowther. Is that correct?"

"That's what he told me. I really have no way of knowing with whom he was speaking."

"Would Mr. Boyd have any reason to lie to you?"

"Well, no, but you know how complex we humans tend to be. All of us fall into bits of prevarication from time to time either through memory lapses or…."

"Let me ask you again. Would Mr. Boyd have any reason to lie to you about who was on the phone?"

Hawkins considered his answer for a long moment. "I do not believe he would."

"In the course of your relationship with him, has he been truthful?"

"I never knew him to be dishonest with me."

"Has he ever shared his feelings with you about his son-in-law, Dirk Lowther."

"After Lynne was shot, he indicated that he thought Dirk was either the shooter, or behind it."

"Before that, did he ever discuss Dirk with you."

"I don't believe so."

"Do you know whether Dirk might have been on the payroll of Magnus Conservus?" Ray asked.

"I don't think so," Hawkins responded, his answer tentative.

"You don't know or…."

"Well, first it's never come to my attention, and I've only been working with Magnus Conservus for about a year. Their HR department handles all employment matters. I know over the years Boyd has run several other corporations, and he has deep roots up here. It's possible that Boyd might have employed Dirk along the way."

"I was a bit surprised when you called me yesterday. In our last conversation you suggested that Magnus Conservus took care of the security needs of its customers."

"Yes, they do that. And in many parts of the world where they operate, civil authority is either incompetent or almost non-existent. Obviously, that isn't the case here." Hawkins paused and sipped his coffee; Ray and Sue made no attempt to fill the silence. "Besides, yesterday we were confronted with a situation that we were not prepared to handle."

"Which was?"

"The simplest of things. We didn't have another boat operational. Which..." Hawkins stopped short.

"Go ahead."

"My job is to look after the legal matters for Magnus Conservus. My specialties are corporate and international law. Yesterday it seemed to me that things might be spinning out of control. I thought the involvement of local law enforcement was appropriate given the situation. I didn't want any of the corporation's employees put in legal jeopardy. I didn't want anyone put in a position where they might end up with a felony charge."

"So you knew he was going to meet Dirk?" asked Sue.

"I thought that was a possibility."

"Did you try to counsel Boyd on how...?"

"I tried to talk him out of going over to the island. I reminded him of his health problems. I advised Mr. Boyd that if he had been threatened by Dirk that he should contact your office. And if Mrs. Boyd had been home, I would have told her that he was planning to go to the island. Perhaps she could have talked some sense into him. But she was here at the hospital with Lynne, and the other children weren't around."

"And you elected not to accompany him?" Sue questioned.

"Boyd said there were things he needed to do on his own. I was specifically not to. And I don't think I would have, anyway."

"Why's that?"

"My job is to provide legal counsel. I'm not his bodyguard. And I wouldn't do anything that might lead to my disbarment."

"So what will be your role now?" Ray asked.

"I will continue to provide counsel to the corporation as long as my services are needed. I've called the firm and explained the situation. One of the senior partners, Nicholas Ovilbee, who oversees criminal matters, will be on the first flight from Chicago tomorrow morning to assess the situation. I suspect Nick or someone he designates will be attending to this matter."

Ray looked across the room. Hanna Jeffers was striding in their direction. She stopped as she reached the table. "I was hoping I would find you here."

"What's happened?" asked Ray.

"Boyd coded shortly after you left the unit. We started a very aggressive resuscitation; we were not successful."

"He's dead?" asked Hawkins, disbelief in his voice.

"Yes," she said, her tone softening. "His damaged heart just gave up. There was nothing we could do. Mrs. Boyd needs you. I'll take you to her." Then she marched away, Hawkins trailing after.

50

John Tyrrell, the Cedar County prosecutor, was sitting at the head of a conference table in a room adjoining his office. His collar button was open and the knot of a muted tartan tie hung several inches below his corpulent neck. A carafe of coffee and mugs were on a tray in front of him. As Ray and Sue entered the room, he folded a copy of the *Wall Street Journal* and moved it off to the side. Sue sat at Tyrrell's right, Ray at his left.

As they exchanged pleasantries, Ray poured a mug of coffee. Sue had brought a Diet Coke with her and a stack of folders that she arranged on the desk in front of her.

"What do you have for me?" asked Tyrrell.

"First there's Gavin Mendicot. He's finally coherent enough that we've been able to question him."

"Does he have representation?"

"Yes. A Chicago law firm that seems to look after Mendicot has retained Keith Birdsall. Mendicot seems to live off a very substantial trust."

"Was Birdsall there during the interviews?"

"Yes, both times."

"Good. Go ahead."

"The prosecutor in Alger County is preparing a warrant for his arrest in the murder of Danny Lowther. They should be able to put together a fairly strong case for first-degree murder. We have the probable murder weapon and evidence that puts Mendicot in the area near the time of the murder. The weapon, clips, and related material are on their way to the State Police lab. We're confident that the brass found at the scene will establish that this is the murder weapon."

"Anything else?"

"A credit card charge at a 24-hour gas station outside of Newberry and an ATM photo at the same location. The station is about forty miles east of the scene of the shooting. We found the credit card receipt the first time we searched his car. The State Police did the legwork that produced the ATM photo and security camera video."

"Date and time?" asked Tyrrell as he freshened his coffee.

"It was after three in the morning, an hour or two after the murder took place. He was on his way downstate."

"So why did Mendicot want Danny Lowther dead?

"We've pieced things together from our interviews with Mendicot. He's told us a lot, far more than Birdsall would have liked. Once you get him started, he just rattles on. That said, he provides a very confused and often conflicting story. But before we get into that I'd like Sue to summarize the evidence we have in the shooting of Lynne Boyd."

"Here's the inventory of the contents of his car," said Sue, passing Tyrrell several pages held together by a blue paper clip. She waited, watching his eyes move down the first page and onto the second page.

"It looks like he had a mobile drugstore and a weapons cache," Tyrrell observed.

"Yes," she agreed. "And in the weapons category you will find a rifle with a high power scope."

"Okay."

"We are waiting for results to come back from the State Police lab, but we believe that the rifle was used in the Lynne Boyd shooting."

"What's her condition, now?" asked Tyrrell.

"Lynne is in stable condition," Ray answered. "She was moved to Cleveland Clinic on Monday."

"What's the prognosis?"

"According to Hanna Jeffers, the young surgeon who treated her locally, the prognosis is good. That said, she probably needs a month or six weeks more in hospital care. Dr. Jeffers suggested an additional surgery might be necessary during the healing process."

"So going back to this rifle," said Tyrrell, "you're pretty solid on having the weapon that links Mendicot to the Lynne Boyd shooting?"

"Yes," Sue responded.

"What was his motive for shooting Lynne?"

"Well, that was an accident of sorts. He was really trying to get Dirk Lowther. Mendicot had obviously been watching Dirk, getting his daily pattern down, so he could take him out. But his plan fell apart. On the day of the shooting Lynne was driving Dirk's truck, wearing his coat, and arrived home about the time Dirk usually did. And to make things even more difficult, Mendicot was several hundred yards from his target in near-blizzard conditions. And God only knows the amount of alcohol and drugs he might have ingested."

"So why was he trying to kill Dirk?"

"He seems confused on that point; he can't seem to remember the chronology of events that led to the shooting."

"Well, I'm getting confused, too," opined Tyrrell.

"Let me explain," Sue said. "When we come in to do these interviews, we're very organized. Granted, these conversations quickly take on a life of their own, but usually you can lead the person back to the topic under discussion. Mendicot is all over the place. In non-clinical terms, his brain seems to be fried, nothing is quite hooked up anymore, or if it is hooked up, the connections are in the wrong places."

"What's Birdsall doing? Is he trying to keep Mendicot quiet?"

"He's given up on that. His client seems completely oblivious to anything he says," Sue answered. "Birdsall's suggested to us that Mendicot might have multiple personality disorder, as well as major addiction problems. That may be the course of his defense, rather than denying that his client committed the crimes."

"Let's go back to Mendicot's motive," Tyrrell said.

"There seem to be several," answered Ray, picking up the story. "First he told us that Dirk was messing with his woman. His language was a bit more graphic."

"I can imagine. Who is the woman in question? Anyone I might know?"

"Donna Bateman."

"Ah, yes, the lovely Donna. That woman is driving me crazy. I think that she would willingly compromise the integrity of a member of the prosecutor's office, if she thought it would get her kid off the hook."

"Are you suggesting that she might try to influence the prosecutor himself?" asked Ray.

"You got it," Tyrell responded.

"We are so lucky you're not easily tempted by her feminine charms," Ray said with a hint of sarcasm in his voice. "So what's the situation with Clay?"

"Remind me to come back to him. I want to know Mendicot's motive, or shall I say motives."

"Well, like I said, he was angry with Dirk over Donna. Mendicot had been living with her for a number of months, and after that incident involving Clay, she kicked him out. The shotgun that Clay used belonged to Mendicot. Donna put the blame on him rather than on her son."

"Then there's the other story," began Sue. "Mendicot said he shot Dirk because Prescott Boyd threatened him, saying he would tell the truth about how Mendicot's stepfather died if he didn't kill Dirk and Danny."

"And what's the truth?" asked Tyrrel.

"This goes back more than twenty years. Mendicot's stepfather died on Round Island during deer season. The story has been that he shot himself accidentally, and that Dirk, Danny, and Orville investigated the death. But one of Mendicot's versions is that everyone out there had been drinking heavily. He and his stepfather got into an argument, a gun went off, and Orville and his deputies said he had killed his stepfather. Mendicot says he doesn't think he shot him, but they convinced him that he had. Then Prescott Boyd paid Mendicot several million dollars for his stepfather's share of the club and promised never to divulge Gavin's secret," explained Ray.

"And there are further versions?"

"Yes," answered Sue. "Mendicot also told us that Danny and Dirk killed his stepfather and told him that they would kill him too, if he didn't sell his share of the club to Boyd. He said he was too scared at the time to go to the law. That Danny and Dirk had a lot of things on him, so even if he managed to get them sent to jail, he would have been going away for a long time, too. He also said that they told him they knew lots of people inside, and they would have quickly made sure he got dead."

"They were a couple of quality guys," quipped Tyrrell. "What do you know about the Boyd connection? Is there any truth to that?"

"We'll never know the complete story," said Sue. "We know that Mendicot lives off the proceeds from a trust fund, and that Boyd was party to establishing the trust. We also know that, based on cell phone records, in the days preceding Danny's death Boyd made a number of calls to him. He also called Mendicot after he reportedly argued with Dirk, also verified by phone records.

"We think this might have been the scenario for the final confrontation on Round Island. Boyd lured Dirk Lowther to a meeting there. He then got Mendicot to rush over in the hope that he would take Dirk out before he got to the warming house. But just in case Mendicot failed, Boyd was ready. As soon as Dirk came through the door, Boyd put a bullet in him."

"Wasn't that pretty high risk, both physically and legally?"

"Yes," answered Ray. "But Boyd was a sick man. He was well aware of the fact that he didn't have much time. We think that Dirk had been extorting money over the years for his silence in the death of Hawthorne, Mendicot's stepfather. With Dirk and Lynne's divorce, it seemed things were coming to a head. We believe Dirk was increasing his demand, perhaps asking for a final big payout."

"If this Boyd is so rich, why didn't he just buy Dirk off?"

"I think he needed closure, he didn't want to put his estate in jeopardy. The only way to be really sure of that was to have Dirk dead," Sue explained.

"Well, that makes sense. He neatened things up and then had the good sense to check out," Tyrrell chuckled at his own joke. "Not many bad guys are so protective of their families."

"If you don't need anything else," said Sue, "tell us about Clay Bateman."

"Donna and Mr. Smiles are doing their best to convince us to treat Clay as a juvenile. Here's their argument. Since he didn't finish the football season, he doesn't have much chance for a scholarship. Now he thinks he's going to join the military. If he has a criminal record, they won't take him. As you know, his juvenile record will be expunged when he turns eighteen. And that will happen in early June. They've already talked to the Marine recruiter, in fact the guy's even come in to talk to me about Clay, how they will turn him into a responsible adult.

"So here's my dilemma," continued Tyrrell. "Will I be able to sleep knowing that I allowed Clay Bateman off the hook to go into the service. How do you feel about him defending our nation's borders? I mean, you've met this kid. Would it be better for all of us if I put him in jail?"

Before they could respond, Tyrrell pulled himself out of his chair. "I've got a lunch meeting. Good work, guys. Keep me in the loop." He started to move away from the table and then came back. "Ray, early on, just after the Lynne Boyd's shooting, you told me about some threatening letters she'd received. What happened with those?"

"We sent them to the State Police Laboratory. And it turns out the sheriff's office in Antrim County had sent them some similar packets—threatening letters sent to a principal and a science teacher. The evidence techs quickly determined the same person assembled those letters and the ones sent to Lynne."

"And," prodded Tyrrell impatiently.

"An eighth grade student in Bellaire got in trouble for bringing a hunting knife to school. When the sheriff was interviewing the student, he asked him about the letters and kid eventually fessed up. They called in the State Police and the boy admitted to writing the letters that Lynne received as well."

"What was his motive?" asked Tyrrell

"The sheriff told me the kid comes from a family of gun nuts. The kid thought Lynne's reports were an attack on his second amendment rights."

"Well, someone needs to tell that kid those rights don't apply to children," Tyrrell responded. "Again, keep me in the loop."

Ray sat and watched Tyrrell depart. He looked across the table at Sue. "How about lunch? It's on me."

"Do I have to watch you eat a tempe Rueben at the Good Earth," she joked.

"You pick the place," said Ray. "You can have a bacon-topped double cheeseburger with fries, and I won't say a thing."

"You're on," said Sue.

AUTHOR'S NOTE

In the process of writing this book I received help and encouragement from readers and friends. I am especially grateful to the early readers of the manuscript for their insightful feedback that helped me grow the story during the many revisions. Special thanks to Heather Shaw, Anne-Marie Oomen, Irene Biber, Angela Williams, and Diane and Danny Carr for that gift. And to Jan Nellett my gratitude for a close reading at the end and decades of friendship.